COLORS
OF
CHRISTMAS

Two Contemporary Stories Celebrate the Hope of Christmas

COLORS OF CHRISTMAS

OLIVIA NEWPORT

SHILOH RUN PRESS

An Imprint of Barbour Publishing, Inc.

Published by Shiloh Run Press, an imprint of Barbour Publishing, Inc., P.O. Box 719, Uhrichsville, Ohio 44683, www.shilohrunpress.com

Our mission is to publish and distribute inspirational products offering exceptional value and biblical encouragement to the masses.

ecpa Member of the
Evangelical Christian
Publishers Association

Printed in the United States of America.

CONTENTS

AUTHOR'S NOTE

Welcome to *Colors of Christmas*, two stories about both the ultimate transformational meaning of Christmas and the things we don't like to talk about at Christmastime because somehow they don't belong in the sort of Christmas we think we're supposed to have.

Both sentiments are true, but we're not always very good at holding them in balance and claiming them both as true. Can *grief* be just as true as *triumph*? Can *loss* be just as sacred as *receiving*? Can Christmas be about the baby in the manger and also be about rending apart how we protect ourselves from the way the world hurts us?

I think so.

Every year when I drag the red crate from the crawl space, open it up again, and see ornaments I don't necessarily hang anymore but which still hold sentiment, I realize it's not hard to buy an ornament that says "Baby's First Christmas" or to cross-stitch the year of a wedding onto a handmade ornament to mark new beginnings. At the same time, I realize many "firsts" also mark the first birthday or anniversary—or Christmas—since a seismic shift of some sort.

The loss of a job that was not easily replaced.

The loss of a home.

The loss of a relationship, even a long-term marriage, by betrayal, breakup, divorce.

The loss, by death, of a dearest friend, sibling, parent, spouse.

The first year with one less place setting at the table. The first year with adjusted—or released—traditions. The first year with no place to go for the holidays. The first year of having your eyes opened to the pain that was always there but that no one talked about.

The second year, the third year, the fourth, the tenth. These are not easy signposts to journey past, especially if we are alone.

Why have I chosen to write about such themes at Christmas? Because they are true at Christmas just as they are other times of the year. Because perhaps we feel them more heavily at Christmas than we do at other times of the year. Because we need Emmanuel— God with us!—nearer to our hearts at a time when it may be most difficult to look and see that He is there.

I pray that in these stories you will see hope. And I pray that after you've read them, you'll linger with the reflection questions at the back of the book, whether on your own or with a group of friends, and take your own heart deeper into hope.

Olivia Newport
2017

CHRISTMAS IN GOLD

DEDICATION

For Astrid, whose faith and hope shine always.

CHAPTER 1

They rode in silence, the murmur of Alex's expensive late-model white SUV lulling Astrid into drowsiness. She preferred an automobile with more clatter, something a person would be sure to hear coming—like her old but faithful beige Buick sedan. Even if it was fifteen years old, it took her where she wanted to go, and as both she and the car aged, they'd become companions who understood each other.

Now someone else drove her car, someone ecstatic to buy a low-mileage vehicle driven by an old lady who went to church, the grocery store, the library, and out to lunch with her friends. She hadn't been afraid to drive farther and occasionally did, usually to see one of her friends who had downsized and moved to one-floor accommodations. Her neighbors, younger and spunkier, were kind enough to check in on her—not that she needed this service until lately. Now it was her turn to downsize and move.

A truck rumbled past them, circumventing Alex's prudent driving and roaring in the left lane. Astrid's eyelids, which had closed, fluttered open. It was an older model—older even than her Buick—and the speed required to pass multiplied the decibels.

She had learned long ago that the oddest things provoked deeply buried memories.

The Americans had come and rounded up all the men, including her father, in the open beds of trucks that sounded like the one that had just cut back into the lane ahead of Alex. She hadn't seen her father again for a year. He came back gaunt and stooped.

Beside her, Alex adjusted his grip on the steering wheel.

"This is the right thing, Mom," he said.

Astrid nodded.

"We've talked about this."

Astrid nodded again, her eyes watching the never-ending shops and businesses that populated the stretch of highway.

"Mom."

"Mmm?" Astrid turned toward her son.

"I know you value your independence," Alex said, "but we also have to think of your safety."

If she had fallen on the steps outside the library instead of coming down from the second story of her own home, would she be in the car with her son at this moment? Astrid had never played the what-if game, and she wouldn't start now. Speculation wouldn't change the fact that she had fallen and two bones snapped.

"I know." Feeble acquiescence was the best she could offer right then.

"You'll be closer to me," Alex said. "I can visit more often—and bring the kids."

When you're not traveling the world, Astrid wanted to say. She held her tongue. Alex was enormously successful in business, and she was proud of him. She wouldn't sully the sentiment with her discontent of the inevitable. She was past eighty years old, after all, and her balance was fraying at the edges. The home where she raised Alex and Ingrid was far more space than she required at this stage of life, even when she invited a few friends in for a simple supper.

And she wasn't afraid of change. If she were, she would have been huddled up somewhere years ago, slowly losing her mind.

"It's fine, Alex," she said.

"It really is for the best."

"Yes, I understand."

"Mom."

His tone grated for an instant. He first used that inflection while speaking to her when he was thirteen or fourteen, caught in that age where children believe their parents understand little of the world and it is their duty to patiently explain. Ingrid had grown out of it more quickly. Alex hung on to it, perhaps believing himself to be the man of the house charged with taking care of her.

She had taken care of him, and Ingrid, too. Every moment of those years. The grief. The adjustments. Moving on. Believing in happiness again. Grasping goodness. Astrid found work first in one bank and then another. Alex and Ingrid went to good schools, earned college degrees, entered careers, had families. If they ever thought of those moments forty years ago anymore, they didn't speak of them—at least not to her.

Astrid turned and mustered a smile. "I'm fine, Alex."

"I hope you don't feel like we forced you to do this."

Astrid chuckled. It was a little late to suggest they could simply back out of the arrangements now. Her car was gone, her house scrubbed top to bottom, staged beautifully, and priced attractively. She had been afraid to touch anything in her own home the last few days. Already the Realtor had brought two couples back for a second look. There might even be a bidding war, the Realtor said. It might be a couple of weeks before they knew for sure. Ten days before Christmas was not peak house-selling season, but after the holidays lookers would be earnest.

"No one forced me to do anything," she said. She'd signed all the papers with a clear mind while her children sat across the table doing their best not to be overbearing. "I am an old lady, and I don't want to be a burden to anyone."

"Mom, you're not a burden. You've been taking care of yourself since you were twelve. It's time to let yourself take it easy."

Astrid nodded. In the mirror on the passenger side of her son's car she could see the hired truck behind them. Strangers had whisked in, sorted her belongings that had not yet been boxed up according to instructions Alex issued, and loaded the truck with basic furniture for a one-bedroom apartment with limited storage.

"We want you to be safe," Alex said. He was repeating himself now.

"Of course, dear," Astrid said.

"And happy. We want you to be happy."

"Have I been putting out vibes that I'm unhappy?" She had just had a pair of bad breaks in her ankle and lower leg. Astrid thought she had borne up rather well, considering the circumstances of the last few weeks.

"No," Alex said. "But we recognize this move will be an adjustment."

We. No one else would have to adjust.

"Of course it will," Astrid said. She'd been through worse, and Alex knew that.

"I wish I could stay longer to help you settle in."

"But you have to go to France. I understand."

"I'll stay long enough to make sure everything gets off the truck and out of my car. I don't want you to have to worry about any of that."

Astrid nodded. Alex would do his best, but she wouldn't hesitate to rearrange if his choices didn't suit her. This was to be her home, after all.

"When I get back we can buy anything you need. Keep a running list."

"Provided we packed pen and paper," Astrid said.

"Mom."

There was that tone again.

"I'll be fine, Alex. It's an all-included place."

"That's what we talked about. You liked this place when we toured."

Astrid didn't deny the statement. Compared to the other "senior communities" Alex dragged her to, this was a fine choice.

"Meals, laundry, housekeeping, salon, exercise room, activities." Alex ticked off the benefits as if Astrid didn't comprehend the concept of "all included."

Astrid wondered what, if she didn't have to cook, clean, or do laundry, she was supposed to do all day. With no car.

"And physical therapy," Alex said. "Most places like this don't have physical therapy on-site."

Places like this. If her son wanted her to feel happy and at home, he might have chosen another phrase.

"The doctor sent his order for physical therapy electronically," Alex said. "I checked yesterday to be sure they have it and there won't be a delay in getting started."

"Thank you." Astrid was quite capable of making those calls, but since Alex had already done it, she had nothing to gain by arguing the point.

Silence resumed. Astrid watched the truck in the mirror. Loading it had happened so quickly that morning. The men were on the clock, after all. Their efficiency had excluded Astrid from being sure that some of the boxes she had packed herself weren't erroneously headed elsewhere. Alex had arranged for someone to pick up items that might have value if sold on commission. Another pile was headed to Goodwill. Forty years in a four-bedroom, three-bath home with a finished basement yielded an overflow of items for both categories. A few things were going to Alex's storage unit for the time being, until they could be sorted properly. Astrid closed her eyes and tried to picture the major items on the truck. The bedroom suite she had treated herself to just five years ago. A bookcase. The couch and a recliner, a matching ottoman, a couple of end tables. Lamps. Cardboard cartons she presumed included items for the small kitchen, bedding, favorite books she had refused to part with, photo albums, a handful of small heirlooms. Astrid had wanted to take another chair, but Alex had whipped out the diagram of the apartment and made a convincing argument that there was no space for it—unless she sacrificed the bookcase, which she was unwilling to do.

"Mom."

Astrid stifled a sigh. "Yes, sweetheart?"

"This really is the best thing."

"Have I argued otherwise?"

"No, but that's not the same as agreeing."

"I'm sure it's going to be perfectly lovely."

"Mom."

"Sweetheart, I know it's the right thing," Astrid said. "I am not wishing it weren't happening. But you will go to France and then to your own home, and tomorrow I will wake up in a strange place without most of my things. Surely you can see that I may be a little unsettled."

Alex exhaled. "I'm sorry. Of course you're right. But Ingrid and I only want what is best for you. I hate the thought of you falling again."

"As do I."

"Next time your cell phone might not be within reach."

Astrid did not reply. They must be nearly there. Alex slowed at an intersection and made a right turn. After another few blocks, Sycamore Hills Community Living came into view, its yellow brick gleaming in the winter sun and the lawn beside its parking lot still covered in last week's snow and the small man-made pond frozen over.

"You can see your window from here," Alex said. "Second floor, third from the left."

Astrid followed his fingers. At least she would look out on the lawn and pond and not the back parking lot.

She gave Alex a smile and said, "Home sweet home."

Chapter 2

H ere we are." Alex turned the key in the lock. "Apartment 231."
Astrid was a couple of yards behind him and nervous
about the cavalier way he was carrying the potted succulent
she'd spent the last six years nursing. Her bent knee was well
accustomed to the cushion on the wide-wheeled scooter that
Alex's son called a "crutch alternative." Alex held the door
open and let her pass directly into the kitchen, which was
about one-sixteenth the size of the comfortable kitchen she
was accustomed to. Glancing at the cabinetry, she feared she
hadn't sifted her kitchen equipment sufficiently for this reality, after all. At least there was a stove, small as it was. Some
of the units they'd toured had only a microwave. Astrid liked
to think she was a long way from not being trusted to turn off
a burner.

The walls had that freshly painted smell, and Astrid wondered whether she would find them still wet if she grazed an
ecru surface with her fingers. The carpet, they had been assured,
was completely replaced after the previous resident's departure.
Astrid pushed away thoughts of what would ruin a carpet in
a building full of aging occupants. The color was a few shades
darker than the walls but still a neutral palette. Already she
missed the jewel tones she always preferred, but once she hung
curtains over the standard-issue blinds and put some pictures on
the walls, it might not be so bad.

"I'll grab that chair from the hall," Alex said.

Astrid didn't object. She was out of her boot cast and wearing a lace-up brace but still instructed not to put weight on the

healing bones for a little while longer. Alex unloaded the plant on the narrow width of counter between the single stainless-steel sink and the white refrigerator, which wasn't as big as what she had at home.

Home. Would she ever use that word to denote Apartment 231 at Sycamore Hills Community Living?

Astrid rolled into the area she would learn to call the living room, well out of Alex's way as he lifted the yellow plastic Adirondack chair that they'd found beside the doorway. He set it down again next to the random spot Astrid had chosen to stand, and she lowered herself into it. Its slant and depth meant she might have trouble getting out of it, but she wouldn't worry about that now.

"Will you be all right?" Alex said. "I should go down and meet the movers at the delivery entrance."

"Go," Astrid said. "I will be right here." Where else would she go? At some point the yellow chair would be in the way, but perhaps her recliner would be in the room by then.

Alex propped the door open as he left, and ambient noises filtered into the apartment. Someone across the hall had a dog with a squeaky bark who would likely be agitated all through the process of getting Astrid moved in. Heavy footsteps approached, passed, and receded. Two female voices laughed.

Astrid gripped the arms of the chair and pulled herself forward. Alex had parked her scooter just out of reach, but if she made sure to put all her weight on her good foot, she could take a valiant hop and reach it. A victory breath passed her lips once she was upright and on the scooter, and she crossed the few yards of the living room to get a good look at the bedroom. It would do. She wouldn't have as much space to walk between the furniture, but according to Alex's sketch, everything would fit.

Alex's voice wafted in from the hallway, and the little dog

across the hall barked its protests from behind the closed door. Another voice, deeper, answered Alex.

"Mom?" Alex said as he came through the open door.

"Here." Astrid turned the scooter back out of the bedroom and into sight.

"You should be sitting down."

"I'm fine." But she acquiesced to the plastic Adirondack chair once again.

Two of the movers rolled in her dresser on a wide dolly. A third carried two table lamps. Including Alex, there were four men to accomplish the moving in. Astrid felt as if she were watching events unfold for someone else's life.

"Knock, knock." The chirpy voice belonged to a petite woman standing at the door.

"Come in," Alex said.

Astrid rather thought granting admittance ought to be her prerogative. She recognized the woman. Dark short hair. Big brown eyes. Smartly dressed.

"Hello, Joy," Astrid said. TRANSITION COORDINATOR, her name tag said.

"Welcome to Sycamore Hills. We're so glad to have you."

"Thank you."

"I thought you might enjoy meeting a few people," Joy said.

"Already?" Astrid said. "We've only just begun unloading."

"Why don't you go, Mom?" Alex said. "We'll get the truck unloaded, and you can sit somewhere a little more comfortable in the meantime."

The glance between Joy and Alex told Astrid that this had been the plan all along. The voice of Alex's son filled her head. "*Resistance is futile,*" he liked to say at every opportunity.

She had no reason to resist. If she couldn't help, she might as well be out of the way.

"That would be lovely," she said, reaching for her scooter again.

"I could bring a wheelchair if that would be easier for you," Joy said.

"No, thank you." Astrid rose to demonstrate mastery over the scooter. She might be aged and injured, but she didn't require a wheelchair.

"I'll find you in a few minutes," Alex said. "You have your phone?"

Astrid nodded. At home she hadn't always kept her cell phone within reach. It had been fortuitous that it was in her pocket when she fell and that it had survived the fall in working order. Now, she supposed, it would be smart to imitate her teenage grandchildren who couldn't be separated from their phones. It was in the quilted bag strapped to the handles of the scooter. Alex's wife had made it, including embroidering Astrid's name on it with her fancy sewing machine.

In the hall, Joy said, "On my way in, I saw Carly. She's the physical therapist who will be helping you. Would you like to begin by meeting her?"

Three times a week for six weeks. Astrid had heard what the doctor recommended.

"Meeting Carly would be a good place to start," Astrid said.

"Right down this hall. We have a fully accredited therapy room." Joy's steps were patient, never moving faster than Astrid could manage. If Alex's boys had her scooter, they would be riding it at maximum speed down the length of the wing. Joy led her down the hall and turned left past the laundry room.

"The staff will do your laundry once a week," Joy said, "but you are free to use the laundry room in between if you need to. Instructions are on the machines."

Astrid nodded. They passed the nurses' office and a small

theater, finally coming to a large brightly lit room fitted with treadmills, stationary bicycles, stair machines, and therapy tables. Two young men in gray scrubs stood guard as two mostly bald men followed instructions on the equipment. Since Astrid had never used this sort of equipment before her fall, she couldn't imagine she would begin now—at least not once her physical therapy was complete.

At a desk in the corner, a young woman lifted her head. Jet-black hair hung in a braid halfway down her back. Green eyes popped from the olive tone of her face.

"Hello, Carly," Joy said. "I've brought Astrid to meet you."

Carly came around the desk and offered a handshake. Astrid balanced carefully to accept it. Carly's eyes took in Astrid's face and then dropped to her left foot.

"I've just been reviewing your file," Carly said. "I'm sorry for your fall, but we'll get you moving soon enough."

"And perhaps teach me to do the jig." Astrid winked. "Can you do that?"

Carly blinked and then laughed. "Maybe we can find a You-Tube video and learn together."

The young woman, perhaps just shy of thirty, had a pretty smile, but the lines in her face hadn't relaxed with the laugh. She carried a burden, Astrid decided. Astrid knew a thing or two about burdens.

"When do we begin?" Astrid said.

"You're on my schedule for tomorrow," Carly said. "I'll do a full assessment of strength and mobility in your leg and foot, and we'll make a plan to go from there."

"I solemnly swear I shall be a dutiful and obedient patient," Astrid said.

Her promise evoked another smile from Carly, once again with strain in her eyes.

"Thank you, Carly," Joy said. "We'll let you get back to work."

"See you tomorrow." Carly turned back to the papers on her desk.

"Let me know if you need to sit down," Joy said. "There are chairs all up and down the halls, and of course the library, the lobby, and the parlor downstairs are good places to go if you are in the mood for conversation. The fireplaces seem to attract groups."

"Especially at this time of year, I suppose," Astrid said.

"I can hardly believe Christmas is only ten days away. Decorating will start soon. You'll meet Penny, our director of fun. She'll be in charge."

They came to a round table in an open space at the top of the stairs. Three women were playing cards. They looked up, and Joy made introductions. The only name that stuck was Betty.

"Do you play cards?" Betty asked.

Astrid laughed. "I don't suppose playing Go Fish with my granddaughters counts."

"We'll make sure you have a better time than that. Look for us in the dining room for dinner and we'll get to know each other."

Joy and Astrid took the elevator downstairs and continued the tour. Astrid had been to the building before, in the process of choosing where to move, but she was grateful for the reminder of where things were. She met the receptionist and a couple of the caregivers in blue scrub tops who would be on hand if she needed something. Joy pointed the way to the dining room and reminded Astrid of the hours when meals would be served. They ended the tour in the bistro adjacent to the dining room, where the gas fire was welcoming and coffee and other beverages were handy all day. Joy sat with her, both of them drinking coffee, probing for any questions Astrid might have.

Astrid hadn't moved in forty years. She was going to need time to adjust.

"There you are." Alex breezed into the bistro.

"You need to be on your way, don't you?" Astrid said.

"I'm sorry, but yes." Alex handed Astrid a key. "I did my best to get some boxes unpacked so you have the basics ready. The main thing is your bed is set up and made, and your clothes are in the closet."

"Thank you," Astrid said. "For everything." As awkward as this transition felt, Alex deserved credit for making it as painless as possible.

"I didn't unpack everything," Alex said. "I thought you might want to do that yourself when you're up to it. Put things where you want them. I stacked the boxes in one corner."

Astrid nodded and squeezed his hand. "Have a good flight."

"I'll be back for Christmas," he said. "We'll all be together, just like always."

"Yes." They would all be together, but not at her home.

"You'll be all right."

The statement rose as if it were a question. For a grown adult and an accomplished business leader, sometimes Alex was still a little boy seeking assurance.

"I'll be fine," Astrid said. "Go, before you miss your plane."

Chapter 3

The engine started. These days Carly was never sure that it would. She needed a new car, but too many work and address changes in the last two years made it impossible to get a loan. The piddly amount of her paycheck she was setting aside to trade up for something a little newer wasn't adding up fast enough. It didn't help that she had to keep dipping into that account to pay for repairs to keep her clunker running in the meantime.

But for today, right now, the car started. The red numerals in the dash chided her for leaving work a few minutes late, which once again meant she would be a few minutes late picking up Tyler and might be exposed to the scowl of the preschool director who monitored the comings and goings of parents far too fastidiously, in Carly's opinion. Carly had mastered walking past the office to her son's classroom without meeting the eye of any staff or the few parents who might also be straggling after the rush toward closing time.

Tyler was in a full-day program now, which theoretically should have made it easier for her to schedule her work hours around dropping him off and picking him up. Somehow, though, she was always late.

And nervous. She had to scan her surroundings six times as carefully as a normal person, and even then she wasn't sure she hadn't missed something. Another parent followed her into the parking lot this time, which relieved Carly from being the last.

At the open door to Tyler's classroom, she squatted and awaited his hurtling body to fill her arms as it did every day. She inhaled the scent of the gentle children's shampoo she had rubbed into his hair during his bath last night. His hair was getting long again. Her mother had begun hinting that it was time for a haircut, but Carly loved the softness of his long blond strands under her fingers and every week decided to wait just a bit longer. Carly looked up at the teacher putting papers in Tyler's backpack. He was supposed to do that himself. She would have to talk to him again, and this time she would make herself sound firm and nonnegotiable.

"He had a good day," Miss Lesa said.

"Was he quiet during mat time?" Carly asked.

"I think he may even have dozed off this time."

Carly put a hand on her son's smooth cheek. "Did you have a nap today?"

"I told you. I'm too big for naps."

Carly stood up, still holding him, and shrugged her shoulders at Miss Lesa. Lots of four-year-olds didn't take naps. As long as he stayed on his mat and was not disruptive, he would earn a sticker.

"He's delightful," Miss Lesa said. "The other children like him. I know you were worried that the transition was a little rough at the beginning, but he seems to have made a wonderful adjustment, considering he transferred in so late in the school year. He knows the classroom routine and is respectful. You have nothing to worry about other than a few misplaced worksheets."

"Thank you." *Nothing to worry about.* This time. Tyler could be in another new school in a few weeks. How long could one child be expected to make seamless transitions to new settings? Carly scribbled her name in the binder, signing Tyler out, before putting him on his feet and handing him his "packpack" as he called it.

Fifteen minutes later, they tumbled through the back door of her mother's home. Tyler hugged his grandmother's knees on his way through the kitchen, no doubt determined to turn on the television. Their stay was supposed to be temporary. A month, two at most, while Carly got on her feet. That was two years ago. Now this house, in a neighborhood of well-kept lawns and fenced-in yards, was the most consistent element of Tyler's existence. And so far they had been safe. Tyler had been in three schools, and Carly had been in four jobs, but this sanctuary hadn't been physically breached. The moment Carly felt her mother was genuinely threatened, she would take Tyler and go. Where? She had no idea. But her mother had nothing to do with the troubles.

She dropped her keys and bag on the counter. Her mother looked up.

"Good day?" Carly asked.

"A very good day." Her mother stirred a pot. "And yours?"

Carly nodded. "I'm busy enough that the day goes quickly. They assigned a new patient to me today. A German woman. At least she sounds German."

"Maybe you can use your high school German, after all," her mother said. "I made corn chowder and biscuits."

"Tyler's favorite."

"Every little boy deserves a gran who will spoil him."

"Well, he hit the jackpot with you. We both did."

Her mother tapped the ladle on the side of the pot and then set it on the counter. "I know circumstances haven't been ideal for you, but I am still your mother. Not being completely on your own is probably the safest thing for both of you right now, and I have plenty of space."

Carly kissed her mother's cheek and took dishes down from the cupboard before calling Tyler back to the kitchen to wash up. When he saw the giant biscuits come out of the oven, he was more than willing to comply.

"Slow down," Carly cautioned in the middle of supper. "You're eating too much too fast."

"But it's my favorite," Tyler countered.

"You don't want your favorite food to make you sick."

Tyler bit into a third biscuit, but he did chew more slowly this time.

After supper, Carly rummaged through his backpack for notes or permission slips. The Christmas program was only a few days away, and she had yet to find Tyler a Santa hat and sew a jingle bell on the tip. She bathed him, letting him play in the water until it went tepid, and then negotiated the books they would read together that night. Tyler proposed thirteen. Carly suggested three. Since Tyler was four and had a limited concept of the difference between three and thirteen, his next offer was four, which Carly gladly accepted. Fed, clean, and sleepy, he didn't resist when she said it was bedtime. He picked out his clothes for the next day and climbed into bed. Carly tucked the quilt around him as he burrowed in.

"Stay, Mommy," he said.

She always stayed. He seldom took more than a few minutes to drop off, especially since he had abandoned regular naps. In those moments, in the glow of his sailboat nightlight, Carly could study the features of his face and wonder how something so good came out of her mistakes. His shoulders rose and fell, and as soon as the rhythm was even, Carly began breathing along with him and counting to a hundred. To Tyler this was an enormous number. To Carly it was enough for her to feel his sweet peace invade her rattled spirit and calm her as well.

In the living room, her mother was working on a sweater she was knitting for Tyler for Christmas, a medley of blues and browns.

"Mom, you must be tired from working all day and making dinner," Carly said. "Why don't you have an early night?"

Her mother lifted her knitting needles for Carly to inspect the project dangling from them. "Do you see any sleeves on this thing?"

Carly shook her head. "Maybe it could be a vest instead."

"It will be a sweater. He needs a good sweater to see him through the winter."

Carly picked up the stack of papers she had brought home from work and once again read the file of Astrid. With both an ankle and a lower leg to rehabilitate, they had some hard work ahead of them. Not many octogenarians would be using a scooter. A wheelchair would be safer to keep the weight off without risking another fall. The doctor's notes indicated that he believed Astrid had adequate upper body strength to use the scooter, and Carly had seen for herself that this was true. Still, she would feel better when Astrid could safely put enough weight on the foot to use a walker instead.

She read files while her mother clicked her knitting needles, occasionally humming a measure of a Christmas carol. Outside, the wind kicked up. During the evening news, the meteorologist said there could be light snow before morning. Mother and daughter drifted toward their bedrooms.

Carly's cell phone startled her out of deep sleep, and she pounced on it before the noise would wake Tyler across the hall.

No one would speak to her. She knew that, but she answered anyway.

"Hello."

Silence. Carly held her own breath in order to hear his.

It was him. It was always him. He was the reason Carly left a perfectly good job doing physical therapy with children. Truman was an assistant who worked with several of the therapists in the pediatric center. Carly was the single mother of a toddler, and Truman fancied himself the answer to all her troubles. In the beginning, they'd been friends. He'd worked at the center for a long time and helped her acclimate. Occasionally they had lunch together, and once they went together to a movie they both wanted to see. That was all it was. But no matter how kindly but firmly Carly discouraged his attentions, he set his romantic sights on her all the more.

Finally, she looked for another job.

And then he found her.

He always found her. He always discovered her new cell phone number. There was no telling what systems he was hacking into to do that, or what stories he spun to persuade someone to give him the information, or how many different numbers he would call from to avoid the block she put on his calls.

With one movement of her thumb, she ended the call. Why wouldn't he just leave her alone?

Chapter 4

Astrid woke. The fleeting disorientation was normal, she told herself, like waking up in a hotel room and not being sure where the bathroom was. Sycamore Hills. She lived here now. This would be her morning view. Sunlight leaking through thin slats in the blinds reminded her that her apartment faced east, and if she got up early enough she would see the sun rise. But she had never been a sunrise person. She was, however, a breakfast person. Most mornings she was content to make a piece of toast in the apartment and spread some peanut butter over it, and the coffeemaker would be right there on the cramped counter. But today—and every day—a hot, full, paid-for breakfast would await her if she could make her way to the dining room in time.

She threw back the bedding and sat up. This was her bedroom with her familiar bedroom furniture. On the other side of the door was the living room with the sofa she had deliberated about for three months before finally buying it. Adjacent to the living room, the small kitchen was barely large enough for a narrow table up against the wall. Through the kitchen was the door to the hallway and access to the entire community.

Community. Astrid was not quite used to the way the term was used in this place. But she was ravenous, and in another twenty minutes the dining room would stop serving breakfast. She stared for a moment at her bare left ankle, the culprit that precipitated the move to Sycamore Hills. Alex had been lobbying for two years. The fall gave him the final evidence that the time had come. Astrid did not disagree, but she was the one to absorb the reality of the change. Her scooter was beside the bed, and she gripped it now and pulled herself upright. Clothes. Hair and teeth. Blood pressure pills. Ankle brace. Then out the door.

By the time she reached the dining room, she was steering against traffic. The few people still in the dining room were merely lingering over coffee. Astrid dropped into a chair at the table closest to the door. Dinner the previous evening had taught her that a server would come to ask what she wanted to eat.

Pancakes, she thought. Lots of pancakes. Bacon on the side. And a tall glass of orange juice. Of course coffee. She grew hungrier by the minute waiting for someone to take her order.

Finally a young man approached, but he was not a server. His uniform clearly identified him as the chef.

"I'm Sam," he said, offering a hand.

"Astrid." She shook his hand in a firm manner. She was never one for wet noodle handshakes.

"Welcome to Sycamore Hills," Sam said. "I like to be sure I meet our new residents."

"I'm delighted to meet you. I'm afraid I dallied too long this morning. Is it too late to trouble you for some breakfast?"

"Not at all. What are you in the mood for?"

She told him, leaving out *lots of* pancakes, and Sam waved someone over to fill her coffee cup.

Sam brought the food himself, setting the plate in front of Astrid and lifting the warming lid. The pancakes were still steaming. Astrid's stomach gurgled.

"Thank you," she said. "I can see you're going to be a handy young man to know!"

"We aim to please." Sam grinned and waved over his shoulder as he strode back to his kitchen.

As she dragged the last bit of pancake through the syrup, Astrid looked at the large clock on the dining room wall. It was time for physical therapy. Mentally she rehearsed the turns she and Joy had taken the day before, certain that she could arrive in the therapy room on schedule and without getting lost.

Two therapists in their telltale gray scrubs were already at work with residents. One looked up.

"Can we help you with something?"

"I believe I am supposed to have a session with Carly," Astrid said.

The therapist glanced at the clock. "Looks like she's running late, but you can come in and wait for her."

"Thank you." Astrid aimed for the nearest chair against the wall. On the seat beside her was a magazine about health and wellness. She flipped through the pages, hesitant to be in the middle of reading an article when Carly arrived.

Carly blew in from a door on the other side of the room. Astrid set the magazine aside.

"I'm so sorry," Carly said. "Give me two minutes, and we can get started."

While Carly shirked off her coat and pulled papers from a briefcase, Astrid used her good foot to push herself upright.

Carly patted a padded treatment table. "If you can sit here, I'll have a look at things."

Astrid crossed the room. Carly pushed a button that lowered the table so Astrid could easily sit and dangle her legs.

"I had to take my son to school," Carly said, pulling a stool toward the table. "Sometimes the teacher gets very chatty, and today was one of those days."

"It's no problem," Astrid said. She had only waited about three minutes. "How old is your son?"

"Four."

"Does he like school?"

Carly's mouth twisted to a half grin. "The teacher says all the girls like him."

"Ah, yes," Astrid said. "It was that way for my brother. We went to a German kindergarten. I spent three happy years there. That was in the 1930s. I suppose now kindergarten is different than it was in those days."

German kindergarten was a place where children learned discipline, good manners, respect, hygiene, and punctuality. Tante Tilde presided over twelve kindergartners. Kindergarten also was a place of imaginative play. When her grandchildren were that age, Astrid had adjusted to saying *preschool* rather than *kindergarten*. American kindergarten was the beginning of serious learning, and children were expected to come into kindergarten with some mastery of letters and numbers. None of that was as carefree as her memories of German kindergarten.

"I'll never forget," Astrid said, "the time on sunny days when we all played on the large balcony. There was a big sandbox with moist, clean sand and many metal forms to make rolls, cakes, breads, and cookies. We pretended to be real bakers."

"That sounds like fun."

"It was. There were even shelves where we could display our wares. Tante Tilde let us play out nursery rhymes. All day long there was laughter and singing."

Astrid gazed past Carly, staring blankly at the far wall. Those three years with Tante Tilde were a safe place for young children unaware of the danger that brewed in Germany in the 1930s. Tante Tilde's school was so well structured that every hour was a fun, unforgettable experience. None of the children in that school had yet learned to feel suspicious. Her parents protected the innocence of their small children. Fearful questions were still years away from stirring in a little girl's mind.

"I hope your little boy loves school half as much as I did," Astrid said. "Perhaps he will even make a friend who lasts him a lifetime."

"Maybe." Carly pressed her lips together. "I'll need every-thing off your foot."

"Of course." Astrid raised her injured leg and gently removed brace, sock, and shoe.

"You also might be more comfortable if you roll up your pant leg," Carly said.

Astrid did so.

"Thanks," Carly said. "Today I'm just going to figure out your baseline for strength and range of motion."

"You're the therapist," Astrid said.

Carly bent Astrid's foot at several angles, watching to see when Astrid might wince or object to the motion. She asked Astrid to push against her hand, curl her toes, and a half dozen other tasks. In between requests, Carly made notations of the measurements.

"Where does your son go to school?" Astrid asked.

"It's not too far from here."

Carly's response came slowly enough that the conversation lost its fluidity, and Astrid probed again, gently.

"Does he like his teacher?"

"I think so."

"Does he talk about his friends?"

Carly shrugged and wrote another measurement.

"What about the girls?" Astrid said. "Does he mind that they like him?"

Here Carly did look up with the hint of a smile. "I think he's clueless."

"Well, he's only four. Did he go to the same school last year?"

Carly shook her head and tapped her chin with the top of her pen. "We've got some work to do. I think the doctor is right to caution you about putting weight on your foot right now, but I don't think it will be long. If it happens accidentally, the brace will help prevent injury. Once we get you into a walker, I imagine it will be easier to get around and do things for yourself."

Astrid nodded. But she would not stall at the walker stage. She wanted her freedom back. She would walk on her own two feet.

"Let's start some trial exercises," Carly said. "Have you ever tried picking up marbles with your toes?"

CHAPTER 5

B y lunchtime, the dining room tables boasted gold tablecloths and white candles and sprigs of blue spruce. In one corner stood an artificial Christmas tree, still naked, towering over a box that no doubt held the decorations that would dress it. Astrid stood in the doorway soaking up the scene. Outside, stores and homes had been lit for Christmas for weeks. Astrid always preferred to wait until closer to Christmas to put up a tree, but the tables looked inviting and might cheer a spirit or two.

A hand shot up from a table in the center of the room and beckoned. Astrid glanced over her shoulder to see who might be the recipient of the summons, but no one was behind her. The fingers wiggled again. The gesture was for her. Astrid rolled her scooter toward an empty seat at the round center table. She recognized the group now—the ladies who liked card games, with Betty at the center of the action.

The summoner stood up to pull out the chair. "You looked a little forlorn standing over there by yourself. Please do sit with us."

Astrid nodded. She was used to eating alone at home, but a little company now and then was welcome.

"I'm Betty, and this is Phyllis, Mae, and Fern."

"Thank you for reminding me of your names." Astrid mentally repeated them as she arranged herself in her chair, hoping her scooter was out of the way.

"Skip the special," Mae advised. "It's always safer to go with the meat loaf."

Astrid chuckled. She'd had the meat loaf the night before.

"Tomato soup today," Betty said. "It's the best soup they have."

Soup and bread appealed. Astrid wasn't used to eating a large meal in the middle of the day, and her robust and late breakfast had served her well.

"What happened to your foot?" Fern asked. "If you don't mind my asking."

"Not at all," Astrid said. "I fell down a few steps in my home."

"So you ended up here," Phyllis said. "There's always something that makes the kids think it's time."

That was exactly what happened to Astrid. Alex had appeared with a list of places to visit, and on the phone Ingrid had urged her to cooperate for her own good.

"Well," Astrid said, "here we are, whatever the reasons."

"Honestly, you're going to love it here," Betty said. "The people are so friendly, and there's always something going on if you want to get out of your apartment."

"I've still got some unpacking to do," Astrid said. "Get things on the walls, arrange the kitchen the way I like it, get the books on the shelves, that sort of thing."

Mae laughed. "Do you mean your kids didn't try to tell you where to hang the clock or that you didn't need all those books?"

Astrid smiled. If Alex hadn't been racing to catch an international flight, he would have done those things and more.

"How can you manage the unpacking with one knee on a scooter?" Betty said.

Astrid shrugged. "I've been using it for a few weeks now. I manage. Carly will speak to the doctor soon about putting weight on my foot."

"The physical therapist?" Fern said. "She helped me when I sprained my wrist. She was very sweet, but she seems, I don't know, antsy. She never seems to relax."

Fern's words confirmed Astrid's assessment of Carly. Something was not right in that young woman's life.

Mae put her hand to her mouth and leaned to one side to speak behind her hand. "Here comes Penny. We know what she'll want."

Penny, Astrid remembered, was the young woman who was the "director of fun" for Sycamore Hills. Joy had mentioned her.

"Hello, ladies." Penny stood between two chairs, one hand on each. "We're decorating today, and we could use your help."

"Ornaments?" Mae said.

"My elf helpers are bringing the boxes out of storage right now." Penny settled her eyes on Astrid. "I don't think we've met."

"I'm Astrid. Just arrived yesterday afternoon."

"Welcome to Sycamore Hills. I hope you'll join in the fun. We're putting up trees in all the common rooms."

Astrid nodded. "Thank you for including me."

"This year's theme is gold," Penny said. "We'll use other colors in some places, but I'm hoping we can do the tree in the lobby completely in gold. I think it will be stunning."

Gold. Astrid pictured the twelve-foot evergreen that had once stood in the corner of her family's living room. Her papa had brought home a box of brand-new gold ornaments, polished gleaming spheres for the tree. She was small, and Papa let her hang the ornaments at her eye level to see her reflection in each one.

"I'm happy to help," Astrid said, "if you've got a task I can do sitting down."

"No problem," Penny said. "After lunch, come to the lobby. All of you. Please join us. It will be loads of fun."

When Penny moved on to another table, Fern rolled her eyes. "For Penny, everything is loads of fun."

"Then it sounds like she's in the right job," Astrid said.

"We'll all help," Betty said. "We always do."

Astrid took in her tablemates, wondering how long they had lived at Sycamore Hills to say things like "always" or predict what is going to happen next. They were at least as old as she was, and likely older. Fern looked closer to ninety than eighty. Astrid looked around the dining room, which had been filling steadily in the last few minutes. Some residents came with walkers, some in wheelchairs pushed by staff in blue scrubs, a few with canes, and many fully ambulatory. A walker would feel like a step up for Astrid, because it would mean she could gently put weight on her foot. She had no reason to think she would not be walking independently within a few weeks—and without settling for a walker.

"Does your family have Christmas traditions?" Betty asked.

Astrid's lips spread in a smile. "When I was small, my papa made sure we had a wonderful Christmas. I always tried to do the same for my children, and now they bring their children."

Papa was fantastic. Mama usually planned the family meals with the cook, but Papa took over on Christmas Eve. The thought of chicken liver sausage pâté made Astrid salivate even all these years later. The tree spanned floor to ceiling. Papa decorated it with gold and silver bulbs and strands of tinsel, hung one at a time, and little wooden angels. And real candles sat on the widely spread branches. Papa took great pleasure in decorating the tree, making his children stay out of the room until he rang the Christmas bell and threw open the French doors. Every year was a wondrous sight for Astrid and her brother and sister.

Then they lined up in front of the tree and sang Christmas songs. Mama knew every verse of every song. After the singing, Papa extinguished the candles on the tree, turned on the lights, and took the children to look at their presents on the table. They weren't wrapped, but Papa tied pretty bows on them. Cookies and chocolate on porcelain trays were a special treat while they opened gifts. Afterward, they went to the dining room for a gourmet meal. Astrid had albums full of photographs documenting her father's holiday flair.

Astrid picked up the menu in front of her, which offered basic American fare. If she got to speak to Sam again, she might ask him if he knew how to cook any German dishes.

The conversation turned to what the other women did at Christmas, where their families lived, what foods would be on their tables. Alex would be back from France; Ingrid would come from Kansas with her family; and they would all be together in Alex's home, where his wife, Gwen, would do her best to make Christmas a delight. This would be the first year they didn't all share Christmas at home—in the house where Astrid had lived for so long and where Alex and Ingrid grew up. Astrid had been making Christmas in America for more than sixty years. It was time for the next generation.

All the talk about holiday meals had made Astrid hungry for more than soup and salad, after all. She ordered trout amandine with herbed rice and vegetables and indulged in a cupcake for dessert. When the others pushed back their chairs, Astrid did the same and they migrated as a group to the main lobby. Next to the fireplace, a bare tree stood. Astrid could see into the adjoining parlor, where another tree was half adorned but lacking anything gold.

Penny lit up at the sight of the volunteers, even if it did feel as if they had been conscripted.

"Here's a comfortable chair for you right here," Penny said, urging Astrid toward a blue wing chair. Beside the chair were three cardboard cartons. "I know there are some gold ornaments in here. Maybe you can pull out the gold ones and sort the other colors so we know what we have to work with."

Astrid sat down and let Penny park the scooter against the wall. Bending over, she opened all three cartons and met with a jumble of ornaments, some spheres, but many miniature items with wintry themes. Clumps of last year's tinsel snagged on hooks. Papa was a perfectionist. He never would have allowed anyone to put away decorations in such mishmash condition. With Christmas music playing softly in the lobby, Astrid settled into her task of sorting colors, picking off tinsel, and examining ornaments for cracks or missing hooks. Eventually she accumulated nearly three dozen large round gold ornaments safely nestled in a box of their own.

Somewhere she had gold ornaments. She had specifically told Alex she wanted to take them to her new apartment. There were only three, but other than faded black-and-white photographs, they were all she had left of her father's exquisite Christmases. Surely one of the unopened boxes in her apartment contained this childhood treasure.

CHAPTER 6

C arly glanced at the time on her phone before shoving it in the side pocket of her cross-body bag. If she hustled, she would have time for some quick Christmas shopping for her mother and her son. Tyler would be happy with anything as long as it was truck-themed. Her mother was more puzzling to shop for. She insisted she didn't need anything. Carly wanted to find something that wasn't strictly necessary and that would evoke delight. And Tyler's teacher. Carly had enrolled her son in enough different preschools to know that many parents offered at least a token gift. Starbucks gift cards were popular, but Carly wanted to do better than that.

Chilled, she paced across the parking lot of the Super Target. If nothing else, she could hit the toy section for a Tonka truck for Tyler, and maybe the book section would have a colorfully illustrated volume about the different kinds of big trucks. Tyler was only four, but somehow he already knew far more than she did about the functions and distinctions of large trucks. When they were out driving and he spotted a truck, Carly just nodded her head into the rearview mirror while from his booster seat in the back he explained to her what he saw.

At the crosswalk, a car approached and Carly slowed her steps to let it pass.

It slowed down. Her spine shivered.

The tinted windows prevented a clear view of the driver, but Truman had often jabbered on about owning a car like this one, a full-size blue SUV with every gadget imaginable.

Carly pulled her gaze away, mindful that even if she couldn't see the driver, the driver could see her. She angled left to walk behind the car. Only when her presence on the sidewalk triggered the store's doors to open automatically did the car increase speed. Truman should be at work two suburbs away. And he was too careless with his money to actually own a brand-new SUV. Lots of people drove cars like that, and the driver might have slowed simply to look down the parking lane for an open spot. Carly shook off the premonition, tugged a red shopping cart from the corral, and turned it toward the toys.

Yellow trucks. Blue trucks. Green trucks. The one Carly went home with had to be child-safe for a four-year-old without being too babyish. The more features, the better, but she didn't want endless parts that could come off and end up in the archaeo-logical layers of her son's room. Carly dutifully picked up one box after another to read the descriptions and parent advisories. After the fifth truck she lifted her eyes from all the small print and glanced down the aisle. At the far end another woman, with a baby in her cart, was pondering Lego kits, and beyond her toward the center of the store, a young couple flipped through a rack of children's clothing.

A man's jacket in motion caught Carly's eye. Brown and worn, in the classic style of a bomber jacket. The man's hands were shoved in the front pockets, and Carly could only see the back of his head, but her gut burned.

Truman had a jacket like that. It had belonged to his father, but Truman wouldn't give up wearing it. And he liked to walk with his hands in its pockets despite the awkward angle at which they were set.

No. Surely not.

Once again, Carly reminded herself Truman worked and lived two towns over. Nobody drove that many miles to shop at Target. Nearly every town in the area had one. She abandoned her truck selection and walked slowly to the main aisle that transected the store. Caution ruled. A better look would reveal if the man was Truman. The knit hat pulled down against winter air covered the man's hair color, but the height was right. He turned his head from side to side as if looking for something.

Or someone.

Her.

Or he might have been an innocent shopper looking for inspiration for Christmas gifts.

Carly wasn't taking any chances. She would have to come back for Tyler's truck, or order online and pay the shipping fee to assure it would arrive in time for Christmas. When the man turned a corner, Carly turned in the opposite direction, dragging her shopping cart in case she needed to get something between her and Truman. She had a restraining order, but turning up in a public place would give him the excuse to claim he was simply shopping and couldn't possibly know she would be in the same store at the same time. It might be Truman, or it might not be.

Once outside, Carly made a beeline for her car.

Trying to unpack boxes and place items around the apartment with one leg bent on the scooter and one hand required to steer was cumbersome at best. Astrid constantly readjusted her own expectations. Alex had done the essentials, leaving the remaining boxes stacked neatly in a corner near the small table and chairs. Astrid opened one box, unwrapped packed items, held them one at a time while she rolled a few feet, and placed them on the table or in a chair. It was a tedious process at the rate she could manage. If she got everything out of the boxes, at least she would know what she had. But the task tired her, and between Sycamore Hills's meal schedule and the staff and the women she'd met rapping on her door to invite her to various activities, progress had been slow. She had barely emptied one box and she was weary.

Her cell phone rang late in the afternoon, and Astrid pulled it from the cloth bag hanging from the scooter's handles. The caller ID announced her daughter.

Astrid pushed the button to answer the call. "Ingrid?"

"Hi, Mom."

Something was wrong. Ingrid made no attempt to color her disappointment as anything other than what it was.

"What is it, Ingrid?"

"Nothing, really. Ellie is home sick."

"Oh, I'm sorry."

"I don't think it will amount to anything," Ingrid said. "But she had me up half the night. We're both worn out, but she keeps coming up with one more thing to ask for."

"What's wrong with her?"

"She has a fever and a headache. I suppose she'll be home tomorrow, too. The school insists students be fever-free for twenty-four hours, so even if it breaks tonight, she'll need another day at home. It doesn't help her mood that she's missing the holiday program."

"That's too bad. I know she worked hard on the props."

"It can't be helped."

Astrid heard running water in the background. Ingrid often called while she was cleaning up the kitchen.

"Anyway," Ingrid said, "I called to see how you're settling in. I feel terrible I couldn't come to help."

"John can't help that he had to be out of town, and there was no need to pull the girls out of school. You'll all be here soon enough."

"The girls are so excited. They think it's such an adventure for Oma to move to an apartment."

Astrid chuckled. "I hope they're not disappointed when they see it. They won't be able to go to the basement to make up plays to perform for us, and the kitchen barely has space to bake a pan of cookies."

"None of that matters," Ingrid said. "Oh, I almost forgot. Ava asked about the gold ornaments."

"Yes?"

"She wants to know if you have them in your new apartment."

"I hope so." Astrid looked at the items strewn on the table and the boxes she had not yet opened. "Not everything is unpacked."

"Will you have a tree?"

"Goodness, no." There was no space for a tree, and Astrid was in no condition to wrestle with one this year. "But there are a half dozen trees around the place. When you come, I'll take the girls around to look at them all."

The sound of water stopped abruptly.

"I have to go, Mom," Ingrid said. "Ellie is fussing about something again."

"Give her a kiss from Oma."

"I will."

Astrid dropped the phone back into the scooter's bag and glanced at the clock. Dinner was early in a senior community, and that was going to take some getting used to. If she didn't go soon, she would miss it. When Alex got back, she would see about getting some groceries to keep in the apartment. It may have been a mistake to sell her car. Her ankle wouldn't be broken forever. Perhaps she would buy another car. She could afford it. Something used, small, and efficient with low mileage.

Checking to be sure her apartment key was in the bag, Astrid steered the scooter toward the door.

In the dining room a few minutes later, Astrid discovered Betty, Phyllis, Fern, and Mae had finished. It was barely five thirty, and already they were on the way out.

"We came down early," Betty said. "They're showing *It's a Wonderful Life* in the theater starting at six. Hurry and eat so you can join us."

Astrid nodded in a way she hoped was noncommittal. In the mood to be alone, she maneuvered to one of the small tables against a window and reached to pull out one of the rolling chairs.

"Let me help you with that." The long arms of a young man pulled the chair clear of the scooter and positioned it so Astrid could sit easily.

"Thank you, Sam," she said. "I was hoping to run into you again."

"Oh, why is that?" His features brightened with inquiry.

"I've enjoyed your food the last couple of days. It must be a busy kitchen that customizes everyone's order as you do."

"I have a terrific staff."

"I was curious whether you ever prepare traditional German dishes."

"I haven't so far, but I just might give that a whirl."

"It would make a good daily special, don't you think?"

Sam cocked his head and smiled. "I think you aren't quite used to being waited on and not having to prepare your own food."

"I have some delicious recipes," she said. "You're a smart young man. I'm sure you could manage the math to offer them on a larger scale."

"I'll tell you what," Sam said, winking. "You bring your recipes down one day and I'll have a look. Right now, I'll make sure a server comes to take your order lickety-split."

She watched him saunter back to the kitchen. He was a charming young man, reminding her of someone she had known—and loved—a lifetime ago. The love she shared with Heinz flamed quickly and was extinguished in the space of a breath more than sixty years ago. But she would never forget him.

CHAPTER 7

The alarm shrieked. Startled, Astrid dropped her head to the library table where she had been reading the newspaper after breakfast the next morning, and covered her head with her arms.

No, that wasn't right.

Even when she was a little girl and bomb sirens blared, she had to do more than simply cover her head with her arms.

Shelter. Where was the nearest shelter? She had known them all as a schoolgirl in Würzburg. If the air-raid siren went off while she was walking between school and home, she knew what she was supposed to do, but in this moment, she could not think where to go.

Astrid sat up straight. She had come to the library for no better reason than getting out of the apartment for more than a meal without committing herself socially. The array of newspapers and magazines was impressive enough that she considered making it a daily habit. A cup of coffee from the bistro across the hall sat half-consumed on the table because she had become engrossed with the editorial page. The siren was not a surprise. She had seen the sign propped up on the reception desk in the lobby announcing a tornado drill at ten o'clock that morning, and at the time she had thought it would be good for her to know where to go in case of a real emergency. She even watched the time as the drill approached.

Still, the siren jolted her, as every siren had during the last seventy-five years.

The British. The Americans. The bombers who did not print out a nice warning of their intended arrival but flew in with as much stealth and severity as possible.

This was not that. She could say those words all day and it would not slow her heartbeat. It never had.

A Sycamore Hills staff member in blue scrubs took long strides across the library and gripped Astrid's scooter.

"It's just a tornado drill," she said, "but we do have to take cover. It's required for everyone."

"It's December," Astrid managed to say as she read the caregiver's name tag. Jennifer. "There's snow on the ground. We're in no danger of a tornado at this time of year."

Jennifer chuckled. "Tell that to corporate. Tornado drills and fire drills. We have to do them year-round so new residents and staff know what to do."

"Like me."

Jennifer shrugged one shoulder and steadied Astrid's elbow as she arranged herself on the scooter.

"Where to?" Astrid said.

"Through the dining room to the kitchen."

"The kitchen?" Astrid pushed off with her good foot.

"You'll see," Jennifer said. "There's a room back there built for this."

They were in the hall now. Traffic came from every direction. Astrid entered the flow.

"Will you be all right now?" Jennifer asked. "I have to check the rooms down the hall."

"Go," Astrid said.

In the kitchen, Sam's was the only familiar face Astrid saw. Where were Betty and the others?

"Right through there," Sam said, gesturing. "You'll get used to this."

Astrid doubted the veracity of that statement. In seventy-five years she hadn't gotten used to the sirens. Smoke alarms, ambulances, fire trucks, city-wide tornado sirens. All of them made her heart race.

In another couple of minutes she was in a room she had not imagined existed. How many did it hold? Was there another? Would the elevator work during a real tornado? Astrid pushed the questions out of her head. She found a spot where she could lean one shoulder against the wall and close her eyes.

This was not that.

For most of the war, the threat of bombs sent the people of Würzburg to the shelters, though the damage usually was light. When the frequency of air raids increased in the final months, though, bombs destroyed parts of the city. Mama prodded Papa to make some arrangements. The family needed to be out of the city, away from the targets. He dragged his feet. What about his *Apotheke* business? Finally, Papa found a place in the countryside where they could go and arranged a truck to transport the family's belongings. They could move to an old unoccupied beer brewery in the village of Wenkheim. Movers disassembled the furniture and packed the entire household except for mattresses and a few chairs. The date was set for the family to travel.

And it was one day too late.

When the sirens howled, Astrid grabbed her survival bag, just as her brother, Harald, did—just as they had both learned to do in the intensifying weeks of air raids. Nanny Paula carried her younger sister, Uta, and Mama and Papa had the other bags. The family ran down the flights of stairs in their apartment building and into the public air shelter next door.

It was cold and damp and dark and crowded. Astrid felt that place now, even as she was in a warm and dry space with calm conversation swirling around her.

Sirens screamed for hours that day. Enormous explosions shook the building. When the shelter's wall and door collapsed,

Astrid reached for the nearest person to hang on to. She wasn't even sure whose hand she held.

Then it was quiet. Eerie. On other days, quiet meant the danger had passed. Not on that day. Not on March 16, 1945.

Papa and some of the men climbed out over the rubble to see if it was safe. Far from it.

"Go," he said. "Take shelter in the park across the street."

Astrid climbed out, taking her brother's hand to pull herself atop the rubble. Mama handed Uta up to Papa. Nanny Paula followed. Astrid's heart raced so fast she feared her chest would break open.

"Hurry," Papa said, though Astrid could hardly make her feet move against her rushing heart.

Every structure was on fire, flaming first from the upper floors. The red sky shot sparks from incinerator bombs in every direction. The building behind her family's apartment building was half gone already.

"Harald and I will check the apartment," Papa said. "Perhaps we can salvage something."

Papa, no, Astrid thought. If he ran into the thick, spiraling smoke, she might never see him again. Uta was crying, her mother frantic. If Papa and Harald didn't come back, who would take care of them?

"Do as your papa says," Mama said, her voice strained but firm. Astrid's heart raced on as she obeyed her mother and covered herself with a wet blanket—she had never been sure where it came from—and ran for the park. The crowd was as dense as the smoke, and Astrid wondered how Papa would ever find them. What if Papa never came? Family after family thickened the throng. No one could go home. Astrid shivered under her blanket, her eyes stinging as she watched the burning sky.

And then Papa came. He and Harald managed to throw the

mattresses out the window to drag to the park, and they saved six chairs and the baby's crib.

In her young life, all of it lived in the shadow of the Nazis, Astrid had never seen such horror. The neighborhood burned, as did every neighborhood in the city. In a matter of hours, the entire city was reduced to what its citizens could carry. No matter whom she looked at, stunned and frightened expressions greeted her.

The next day, while the inferno raged, families clambered for limited transportation to the countryside. German soldiers, stationed in barracks nearby, were allowed to assist with a few trucks, not nearly enough to move families out as quickly as they wanted to go, even if they had no destination. Papa was determined to check on the Apotheke, his downtown pharmacy business. Flames and smoke were still spreading, and entire blocks had turned to smoldering rubble.

Papa, no, Astrid thought again. *Don't leave us.*

They waited and waited. When he returned, Papa had a hand trolley loaded with a fifty-liter bottle of olive oil and a large box of powdered and crystallized sweetener.

"For the soldiers," he said. If he had something to offer them, they might help him return to the Apotheke and retrieve more of value. The plan almost worked. But it was too late. By the time they got there, the building had burned beyond recognition.

"It's gone," Papa said when he came back to the park, his shoulders slumped. "Everything. Gone."

Too late. Everything was too late. They'd lost their expansive apartment, and now Papa's downtown office building was gone as well.

For three days Astrid was terrified. Of the fires. Of losing sight of her family. Of what the future held. Of whether she would ever feel safe again.

Finally, they left in the open bed of a German military truck. Astrid watched the burning city recede. She twisted around to face the other way, toward wherever they were going.

Someone touched her, and Astrid jumped, her eyelids flying open.

"Are you all right?" Sam said. "The drill is over. You're free to go."

This is not that.

Astrid swallowed, watching everyone making their way out of the safe room.

"Do you need help?" Sam said.

Astrid gripped the handles of her scooter. "Thank you. I can manage."

She was one of the last to leave and went straight up to apartment 231, any appetite she might have had for lunch consumed in the destruction of Würzburg.

CHAPTER 8

Tyler was particular about his breakfast cereal. A preschool-style nutrition unit now made him ask a lot of questions about food. He couldn't read yet, but he recognized the nutrition label on the packages and demanded his mother interpret them. Sugary cereals were out, and high-fiber cereals were in. Carly chose something and dropped it in the grocery cart. She had only come in for three items—cereal, yogurt, and bananas—but had a dozen already and decided to stop there. Tyler was in school, and Carly's morning was free of appointments. If she checked out now, she'd have time to go buy that Tonka truck that would amaze her son.

She pushed her cart toward the checkout and chose a line. The cart in front of hers contained the makings of a holiday meal and enough baking items to underwrite a massive Christmas cookie exchange. Finally the checkout belt rolled forward, and Carly put her reusable canvas bags and distinctly non-holiday items on it. Her mother liked the little holiday touches. Carly could wait to see what her mother had in store for Tyler before committing to baking. She fingered her debit card while the checker scanned her items, quickly punching in her PIN when the time came and muttering her thanks as she gripped the handles of two bags.

At the store exit, Truman stepped into her path.

"Holiday shopping?" he said.

Carly gave no answer but stepped to one side to go around him. Truman moved as well.

Carly stopped, braced her feet, and imagined swinging a grocery bag at his head, followed by an uppercut swing of her fist.

"What a coincidence running into you at the grocery store," Truman said.

Carly adjusted her grip on the bags. "I have a restraining order, Truman. You're standing way too close to me."

"Am I?" He stepped closer.

Another couple of feet and he would be close enough for a direct punch to the stomach.

"Anybody can come in a grocery store on an ordinary Thursday morning," Truman said.

Carly eyed him—the brown bomber jacket, his hands in the pockets. She could put her groceries down and get her phone out of her purse. The police number was on speed dial. Carly moved both bags to her right hand, freeing up her left either for a punch or a phone call.

The doors slid open as another customer entered the store, excusing himself as he walked around them as if they were an ordinary couple or two friends who ran into each other.

"You're not supposed to be here," she said.

Truman shrugged. "I need a loaf of bread."

"I'm sure they sell bread at the grocery store down the block from your apartment."

"I should have dropped you a note to tell you I moved to a new apartment," Truman said. "About half a mile from here."

Drop her a note? Would he really send her mail? He was taunting her. He wouldn't give her written evidence that the restraining order meant nothing to him.

"You always said you didn't want a long commute," Carly said.

"It turns out it's not so bad." Truman extended a hand. "Can I help you with your groceries?"

"No, thank you," she said. "Shouldn't you be at work?"

"Shouldn't you?"

"I'm trying to get there on time. You're not helping."

"What happened to us?" Truman said. "We used to be so good together."

"Truman," Carly said, "we were never together. We worked at the same place and had lunch a few times. That's not the same as being together."

"We could be together. We're compatible. We have the same taste in movies and music. We both like a good run."

"Truman." The bags weighed heavy, hanging from Carly's hand. In another minute, she would have to shift her grip. This wasn't the first time Truman violated the restraining order. The night calls were bad enough, but showing up in person was the worst.

"Did you follow me in here?" she asked, though she felt certain how he would answer.

"Like I said, I need bread. This is the closest grocery store."

If he lived close to this store, then he lived within three miles of the home Carly shared with her mother. Carly racked her brain to try to remember if she had ever told Truman her mother's first name. With the exception of one movie, they'd never seen each other outside of the physical therapy center where they both worked, and she had met him at the theater that night. How did he know to move to this town under a guise of innocence? The phone book was no friend in situations like this.

"Then maybe you should go on and get your bread," she said. "As you can see, I'm on my way out. I don't have time to chat."

"At least tell me how Tyler is doing."

Carly stiffened. "My son is fine." He was a happy little boy, and Carly was going to make sure he stayed that way.

A man in a blue shirt and navy tie came out from behind the customer service desk. His tag said he was Nate, the assistant manager.

"I have to ask you not to loiter here," Nate said. "You're blocking the entrance and exit. Perhaps you haven't noticed that you're making the door open and close."

"I was just leaving," Carly said, taking the fleeting distraction to step around Truman. Surely he wouldn't inflame the incident with a witness standing so near.

Without looking back, Carly raced through the open door and to her car. Fortunately it was only four parking spaces away from the store. Several items tumbled to the floor as Carly dumped the bags on the passenger seat. She ignored the cascading groceries, started the car, and drove. Truman hadn't exited the store by the time her tires squealed out of the lot.

His calls at night were so frequent that Carly had given up reporting them to the police, but she did call in every physical encounter. She took a random turn and drove six blocks into an unfamiliar neighborhood before stopping to pull out her phone and dial. Reporting one confrontation never stopped the next one from happening. If Truman really had moved, they might even have his latest address in order to stop by with a friendly reminder about the terms of a restraining order. Truman wasn't stupid. So far, he stuck to public places where anyone was free to go and it would be impossible to prove it wasn't coincidence. Even if Carly managed to call the police, Truman would be gone by the time they arrived. It was as if he could smell a squad car coming from a mile away. But once again she reported the circumstances of Truman's behavior.

Carly scanned the street. Presuming that the man she'd seen in Target was Truman and that he owned the vehicle she'd seen that was his dream car, she watched for the SUV. She didn't know this part of town well, but he would know it even less. Truman said he moved to a new apartment. This street was all single-family residences. Nevertheless, she wouldn't take a direct route home. The last thing she wanted to do was lead him to her house or to Tyler's new school or her new job. This was the third job change in two years. The more she moved around, the harder it would get to find another job. She certainly hadn't expected to work in a senior community where all her patients were at least seventy, but she wanted Sycamore Hills to work out.

When she first met Truman more than three years ago, they bantered around the physical therapy center like old pals. Tyler was just a baby, not even walking yet, but Carly was never without fresh pictures of him. Truman was assigned to be Carly's primary assistant in executing the therapy plans she crafted for her patients, and he was ready and able to do what she asked—and plenty more than what the job required. Truman asked how Tyler was, offered to bring Carly a cup of coffee while she did paperwork at a desk, made sure she got safely to her car on dark wintry nights, bought a bigger lunch than he needed so he could share with Carly.

He'd been so different than Tyler's father—who was a huge mistake. That relationship had moved too fast and had no legs underneath it. By the time Tyler was born, Carly didn't know where his father was anymore.

Under other circumstances, Carly might have received Truman's overtures on another level. But she was a single mother, and her focus was on her child. The mistake with Tyler's father was hers alone, and her son was not going to pay for it the rest of his life. Figuring out how to be a mother was complicated enough without the complexity of a romantic relationship that might or might not work out. Truman was a thoughtful friend, but that's all Carly wanted at the time—a friend. She'd told Truman this several times, and it hadn't stopped his kindnesses. In fact, his gestures increased.

Then came that Thursday in the third week in April.

Truman had taken the day off work, something he rarely did. Their manager was always reminding him that he was going to lose his vacation hours if he didn't start using them. At the end of the day, Carly left the building and her heart nearly stopped when her car wasn't parked where she'd left it that morning—in the spot where she left it most mornings. She didn't see it anywhere in the employee section of the lot. It was a no-frills car that was only slightly more reliable then than it was now. Who would steal a car like that?

But it was gone.

And then Truman rolled into the lot with it, grinning. He resisted answering her questions about how he'd gotten a key, waved off her indignation about his deception, and awaited her effusions of gratitude for changing her brakes and replacing her starter and battery without asking for a penny. The next day, she gave him a check and started looking for a new job.

And then one day Truman turned up outside her new place of employment.

She changed jobs and changed Tyler's preschool.

And Truman dropped by her workplace just to say hi.

She changed jobs again.

If Truman didn't get the message this time, with a restraining order in place, she might have to move out of her mother's house. That would break Tyler's heart and would certainly complicate the question of reliable childcare when Carly needed to work late or go in early. Despite the circumstances of Tyler's birth, her mom was over the moon for the boy and sometimes rearranged her own work schedule to be with him when Carly couldn't. Three generations in one household had its advantages. Everyone was happy. It was working.

And now this.

Even in the face of a restraining order, Truman had morphed from kind to creepy.

CHAPTER 9

Astrid couldn't remember the last time she played a real card game with other adults. Since Alex and Ingrid became parents, she had played Go Fish and Old Maid too many times to count. When Betty knocked on her apartment door with an invitation to play, Astrid politely declined. But Betty persisted, and now Astrid sat at the round table in the wide second-floor landing trying to remember the rules of Rook. Poor Fern was her partner. No doubt Fern was more accustomed to a partner who knew what she was doing.

A middle-aged man made his way down the hallway, pausing to greet, touching a shoulder gently, laughing, offering a somber nod. It all depended on the person he encountered. The distraction he provided Astrid was no help to her Rook game. When he came close, he placed his hands on the backs of two chairs and leaned in to observe the game.

"Hello, Pastor Russell," Mae said, not taking her eyes off the game.

But Astrid glanced up. Pastor Russell?

He met her glance and offered a hand. "I'm Russell Gaines, the chaplain around here."

Astrid had always pictured chaplains as elderly men in dark suits who made the rounds visiting people in the hospital. But Russell couldn't have been more than fifty. His dark hair had only the faintest suggestion of graying, and he wore tan pants and a navy polo shirt.

Astrid shook his hand and introduced herself.

"She's new," Fern said, shuffling cards to deal for a fresh

round. "She's only been here three days."

"Then I'm doubly glad to meet you," Russell said, his eyes on Astrid. "I'm always available for conversation, and we have a simple morning service on Sundays and Bible studies on Thursday afternoons in the community room. We'd love to have you join us."

Astrid nodded. "Thank you." Sunday mornings, without a car and the church she had called her own for decades now miles away, would never be the same. She could at least give Russell's service a try.

Her gaze shifted past Russell and down the hall, focusing on nothing in particular.

Growing up, Sundays were family days. Papa always planned outings in advance. They might walk around Würzburg or ride the train out to the forested area, where they tried never to follow the same trail two times in a row. Papa always had his harmonica at the ready, and Mama sang. During the summers, Sundays might find the family at relatives' homes in a tiny village in the Bavarian Forest or on the Inn River in Mühldorf near Munich. In both places, Astrid and Harald—Uta was still too little—found endless ways to amuse themselves. A weathered trunk full of old pictures. Gathering blueberries for a pie. Playing with their cousins. Swimming in an icy stream.

The one thing the family didn't do on Sundays was go to church. Astrid's parents had soured on church before any of the children were born, and their choice had nothing to do with Hitler's opposition to any organization but his own.

Mama and Papa did their best to protect the children from the deteriorating conditions around them. If one of the men on their block hadn't been seen for a few days, they said he was away on an important trip. If Harald asked questions—the same ones Astrid was too uncertain to ask—Mama would go to the grand piano and play a lively tune that the children knew. Checking their survival bags became a game. Astrid never told Mama about the friend at school who cried every day for a week. No one had to ask why. Her father was gone, and Astrid didn't believe he had gone on an important trip. She watched the clock every day after school, her own heart ticking toward the moment her father would safely return for supper.

The family had a radio, but it was rarely on. It was bad enough that the children were familiar with survival bags and bomb shelters. They didn't need the barrage of Hitler's language and German war news when they were in the relative safety of their own home. As hard as they tried, Mama and Papa couldn't control everything.

Every family lived in fear in those days, whether the parents talked about the war or not. Windows had blackout shades. Sometimes Astrid stood with her back pressed against the wall and her head turned to the side, her eyes squinting as she tried to see through the tiniest of slits in the shades. There were no streetlights. Sometimes, when he came home from work, Papa paused to greet one or two other men before slipping into their building at the last minute. Every time he did that, Mama made Astrid move away from the window. No one was allowed to be out after dark, and interior lights went out at suppertime. Everything was subject to inspection. The German SS officers arrested fathers in the neighborhood who might have whispered a word against the Nazi regime, and they were never heard from again. One hushed phrase or inflection could destroy a man's future, and no one could be sure who had given him away. That was more than enough to make families hunker down to keep their families safe and not voice a political stance. Not ever. Astrid and Harald never dared to ask a question about what they saw happening around the city, even at school. Though her family had a lovely home, the increase in shrieking sirens sending people to shelters caused Papa to clear the living room and put down mattresses so the family slept together with a survival duffel for each person packed with food and clothing to last a week—and the photograph albums Mama insisted were an emergency item. They went to bed with sweat suits beside the mattresses so they could scramble into the clothes on top of their pajamas if a siren sounded, and then run for their lives down three flights of stairs. No one had a decent night's sleep. Even school hours were interrupted by racing for an air-raid shelter.

In the park that wrapped the city, where the ancient wall had once stood, some children had the yellow Star of David pinned to their clothing. *Jude.* One day the students with stars were not there anymore. No one explained where they went, and Papa and Mama had drilled into Astrid and Harald that they must never ask about such things. At school, mornings began with all students facing the framed picture of Chancellor Adolf Hitler and saluting.

Astrid never told her parents that by the third grade she hated school. It wasn't that she wasn't interested in learning, but something as simple as an incorrect answer could provoke the humiliation of having to go to the front of the class, extend an open palm, and suffer several strokes of a bamboo stick. School was one more place where danger lurked.

Starting at the age of eight, all children had to belong to the Hitler Youth. There was no choice. Even Mama and Papa could not protect their children from this. Youth training included hiking, camping, sports, marching, and singing the songs Chancellor Hitler approved. In particular, teenage boys had to be ready and strong to join the military when the time came. No other youth organizations were permitted, not even in church. Boys barely older than Harald were conscripted and sent to the front lines.

Despite the regime, religion classes at school continued. Twice a week for one hour, Catholic and Protestant instruction was held. Astrid had no religion and had never been baptized. Her parents never talked about God. But in the hall, where her feet sometimes got cold as she occupied the lone chair and watched the religion teachers close the doors behind them, shutting her out, she had no doubt. Even without religious training at home, she believed in God. Surely He was within reach. Maybe God was just on the other side of one of those doors. In her school clothes and warmest socks and sweater, she inched her chair toward one of the doors. Her heart throbbed on the day she mustered courage to ask the Catholic priest if she could sit in his class.

He agreed. That's where it began.

Someday, she hoped, she could be a Catholic, but her interest in religion was one more thing that she knew better than to ask her parents about.

Papa kept his Apotheke business open and constantly sought to improve it. Sundays brought the delight of his attention. School continued. Mama went out every morning with two cloth bags to fill with vegetables at the market. Nanny Paula cared for little Uta. Lina, the other familiar domestic help of Astrid's childhood, helped Mama with the housework and cooking. Papa planned the family outings. Mama played the concert grand piano and made sure Astrid and Harald got piano lessons. Harald learned to play properly, while Astrid played by ear because she couldn't seem to learn to read music fluently.

Life went on.

It was life on the outside, bottling up what was on the inside. The unanswered questions about what happened to the children with yellow stars or the fathers who never came home. The impossibility of saying, "No, I don't want to be in the Hitler

Youth." The secret of taking religious instruction when Astrid knew her parents were no longer religious. The silence of the radio that ought to have cheered their home. How long they would have to sleep on mattresses on the living room floor. And, eventually, what would happen to them all after the city burned?

And the survival bags were always there, a constant reminder that the air raids might one day strike their neighborhood. The position of her sweat suit was the last thing Astrid double-checked before she kissed Mama good night and stretched out on her mattress.

"Astrid."

She blinked and returned her gaze to the table and met Betty's eyes.

"Are you all right?" Russell asked.

How long had she been daydreaming—if that's what you call remembering events from a lifetime ago? Surely she had held up the game. She shifted her eyes to the inquiring chaplain.

"Have I completely frightened you with the suggestion of a Bible study?" Russell said. "My apologies."

"No, of course not," Astrid said. "Thursday afternoons in the community room."

"That's right. And if you want to talk. . ."

"Thank you, but I'm quite fine," Astrid said. Ever since she arrived at Sycamore Hills, her thoughts filled with events she hadn't entertained for decades. She was stiff with the effort of it. Perhaps the people who said we carry our memories in our bodies and not just our minds were right.

Russell pointed to a tiny office across the landing. "If you ever need me, I share space with Penny, right there."

Penny. The director of fun. The one determined to have a Christmas in gold. Astrid's penchant for reverie had begun there. She still hadn't come across the missing gold ornaments.

Chapter 10

Carly zigzagged through neighborhoods, glancing in all three mirrors in a regular rhythm. Periodically she pulled into a driveway, turned around, and cut across a corner she had passed earlier.

One thing was clear. She was not made for this cloak-and-dagger stuff. All she wanted was to give her son a safe, loving home. How could she have misjudged Truman's character so drastically? Or had his character changed? Was it the onset of mental illness with no one in his life to tell him what they observed? He always said he didn't have family nearby, and except for Carly, he had held his coworkers at a distance. Carly blew out a breath. That should have been her first clue. He didn't say more than hello to anyone else at work, but he had managed to pull Carly's life story out of her as soon as she put a picture of Tyler on her desk.

By the time she altered her course to head toward home, she was four times as far from the house than she should have been. The yogurt was getting warm, and the ice cream sandwiches she had bought for a treat would be mush. She'd have to get rid of the box before Tyler ever saw it.

And she would be late for her afternoon patients. At least stopping off at home to put away a few groceries was in the same direction as Sycamore Hills.

Her mother thought she should tell somebody at Sycamore Hills about Truman and the restraining order. Carly had one photo of the two of them together, a selfie Truman took on the night she met him for a movie. It seemed harmless at the time, just two friends seeing a film. If only he'd left things alone. Her mother's argument was that it wouldn't hurt for a photo to be available at the reception desk of Sycamore Hills. It wouldn't be on display, just stuck in a discreet place where only the receptionist on duty would see it. She'd have to cut his face out. She'd never let anyone see what he'd done with the photo. It was bad enough showing it to the police to prove there was reason for a restraining order.

Carly didn't want the fuss, the explanations that would be expected, the murmurings among the administrative staff if she left a photograph at the front desk of Sycamore Hills. It would be better if she simply made sure Truman never found out where she worked. As far as she knew, he still had a job, so he couldn't be stalking her every minute of the day.

At home, she went through the back door into the empty house. Her hand hesitated over the lock. She was only going to be there a few minutes. In the past, neither she nor her mother worried about locking the back door when they were home.

Carly turned the deadbolt and shoved groceries into their proper places before she picked up her keys again. Four minutes was the length of her stay in the house. Outside, she scanned in a manner that had become her new normal.

The Sycamore Hills employee parking area was full, and she had to park farther out and rush into the building.

"There you are."

Carly cringed at the voice. She had hoped Patricia would be occupied in another part of the building, not at her own desk at the far end of the therapy and exercise room.

"I'm sorry." Carly stuffed her handbag in a drawer and shirked off her winter jacket.

Patricia waited. Carly swallowed. What could she say?

"You missed an entire appointment," Patricia said, "and

now you're ten minutes late for your second appointment. Mrs. Donahoe is waiting for you in her room."

"I'll go immediately." Carly pulled Mrs. Donahoe's file from the rack and snagged Mr. Thompson's as well. "I'll find Mr. Thompson and see if he's available at the end of the day to make up the session."

"You might have called," Patricia said. "I understand that things come up. It happens to all of us. But it's simple courtesy to call."

Things come up. Carly fished a pen out of a cup of writing utensils. Somehow she doubted any of the other therapists had a restraining order against a former coworker.

"I'm sorry." What else could she say? "I'm going to try to persuade Mrs. Donahoe to start coming down here for her therapy. She could make faster progress if we used some of the resistance equipment."

Patricia shrugged. "She's pretty good at resisting suggestions."

"I really want to help her."

"I know. Good luck. And next time, call."

Next time? Carly didn't want a next time. She needed this job, and she liked it more than she had expected to. But talking to anyone at Sycamore Hills was out of the question. They couldn't know how complicated her life had become.

CHAPTER 11

Astrid rolled herself into the physical therapy room the next morning, having steeled herself for the challenges Carly would inflict on her. Picking up marbles with her toes, if she could master it, was a skill she wouldn't use frequently, but it might amuse the grandchildren when they were all together for Christmas. So far, she'd gotten no further than concentrating on making her toes curl and paying attention to all the parts of her foot that were involved in that simple task.

Carly looked up and wagged a few fingers before wiping down a machine someone had just used. It was a bulky machine, and Astrid hoped that Carly didn't have it in mind for her. Curling her toes and having her foot massaged seemed far preferable. Astrid transferred herself to the nearest chair to await instructions and watched the movements of the young woman. On one hand, they seemed ordinary—running a rag across equipment, opening a folder, picking up a pen and then dropping it, bending to retrieve it, pushing a couple of keys on a computer keyboard, and finally turning to meet Astrid's eyes. On the other hand, the movements were stilted, clumsy, and plagued with trembling.

What on earth could be wrong?

Astrid certainly would do her best to cooperate well and perhaps ease the girl's troubles in some small way.

Carly approached. "How are you today?"

"Ready to work," Astrid said, making a point to smile.

"I think I've put together a plan that will bring good results—as long as you practice the exercises between our sessions."

"Of course," Astrid said. "I will learn to pick up marbles and then shoot them with just my toes. Wait and see."

Carly cracked a smile and extended a hand to help Astrid up. "Come on over to the therapy table. We'll start with some heat to loosen up the muscles in your foot."

Astrid arranged herself on her rolling scooter and followed Carly across the room, where Carly lowered the table. A few minutes later, Astrid's injured foot was wrapped in warmth. She rather liked the sensation.

Carly pulled a backless stool over. "I don't think your file contains a clear description of how you injured yourself."

"Being foolish," Astrid said. "I should have left a hand free to use the stair rail, but my hands were full of clothes I cleared out of my closet, and I didn't want to make two trips down the stairs. I couldn't see my feet."

"How many steps did you fall?"

"Just three." If she had fallen from the top of the stairs, it would have been twelve and she would have broken more than two small bones. "But I suppose the step I missed is the one that counts."

Carly's dark head bent to make notes. "Someone left a note here that you speak German."

"I thought my accent would have given me away," Astrid said.

Carly shrugged only one shoulder. "I wouldn't say you have a heavy accent."

"When I was your age," Astrid said, "I was very self-conscious about speaking English, but I tried hard every day to disguise my accent."

"Why did you feel you needed to disguise it?"

"You are young. But when I came to this country, people were wary of Germans. It was in the years after the war."

"Oh. I hadn't thought about that."

Carly began to unwrap Astrid's foot and moved into a

massage. Astrid closed her eyes. Nothing about Sycamore Hills was anything like Germany, yet she seemed to think about the old days more than she had in years.

"We lost our home," she said, eyes still closed. "Our city was not a primary target until close to the end. I heard once that the bombs they dropped on us were left over from an air raid of Nuremberg. Incendiary bombs. Everything burned. We went into the countryside with next to nothing."

Carly's fingers pressed into Astrid's heel. "Are you Jewish?"

Astrid opened her eyes. "No. I don't compare my suffering to what the Jews endured. No one I knew truly supported the Nazis. Life was more precarious than I realized as a child. My parents did everything they could to protect us, but when your city is destroyed in the space of twenty minutes, everything changes."

"I can't imagine." Carly's fingers moved to Astrid's arch.

"We stayed in the empty restaurant space of a brewery. We had a woodstove to cook on, but no wood. No pots and pans, no food to cook. No furniture but the mattresses and chairs my father saved from the wreckage the night of the bombing. A cellar went deep into the mountain, and that is where we hid when we heard the planes coming."

"You must have been very frightened."

"I suppose I was. I was only eleven, but that was old enough to see for the first time that even the best parents cannot prevent everything." Astrid could smell the damp earthen floor of that place where they huddled beside old beer barrels. "If it hadn't been wartime, the village would have been quaint. Most of the streets were not paved, and the farmhouses made of mud and twigs needed repairs. We couldn't afford to keep a maid or a nanny anymore. My parents went house to house bartering for what we needed. Finally we had a used pot and a few dishes. We ate farina and cooked apples that my brother and I found in an orchard. No one had any food to sell, even to someone who had a little money."

Mama had walked miles to barter the saccharin sweetener Papa had saved from the Apotheke for the farina and to beg for milk. The farmers barely had enough to feed their own families, so it was a treat when Astrid's family had milk with their cereal. Astrid had looked after Uta while Mama was gone, never knowing if she would return with food.

"But if there were farms, weren't they growing food?" Carly asked.

"Most of the men were conscripted into the German military," Astrid said. "The women only planted what they could manage on their own so they could feed their own children, but suddenly the countryside was flooded with refugees from the bombed-out cities."

"It's like a movie." Carly indicated Astrid could sit up.

"A horrible, horrible movie. Believe me, you wouldn't want to live through it."

Papa had borrowed a bicycle to pedal back to the rubble that was Würzburg and see if his business property was salvageable. Astrid had insisted on going along. Her unrelenting begging wore Papa down and he found another bicycle and warned her she would have to keep up and she must not leave him. The outside walls and massive foundation were intact, but the four-story building had crumbled down in on itself. Coals still smoldered, throwing heat upward through the rubble. Papa could do nothing. Somewhere in the debris was his safe, and in the safe were the papers proving the property belonged to him. If he could find that, he could plan how to rebuild. But the search would have to wait until the fires burned out. His shoulders slumped so steeply that she did not dare voice the other question on her childish mind. Would they ever get the gold ornaments back?

"I want to measure your mobility," Carly said, "to see if you're progressing. Bend your ankle as far to the left as you can."

Astrid complied, and Carly made a note in a chart in the file folder.

"You had a maid and a nanny," Carly said. "You had a nice home, and your father had a business. It must have been hard to lose all that so suddenly."

"I held on to God in those days," Astrid said. "I had taken some religious classes—only the ones the Nazis permitted—and the village had a priest. One day, I took my little sister to see him and tell him I wanted to become Catholic. Mama gave her permission, and we went for lessons and were baptized. A few months later I had my First Communion along with children who were much younger. I didn't care. I knew I wanted to hold on to God. I didn't know what the Nazis would do, or whether the next night a bomb would take us all, or when the war would end. But I knew God wouldn't change. I've been so grateful that God would give me the faith to believe."

"Now point your toe and extend your ankle as far as you can," Carly said, one hand lightly on Astrid's foot.

The foot didn't move easily in any direction. To Astrid it looked withered.

"Don't worry," Carly said. "You'll get there. It just takes time. The exercises are important to do every day, two or three times."

"I will," Astrid said. "I will get back on my feet this time just like I have every other time—with God's help."

"I admire your faith." Carly picked up a tool that measured the angle of Astrid's foot.

Astrid wanted to say that of course Carly could have faith in God as well. But there would be plenty of time to ease into that encouragement. After all, they would be spending an hour together three times a week for the next six weeks.

The door opened, and Sam, the cook, entered.

"Hello, Sam," Astrid said. "Do you know Carly, physical therapist extraordinaire?"

Sam and Carly nodded at each other.

"I don't think I've ever seen you up here before," Carly said. "Aren't you out of your element?"

"Mrs. Costineau is my great-aunt," Sam said. "I try to pop up when I can, though I usually take the back stairs."

"That explains it," Carly said.

"When I glanced through the glass and saw the two of you together, I couldn't resist sticking my head in."

Carly looked away as Sam's gaze settled on her. Astrid watched. Sam was interested. Carly was guarded.

Therapy sessions would also allow time for Carly's story to come out.

"I'm trying to persuade Sam to offer some German dishes," Astrid said.

He winked at her. "Will you pass on your mother's own secret recipes?"

Astrid laughed. "My mother wasn't much of a cook when I was a child. I learned from Mrs. Schmidt, the landlady."

"Before or after the bombs?" Carly asked.

"After. When we were in the village. Cooking, baking, cleaning, sewing, laundry. Mrs. Schmidt's husband was off in the war. Even after the war, he didn't come home for a very long time. I liked learning to keep house, and she liked help with her two boys."

"Then I'd like to learn Mrs. Schmidt's recipes," Sam said.

"Once Carly has done what she is trained to do," Astrid said, "and I can stand on my own two feet, we shall have some lessons in the kitchen. I'll even wear a hairnet."

Sam laughed and said good-bye, lingering longer when he

caught Carly's eye. Astrid watched both their faces as Carly watched Sam leave the room and let the door close behind him.

"I like Sam," Astrid said.

Carly nodded as she got out the marbles and a rocking board. The rest of the therapy hour would consist of trying to get her foot to comply with curious tasks.

Mrs. Schmidt. Astrid thought of her often and warmly, despite the circumstances in which they had known each other. Astrid only met her because the Americans came through and moved into the brewery, forcing the family to find other lodging. They ended up in Mrs. Schmidt's barn.

Before the Americans were hundreds of German soldiers. They knew the end was close and begged the farm families for civilian clothes so they could try to get home to their own families without notice. Their uniforms piled up in an empty stable. Astrid began going to look at the heap every afternoon to see how much bigger it had become. For the first time, she wondered what it was like to be a soldier at war. When she sat in a rickety chair in the brewery eating an egg her mother had bartered for with some of Papa's sweeteners, she fretted about those uniforms. Wouldn't the village get in trouble for helping the soldiers? Shouldn't somebody hide them—even just under the hay instead of on top of it?

And then one day the heavy rumbling started. Curious children came out of the small homes to see for themselves. Frightened children squeezed their mothers' hands. Tanks and trucks and jeeps and every kind of military vehicle came over the hill not too far off. Soon the rumble would become a full-throated roar. The village mayor ordered everyone to take shelter in the damp, dark cellar of the brewery. The entire village squeezed in— infants, children, the elderly, men, women. They feared for our lives. Once everyone was in, the heavy wood and metal door was slammed shut and secured from the inside. Only two lanterns lit the awful hole of darkness.

The mayor was the sole person who remained outside. He waited at the entrance to the village with a white flag, ready to surrender his town to the invading Americans in the most peaceful manner possible—or at the risk of his own life. Inside the mountain cellar, the villagers held their breaths, not speaking but only listening for the rumbling that had sent them all scurrying. The convoy of tanks and trucks seemed endless, but eventually the sound halted. Inside the cellar, they heard nothing. Papa was the first to dare leave the cellar, go into the family's adjoining living quarters, and peek out from behind curtains. So far the Americans hadn't left their vehicles. But neither did they aim their weapons at the mayor.

The mayor urged his wife to offer a basket of fresh eggs to the soldiers in one tank. Satisfied there would be no shooting, people straggled out of the cellar. Papa and Harald went first, as they so often did in those days. When the American soldiers saw the children, they threw candy—their own rations—to them. Children shrieked in joy.

The relief was temporary. The Americans occupied whatever structures they chose and filled all the best buildings, displacing the occupants. The streets filled with people with nowhere to go. The mayor went from house to house demanding that anyone still in their own homes make room for others. Astrid's family lost the brewery and ended up in the back part of a farmhouse, above the stable, once again starting with nothing they could call their own for the third time in six weeks.

The Americans quickly got down to business. All the men in the village were interviewed.

And then Papa was taken. He was in his house slippers when they came for him. Astrid ran after them trying to give Papa his warm coat, but the Americans didn't slow down. When a large army truck passed by, loaded with German men, Astrid knew her father must be on that truck. Mama stood beside her, shaking, and Astrid put Papa's coat around Mama's shoulders. Papa hated the Nazis, but he held membership in the party. It was the only way he was allowed to do business in Würzburg. If he hadn't paid his membership dues, his business would have been closed. He would have been shot for not following orders, or sent to the Russian front or a concentration camp.

Villagers had little information about where the Americans took the men or when they might return. The village swelled with evacuees from bombed German cities, and hundreds of Hungarians lined the streets with no food and no place to live.

If it hadn't been for Mrs. Schmidt, the farmer's wife whose own husband was a prisoner of war in the custody of the Americans, Astrid wasn't sure how her family would have survived the end of the Nazi regime—the only world she'd ever known.

CHAPTER 12

S lowly the apartment was coming together. Alex had hung all the clothes in the closet, but Astrid didn't find his system— or lack of one—helpful, and she reordered her clothing the way she preferred, with the current season easiest to access. There weren't many options in the kitchen, but she flip-flopped the contents of two drawers. The apartment had two large windows with sills wide enough for a collection of knickknacks. Peter had given her many of them—a tiny musical carousel, glass bottles in colors that caught the sunlight, a hand-painted teapot, a slender wooden giraffe. After forty years, choosing which items to bring to a one-bedroom apartment hadn't been easy. Alex and Ingrid took some items of sentimental value, and more were packed in boxes in the storage unit until Alex could go through them. An estate sale that involved allowing strangers to wander through her house dispensed with several bedroom sets, excess kitchen and decor items, and patio furniture.

In the apartment, the refrigerator remained empty, and the only food on the shelves were a few slices of smashed bread, half a box of crackers, and dried dates that turned up in a box of utensils. Even when it came to the contents of Astrid's kitchen cupboards, only what would stage well had remained until the day she moved out. On moving day, Alex had cleared the cupboards, likely reasoning she didn't need food because her meals were included in the monthly fees. Again Astrid wondered if she'd given up driving too soon, though even if she had a car right now her injured foot would have prevented her from driving. Astrid's apartment was in the "independent living" section of Sycamore Hills, but how independent could a person be if she couldn't even whip up a couple of scrambled eggs?

She wouldn't complain. A bus from Sycamore Hills went to a local shopping center twice a week and the mall once a month. As soon as she was fully ambulatory, she could buy a few groceries as often as she liked. Apartment 231 at Sycamore Hills would be her final address, and she would live simply. Even this small apartment was a palace compared to some places she'd lived.

Two unlabeled boxes remained for her to sort. She lifted one to the table and opened the flaps, hoping the gold ornaments of her childhood would turn up. Instead she found photo albums. The efficient approach would have been to simply put the albums in the bookcase, but Astrid opened the first one—the oldest one. Her father had loved his camera. He was never without it on vacation or the family's Sunday recreation, but it was a wonder any of the photographs had survived the family's destitute moves after the war.

Christmas was Papa's favorite time to take photographs of his children. After he trimmed the tree with fresh wonderment every year, Harald, Astrid, and Uta lined up in front of it for pictures. Other photos showed the delight on their faces when they saw their gifts, and still others the holiday table laid with great care.

Christmas of 1945 was missing because Papa wasn't with the family that year. They had no word where he was taken, but surely after the Americans met Papa they would see he was no threat and never had been. He only wanted to care for his family. In time he would return, but that Christmas was gone forever.

Days passed, then weeks and months. The space at the back of Mrs. Schmidt's farmhouse was connected to the hay barn. When they moved in, a stove for cooking and heating was the only thing there. They had to be resourceful. Even if they'd had any money, currency was drastically devalued after the war. Astrid hadn't felt sorry for her family in particular. How could she? There were millions just like them who also lost everything overnight during air raids or at the hands of the Russians. Now the Americans had all the men, even if they hadn't been active in the military.

Harald was a slight fourteen-year-old, but he found work on a large farm in exchange for food and a place to sleep. Mama, Astrid, and Uta stayed with Mrs. Schmidt, venturing into the nearby forest daily to gather sticks and pinecones to burn in the stove so they could cook what little food they rummaged up or to heat water to clean up in a borrowed large tin. Astrid took on the family's laundry once a month and soaked up everything she could learn about housekeeping from Mrs. Schmidt.

Papa was taken in the spring, and the harsh demands of an uncertain, primitive existence for the family passed the months quickly. For Christmas, they found a little tree and made a wooden stand. There were no gold ornaments and tinsel and candles that year. Pinecones, nuts, and little apples were the makeshift decorations. Even without a photo, and all these years later, Astrid could picture that little tree in the frigid room above the stable. For many years that Christmas memory made her picture what kind of stable Jesus was born in. Perhaps there hadn't even been a stove to warm the Holy Family.

Astrid turned the pages of the photo album slowly, lingering over each memory they evoked. She left it lying open at the gap where 1945 should have been.

A rap on the door redirected her attention. If it was Betty or one of the others looking for another hand at cards, she would decline. She wanted to be done with these boxes and concentrate on thinking of Apartment 231 as home.

"Just a minute," Astrid called out. Transferring herself to the scooter and getting it turned in the right direction wasn't a swift task. It was Carly at the door.

"Did I forget an appointment?" Astrid asked.

Carly shook her head. "It's just paperwork. I should have had you sign a few things yesterday, and it slipped my mind."

"Come in." Astrid rolled away from the door. "I have a pen here somewhere."

Carly looked around. "It looks nice in here."

"I'm not quite finished unpacking," Astrid said, "and I'll have to get help putting things on the walls."

"Maybe I could help," Carly said. "I'm pretty handy with a hammer and nails."

"So far a hammer and nails haven't surfaced. I suspect my son didn't think I would need them."

"I could bring some from home."

Astrid had rolled back to the table and returned to the chair. Carly stood beside her and put the forms in front of her.

"It's just consent for us to treat you, HIPPA notification, and all the usual papers," Carly said. "Documentation will be my undoing."

Astrid picked up a pen and began glancing at what she was about to sign.

"Wow," Carly said, "that looks like an old album."

"It is. I brought the photos from Germany as a newlywed and bought the album with some of the first money I earned in the US"

"May I?"

"Please." Astrid signed four papers as Carly flipped a few pages.

"Childhood memories?" Carly said.

Astrid nodded. "You could say so, though my childhood ended the night the British bombed Würzburg. All the things I took for granted as a child that adults would do for me were suddenly mine to do."

"I can't imagine what it must have been like for you."

"I had never known a Germany without the Nazis in power," Astrid said, "and the Germany that was left after the war was no country at all. Cities were piles of rubble. Roads were destroyed. No one had any money. There were no jobs because there were no businesses. Hard times leave you no time for childish fun."

"What about school?" Carly picked up the signed forms and tapped them in one stack against the table.

Astrid shook her head. "No schools that year. They opened again the next year, but I never really got to go back to school for any length of time. I was no longer a child with the freedom to decide I didn't like my strict teachers. I had to make my way like everyone else."

"What about your father?" Carly sat in another chair and leaned in for more of the story.

"He was gone for about a year, and then one day he turned up. He had lost so much weight we almost didn't recognize him. He was in terrible health and never wanted to tell us about what happened after the Americans took him. Even Mama didn't press him. We were just glad to have him back."

"I'm sorry you all had to go through that."

"My aunt came and nursed my father back to health. After a few weeks, he wanted to go back to Würzburg to check on his property. We didn't know what things would be like after more than a year, but I didn't want him to go alone. I didn't want him out of my sight."

"So you went with him?"

"Yes. His plan was to rebuild. But first he had to find his papers. Then he could start again at the beginning."

"Such courage," Carly said. "All of you. Such courage."

"We didn't think of it as courage. It was just what we had to do. Just take the next step, do the next thing."

The difficult years were hardly over. But the stunned look on Carly's face told Astrid the young woman had heard enough for today.

"My faith got me through," Astrid said. "Faith fed my hope."

"I don't really have faith these days," Carly murmured. "Hope is for other people."

"Hope is for all people," Astrid said.

"I'm not so sure." Carly's phone buzzed in the holder at her waist, and she bent her head to look at the message. "They're looking for me. I have to go."

"Of course," Astrid said. "You came for simple signatures and I prattled on. I'll see you for our next session."

Carly stood, walked to the door, and turned as if she wanted to say something. Astrid waited, sure she saw a tear in the young woman's eye. But Carly only waved and went into the hallway.

CHAPTER 13

Morning number six. How many mornings would it take for it to feel normal to wake in this unfamiliar room and navigate unfamiliar mental paths? Astrid's brain still wanted to get out of bed on the other side and take twelve steps across the bedroom to the adjoining bath. Everything felt backward. And once she could manage an outing to the grocery store, she would buy breakfast options to keep in the apartment. No one who was more than eighty years old should have to set an alarm clock in order not to miss breakfast.

Astrid caught the tail end of the Saturday breakfast service and asked for oatmeal and fruit. Six days of meals in the Sycamore Hills dining room were sufficient for her to have developed table preferences. Betty's Brood, as Astrid thought of the group of friends where Betty was the instigator, always welcomed her to their preferred round table, but when she came in off their schedule, she was happy to sit on her own at a small table near the window and look outside. The ground was white with yesterday's snow, but Astrid could see the outlines of the flower beds and vegetable garden that would return in spring strength.

After breakfast, Astrid rolled her scooter into the lobby. Gas fireplaces throughout the building burned from before breakfast until late evening, and Astrid eased herself into an armchair beside the lobby's enticing blaze with a view of the enchanting, towering gold Christmas tree. It was as good a place as any to ponder what she would have been doing at home and how to fill her days here in this strange place.

She nearly didn't recognize Carly when she strode down the

hall bundled in her winter jacket, the hood still up and gloves hiding her hands. Astrid offered a smile, and Carly caught it.

"I'm not so old that I don't know this is Saturday," Astrid said. "Do you do therapy even on the weekends?"

Carly shook her head. "I'm behind on my documentation. If I don't get caught up before Monday, I'll be twice as behind."

"Ah." Astrid turned her palms up. "The quest for a fresh start to the work week."

Carly laughed. "The bane of my existence."

"Paperwork. A universal dilemma, it seems to me."

"It used to be actual papers," Carly said, removing her gloves and flipping the hood off her head. "We still scan in a few things, but a lot of it is electronic, and the system knows when I had an appointment and whether I entered any notes afterward."

"Big Brother," Astrid said.

Carly laughed again, and it struck Astrid that the young woman didn't often have a smile on her face. It was Astrid's conviction that everyone should laugh at something every day, and if she could evoke mirth in the people around her, she would.

The automatic front doors to Sycamore Hills opened, allowing a blast of crisp winter cold. Sam, the cook, paused just inside to stamp gray parking lot slush off his feet. Astrid lifted a hand to wave, and Carly rotated toward the door.

"Well, if it isn't the German cook," Sam said, grinning.

His words were meant for Astrid, but his eyes went quickly to Carly, whose long wavy dark hair now sprawled across the limp hood of her jacket. Carly's cheeks pinked. One corner of Astrid's mouth pulled away in a smile. She and Heinz had looked at each other like that—and she'd been much younger than Carly. Maybe it was Sam who could get to the bottom of why Carly didn't often smile.

"I thought perhaps the B squad did the cooking on weekends," Astrid said.

"That's the theory." Sam shoved his gloves into his jacket pockets as he glanced between Astrid and Carly. "I left menus, but my assistant cook is having trouble finding the ingredients I listed. I'm sure I ordered everything she needs, so I figured I would just pop in and sort it out."

"Do you live nearby?" Astrid said.

"Only a mile or so away," Sam said. "Carly, what about you? Do you have to come far?"

"About seven miles," Carly said. "It's not too bad."

Carly looked at Sam as she spoke. Astrid's smile tugged that corner of her lips again. Even an old lady could see the spark Sam's attention stirred in Carly.

"The fire looks cozy," Sam said. "Penny's trees are spectacular."

Astrid and Carly nodded.

"You should see the photos Astrid has," Carly said. "Her father trimmed a beautiful tree."

"Oh?" Sam moved his glance to Astrid.

"He did indeed," Astrid said. "The photos are only black-and-white, but it takes little imagination to add color."

"I'd love to see the photos sometime," Sam said. "How many trees did Penny do?"

Astrid ticked off her fingers. "Lobby. Parlor. Library. Community room. Landing. Dining room."

"Six trees!" Carly said. "I really should make a point to go around and look at them."

"I was just about to say that," Sam said. "Maybe when I'm finished in the kitchen, I can come find you to see the trees together."

Carly blushed. "Maybe if I'm not too engrossed in my documentation."

"It won't take long," Sam said.

The corner of Astrid's mouth twitched. She must not let on that she noticed the two of them dancing around the edges of flirtation.

Carly tilted her head back to take in the height of the lobby tree. "I haven't seen them all, but it's hard to imagine another one could be as striking as this one done in gold."

"My father did one in gold one year," Astrid said. "Somewhere I still have some of his gold ornaments. They came from his mother, actually. They were quite old even when I was a girl. I loved them best of all."

"I'd like to see them," Carly said.

"Don't leave me out," Sam said.

Astrid gave into the full smile. "As soon as they turn up, I will let you both know."

Surely Alex wouldn't have sifted them out. Astrid had specifically asked for them, and he knew they held great sentiment. Yet she had opened the last box yesterday, and it held only more towels than she was likely to need. If he called, she would ask him about the ornaments, but she might have to wait until he returned from France.

"I'd better get to my work," Carly said. "I promised my son we'd play in the snow today."

"You have a son?" Sam said.

Carly nodded. "He's four."

Astrid's eyes went to Carly's left hand. No wedding band. Had Sam also noticed?

"If I don't get to the kitchen," Sam said, "there might be no lunch."

The pair disappeared into the hall behind Carly, walking in the same direction. Astrid would like to have heard their conversation. Instead, she stared into the gold tree on the other side of the fireplace. So much gold made for a stunning entrance.

The memory of her father's trees shifted to the three days she had spent with him in the rubble. It had taken her three days of persistent nagging to convince her father to take her with him. He had wanted to take Harald, but her mother had argued that Harald could ill afford to put his employment at risk with an extended absence. Then Papa said he would go alone, but Astrid had kept her foot propped in the opening of her father's intention. He had meant to take someone. Why not her? She was old enough.

Papa's acquiescence gave way to a steady stream of caution. *"Be careful what you touch." "Stay where I can see you." "Don't put your weight down on anything you're not certain of." "Don't slam the shovel."*

The stench assaulted her nostrils as soon as they rode into Würzburg, and her heart clenched. The devastation of the bombs left little untouched in the city that dated back a thousand years. Here and there were pockets of people hoping to rebuild, but Astrid's twelve-year-old mind couldn't conceive that this place might once again be a thriving home to thousands of people. Unbridled grief made her tremble.

"You asked to come," Papa said softly. "You must be strong enough to be helpful."

She wiped the back of one hand across her face. "I am strong, Papa."

Astrid couldn't even determine where the Apotheke had once been, with its impeccable shop windows at street level and stories of doctors' offices above. But somehow Papa knew.

Jagged edges of glass, chunks of brick, random remains—a table leg, the back of a chair, a headless doll, rags that had once been clothing, powders that could have been anything, shards of wood, crumbled and unrecognizable gray bits everywhere.

Rodents scurried through the rubble. Astrid's chest had burned, both with the dust that rose from the rubble and the disappointment that this was what their previous life had been reduced to.

"We are looking for the safe," Papa reminded her, handing her a shovel. "That is all that matters."

"The ornaments," Astrid said. "Can't we look for the ornaments?"

Papa shrugged. "Don't get your heart set on that. We must accept they are gone."

Astrid didn't argue. But as she methodically helped her father shovel through the detritus of their city, her eyes searched not only for the black of her father's safe but also the brown of the wooden box that had sat in his office. It was a strong box. Papa had always said so. It was possible it had survived both the blasts and the burning.

Anything was possible. If she couldn't believe that, what good was it to believe anything? *With God all things are possible.* Wasn't that what the priest in the village always said to people grasping for hope in the time since the war ended? Astrid wasn't simply grasping for hope, she was digging for it with a strong shovel.

For three days they dug. Others dug up and down the block, and Papa seemed to recognize some of them. Wheelbarrows carried away load after load of jumbled, worthless debris, and Astrid wanted to cry out to be allowed to look in the passing loads for her wooden box. Even if all she found was a shining bit of gold glass, she would at least know what happened to the ornaments. When her eyes drifted, though, Papa spoke her name and she returned to the spot he had identified.

Three days.

At night they huddled in an old bomb shelter. The door had

been blasted off, and Astrid's mind filled with every instance of seeking refuge from the bombs. She slept little, waiting for daybreak.

Two nights and three days.

On the third afternoon, they uncovered debris they recognized from the Apotheke. The bent metal frame of a display case. The wooden slab that had been Papa's desk. A black metal handle from the filing cabinet. Shreds of the packets he used for dispensing medicine. And then the tilted plane of black. Papa's efforts intensified, digging and tossing aside anything in his way. Astrid cringed. He might toss away the ornaments.

The safe was sound, still closed tightly. Papa turned the combination lock and tugged at the door. It swung free. His concern wasn't for the safe but for the papers it held. Relief colored his face, and in that moment Astrid saw hope. Papa took all the documents the safe had held and jammed them into his coat.

"If we go now"—Papa said, beginning to climb back off the debris toward the street—"we can be back to your mother before dark."

"But the box," Astrid said.

"We will not find the box," Papa said. "How would a small wooden box of glass ornaments survive what we have been digging through?"

"Please, Papa. Just a little while longer?"

Papa blew out his breath, but he picked up his shovel once again.

Papa wouldn't pray, but Astrid did. For the ornaments. For more time to search. That she wouldn't put her shovel down in the wrong place and destroy precisely what she was hoping to save.

"Papa!" Astrid went to her knees and began moving rubble by hand. "I see it."

He knelt beside her, and she pointed.

"That's the corner," Astrid said. "With the brass hinge."

He nodded, and with a huff, he moved the largest piece of jagged concrete that remained in the way.

Trembling and grateful to find the box whole though covered in soot, she opened it. Most of the ornaments had shattered, but three survived whole.

"Thank you, Papa." Astrid threw her arms around her father's neck. "Thank you. I promise I will never lose these again."

Everything about her young life was broken—and probably always had been because of Hitler's rise to power in the years of her childhood. But with three ornaments cradled in her grimy hands, she believed with her whole heart that not everything must break.

Astrid now pushed herself out of the chair and onto her scooter. She had kept the ornaments safe for sixty-eight years.

And now they were lost again in the debris of her move.

CHAPTER 14

There was no point in answering her cell phone. Didn't Truman ever sleep? Or maybe he'd figured out a way to schedule a call to go through while he was in dreamland and Carly lay in her bed resisting sleep because she knew it would be interrupted.

Tonight was different. He'd called four times already, and it was only three in the morning. After the third call, Carly put the phone on vibrate, but she was so accustomed to interrupted sleep that even the slight buzz her phone made on the nightstand jolted her. Now, after the fourth call, she turned it off completely, crossed the room, and stuffed the phone between the cushions of a chair. It couldn't ring now, and in the morning she would take a screenshot of the list of missed calls to send to the police as evidence that Truman was still harassing her. The only reason she ever answered was that one of the officers had suggested that if she didn't answer the call and hear his voice, she couldn't testify credibly that it was him.

Carly was sure. Blocking the number was pointless. He just got another number, probably prepaid phones that he could change as often as he wanted to. Carly even changed her own number twice and was very careful whom she gave the numbers to—her mother, Tyler's school, the supervisor at whatever job she had at the time—and somehow he found the new numbers. That was the creepiest part of the whole travail.

She was entitled to sleep with her phone on if she wanted to. Anyone should be free to make that choice. The level at which Truman violated her space intensified, aggravating her chronic agitation. No one, not even her mother, knew how hard Carly worked simply to appear calm, or that if she could save enough money—which seemed unlikely with the way car repairs and day care ate up her paychecks—she contemplated moving halfway across the country. But that might make her mother vulnerable, and Carly couldn't abide that thought. She would just have to turn the phone off and shove it out of earshot.

Back in bed, all she'd accomplished was not hearing the phone. Falling asleep—deeply enough to feel restored—remained out of reach, and she entertained the thought that she might as well get up and do something productive.

The house phone interrupted this consideration. It rang three times and stopped. Almost immediately it rang again. And stopped. The third time it began to ring, Carly threw back the quilts and went out into the hall. She had no extension in her room, but her mother did.

Carly knocked on her mother's door. "Mom?"

"Come in."

Carly opened the door, to find her mother sitting on the side of the bed, lamp on and the cordless phone in her hand.

"I'm sorry, Mom." If Carly lived somewhere else, even in an overpriced apartment the size of a shoe box, this wouldn't involve her mother.

"No one was on the line," her mother said.

"There never is." Carly took the phone from her mother's hand and set it back in the cradle. She could complain again to the police about the nocturnal calls, but if Truman never spoke and used prepaid phones, what could they do? Track down his new address or his place of employment to make accusations they couldn't substantiate?

"So you think it was him," her mother said.

Carly nodded. "Who else? I had four calls on my cell, and now this. It's no coincidence."

"This is getting out of hand. It's always been out of hand, actually."

"We could turn off the ringer on the phone in here."

"Suppose someone really needed to reach me?"

Her mother's best friend had a husband ailing with advanced Parkinson's. Carly's grandmother was in a nursing home, and this was the number they would call if something happened. Her uncle was fighting cancer, and his wife sometimes called at odd hours. All of them would call the house line out of habit if they needed her mother.

"You could ask everyone to call your cell number if they need you at night," Carly said.

"I shouldn't have to. He's the one who should be stopped. If I have to give my cell number to half the world, they'll want an explanation I don't wish to make."

Her mother was right, of course.

"I'm sorry, Mom." The response was feeble and repetitive, but Carly could think of nothing else to say.

The thump against the door made them both jump.

Tyler, rubbing his eyes and walking unsteadily, entered the room. "I had a noisy dream. Make the telephone stop."

Carly exchanged glances with her mother before picking up the phone and sliding the ringer button to the off position. Tyler burrowed into her hip, and she picked him up.

"There," she said, "I turned off Nana's phone."

He wrapped his legs around her waist, almost too big for her to keep lifting him to carry.

"Will you sleep with me?" he said, his chin propped on her shoulder.

"Sure, baby," Carly said. "Let's go lie in your bed so Nana can go back to sleep."

Tyler might be the only one to return to slumber that night, but Carly hoped her mother would at least try. She crossed the hall to the small room with a twin bed, an upright dresser, and shelving that held the toys and treasures of a little boy. He was reluctant to let go of her neck when she bent over the bed.

"It's all right, Tyler," Carly said. "I'll stay with you until you fall asleep.

She lay beside him in the narrow bed and pulled the sailboat-printed quilt over the two of them. How much had he heard? Could he have heard her cell phone or only the landline? With his head against her shoulder, Tyler's breathing soon was deep and even. Carly's mind raced. The landline account was in her mother's name, and Carly wasn't authorized to request changes. But she would urge her mother to ask the phone company to block the particular number these calls were coming from now. Suggesting that they get a new number and keep it unlisted would meet resistance, and Carly wouldn't blame her mother. If television shows were to be believed, he never stayed on the line long enough to be traced, but the police might be able to search a proprietary database and find out where his new apartment was.

The day Truman had shown up at her new job and casually handed her an envelope, it was all she could do not to tear it in half in front of him.

"I came across this and thought you'd like to have it," he'd said.

"Thank you," she'd managed to say, refusing to make a scene in front of the receptionist.

Once he'd left the building, she almost dropped the sealed envelope in the nearest trash can, but she could just see the police officer who helped her from time to time shaking his finger at her at the inadvisability of that choice. Instead she slit the envelope open and peered at its contents.

The photo of her and Truman on the night of the movie.

Only this version had Tyler's face in it, like a cozy little family.

It was after four when Carly returned to her own room. Rather than crawl into bed—pointless, because she wouldn't sleep—she instead closed the door behind her, flipped on the overhead light, and slid the closet door open. The items she sought were crammed in the back on the floor. She hadn't thought about her high school softball team for years, but in this moment the purpose of that effort proved fruitful. The duffel had long been unused, but now she pulled it out, put it on the bed, opened the zipper, and turned back to the closet. It was time to take matters into her own hands and make sure Truman left her—and Tyler and her mother—alone. Fear would not be a new normal Carly would accept any longer.

Astrid's daily activities were caught between the independence she had taken for granted before her fall and thoughts that began, *Once I am mobile again. . .* On Sunday morning, reconciling that neither of those conditions were true at the moment, she decided to give the chaplain's Sunday morning service a try. Billed as nondenominational, the service struck her as a generic Protestant offering without the passing of the offering plate. The order of service printed on the handout was simple: a couple of hymns sung to the accompaniment of a spinet piano in the community room, a brief sermon, a time of prayer, and a closing hymn. The front of the room had been rearranged and draped with cloths the color of blue that more progressive churches had begun using for Advent, the weeks before Christmas, and Astrid appreciated that someone—she supposed Russell—had given thought to how to make this multipurpose space appropriate for a worship gathering.

The crowd wasn't large. Others still drove cars or could take the buses Sycamore Hills provided for transportation to several larger churches in the area. Then there were those who would rather do without a service if they couldn't attend their own churches. And of course, not everyone was inclined to go to church at all. But nothing about the service made her feel that Russell took any shortcuts simply because the group was small and the service generic. *Heartfelt* was the word she would use to describe it.

Russell's sermon was on one of the familiar Advent texts that Astrid would have expected to hear in a church service. This passage was a glorious text and one of her favorites:

> *"Comfort, comfort my people, says your God. Speak tenderly to Jerusalem, and proclaim to her that her hard service has been completed, that her sin has been paid for, that she has received from the LORD's hand double for all her sins. A voice of one calling: 'In the wilderness prepare the way for the LORD; make straight in the desert a highway for our God. Every valley shall be raised up, every mountain and hill made low; the rough ground shall become level, the rugged places a plain. And the glory of the LORD will be revealed, and all people will see it together. For the mouth of the LORD has spoken'"* (Isaiah 40:1–5).

Many people would hear in their heads the great solo from Handel's *Messiah*, but Astrid heard the soft voice of the priest who had welcomed her into his church so many years ago when the ground of her life was anything but smooth and level. He had put her on the highway for God, and it had seen her through the valleys she hadn't imagined could still lie ahead, much less that she would come through them to see God's glory.

A brief litany of prayer followed. Astrid's lips moved for the congregational responses while in her heart she pondered one person: Carly. She was a physical therapist. Presumably within a few weeks Astrid would be walking again and the two would have no reason to meet. A sense of urgency gripped Astrid's heart. Carly was walking through a valley. Astrid didn't know its terrain—yet—but she recognized it nevertheless.

Hope would be the only answer.

Chapter 15

Astrid rolled into the therapy and exercise room just after breakfast the next day. When Carly's head lifted from the laptop on the desk, Astrid exhaled relief. All day yesterday, after the church service, she couldn't shake the feeling that something was amiss. But Carly was there and put a smile on her face as she waved Astrid over.

"We'll start with some heat again," Carly said. "It seems to loosen you up pretty well."

"Truth be told," Astrid said, "having my feet wrapped in heat is my favorite part of therapy."

"I have all kinds of fun for you today. Pushing a rolling pin with the arch of your foot, rocking a board back and forth."

"And the marbles," Astrid said. "Don't forget the marbles."

"Never." Carly moved to a therapy table and lowered it. "But in fact, I was reading an article about some new exercises that made me think of you. Are you game for being a guinea pig?"

"But of course." Astrid wiggled her eyebrows.

"I put the magazine in my bag. Give me a minute."

Astrid's eyes went to a small rack of narrow lockers, expecting Carly would have stowed her personal belongings, but instead Carly went to a duffel against the wall that had seen better days. She unzipped it and rummaged around.

"Are you planning a trip?" Astrid ventured.

"No." Carly's arm went into the duffel up to her elbow. "Just some stuff."

It was none of Astrid's business what was in Carly's bag or why she had brought it to work, but it was a curious sight. When

Carly lifted a baseball bat out of her way, Astrid's eyes narrowed. What in the world? If the calendar showed mid-June rather than mid-December, she would have supposed Carly was the athletic type and played in a softball league. But a baseball bat in a scruffy duffel was a peculiar thing to carry around a week before Christmas. Of course, people did a lot of peculiar things right before Christmas. As far as Astrid knew, the bag could hold assorted gifts for Carly's four-year-old son. But the baseball bat was full size, the sort that Alex's eldest son used on his school team.

Carly pulled out a magazine and shoved the bat back in.

"It was a pleasant surprise to see both you and Sam pop in on Saturday," Astrid said, eyeing the bag as Carly zipped it closed.

"As hard as I try," Carly said, "I never quite get my notes finished. I can take stuff home to read and plan, but I can't access the system from home to enter anything. At least I'm caught up for now."

"I suppose the therapists don't cross paths with the kitchen staff too often."

"Not too often," Carly said. "I think Sam is actually an employee of Sycamore Hills. Technically the therapists work for an outside agency contracted to provide services here, so we don't go to staff meetings or employee events."

"Sam seems very nice," Astrid said.

"I've only talked to him a few times. Once we walked out together at the end of the day and discovered we had parked next to each other."

"A serendipitous moment," Astrid said. Carly began to wrap her foot in warm cloths.

"I suppose." Carly chuckled. "He did come to my rescue when I was about to spill a pile of ill-balanced reading material all over the parking lot."

"So he's thoughtful. I suspected as much."

"He seems like a sharp guy."

Ah. So Carly had noticed.

"Friendly, too," Astrid said.

"No question about that."

"Helpful and responsible," Astrid said. "He came in on his day off, after all, just to be sure the meals were right."

"I hear people mention him now and then," Carly said. "He gets out and about for someone whose job is overseeing the kitchen."

"One must never let one's job confine one," Astrid said. "I learned that lesson when I was half your age."

"Did you have a job you didn't care for?" Carly repositioned a pillow and gestured that Astrid recline if she wanted to.

"Several," Astrid said, "but never a job I wasn't grateful for. Life wasn't easy after the war. My father wanted to rebuild, but he lost his property."

"Lost it? How?"

"The building had belonged to a Jew before my father bought it. Papa had all the documents to prove that he had paid the owner in full through the bank, but the bank said none of the money reached Jewish owners. It had all been confiscated by the Nazis without notifying anyone. Many Jews returned to Germany after the war, and the previous owner of Papa's building was one of them. Since he had never been paid, he was entitled to the property."

Carly dropped onto a stool. "So your family still had nothing?"

"Nothing. Most owners received money from the Allies to rebuild, but we were not so fortunate. Papa was fifty-six and had to start from scratch."

"My mother is fifty-six," Carly said. "My dad passed away a few years ago, but he left some life insurance, and she has a home and a job and a retirement account. I hate to think what her life would be like if she lost everything now."

"Papa was shocked. We all were. But he would have started over."

"Would have? What happened?"

"A year later he was accused of a crime—the crime of speaking without thinking of the consequences. He had trusted the wrong person, after all, and because of one sentence, a friend was sent to the Russian front, where he was killed."

"Surely he could not be held responsible. He didn't know. And the war was over."

"Nothing made sense in those days. When the summons for his arrest arrived, my aunt helped him get false papers and escape with a group of refugees. Eventually he found work—nothing like having his own Apotheke—but my parents lived apart for ten years. We couldn't tell anyone."

"Oh, Astrid!"

"It was hard," Astrid said. "Papa's dreams for us never came true. I do not make light of it. But I joined the church during those difficult times in the countryside, so I would never take them back. My faith gives me such hope."

She had barely finished elementary school at age fourteen when Mama found a job for her. She was up every day at four in the morning to take a workers bus into Würzburg, surrounded by grimy railroad workers who smoked. No other girls or women rode this bus, but Astrid had no other way to get to the job her mother had arranged for her with the woman who had designed Mama's dresses in better times. Once, she missed the bus back to the village in the afternoon and had to walk the twenty-four kilometers. It took seven hours.

The next year she worked for a dentist's family as domestic help—scrubbing floors, harvesting fall vegetables, pulling up weeds, running errands, looking after the baby. Every two weeks she had a weekend off. Papa was away all those years and Harald had moved to Munich. Mama became ill, and Uta was too young to look after her. Astrid pedaled back and forth on a bicycle, losing weight by the week, until her aunt had to come and nurse them all back to health. But in postwar Germany, Astrid was grateful to have any work at all that might contribute to the welfare of her family.

Later, a toothache took Astrid to her aunt's dentist, where she met the dentist's son, who was also a dentist. He wanted to marry, and if it hadn't been for Heinz, they might have wed.

"I find Sam charming." Astrid made a minute adjustment in the wrap on her foot. "I once knew someone very much like Sam. Married him, as a matter of fact."

Carly's eyes widened.

"I took my brother's fresh laundry to him in Munich," Astrid said. "He was at the university there, living on bread and cheese. Heinz was his friend. He was a refrigeration engineer for the Americans, setting up refrigeration for the snack bars all around Munich. One day I arrived just as Harald and Heinz were getting ready for a bicycle outing. Heinz insisted I should come and scrounged up a bicycle for me to borrow."

She would never forget that day. The ride through the lush, green, wooded area. The spring sun. The ancient tower that was all that was left of a medieval castle. Walking along the Isar River talking. The very day that Heinz said he was falling in love with Astrid. He had just received a visa to immigrate to America.

America!

Heinz looked her in the eye and asked if she would like to join him there someday.

How could this be? They had just met!

Emotions kicked into high gear, though. They got engaged on her eighteenth birthday a few weeks later, in May, and then married in September. They managed a honeymoon in a mountain resort, and then lived in Munich for three months before it was time for Heinz to leave. A married woman whose husband was an ocean away, Astrid moved back in with her mother and sister to await news that she could join Heinz. Finally he found someone to sponsor her immigration. Though this meant she was leaving her mother and sister, still in destitute circumstances after eight years, nothing could have stopped Astrid from boarding the boat. After all the Nazi years, after all the circumstances that took her father away and altered the family's financial and social standing, life in Germany remained arduous. She shed no tears when she left Mama and Uta. It seemed that members of the family had to find their own ways to a better life. No one earned enough to keep the family out of poverty. After a year apart, Astrid and Heinz were finally together again in Cleveland, Ohio.

Heinz had rented a room for the two of them with a German family. After three happy months, Heinz received a draft notice into the US army. There was no choice. Heinz would go into the army, and Astrid would work in a candy factory and try to learn English.

One morning just after five, as she was getting ready for work, the doorbell rang. Astrid opened the door, and an army officer handed her a telegram.

WE ARE SORRY TO INFORM YOU THAT YOUR HUSBAND HEINZ ASMUS WAS KILLED DUE TO A HAND GRENADE EXPLOSION THIS MORNING, THE 18TH OF JANUARY, 1954. *STOP*

She screamed.

Heinz was gone.

Carly's eyes were saucers as she listened. The wraps around

Astrid's foot had gone cold during the telling.

"But you hardly had any time together." Carly's voice caught.

"Just a breath," Astrid said. "I choose to believe we would have been deliriously happy for the rest of our long lives."

Carly removed the wraps and began manipulating Astrid's foot, gently testing progress in range of motion.

"And Sam reminds you of your husband?" Carly said.

"Yes. At least in how I remember him. It's been nearly sixty years. Sam has the same light in his eyes Heinz had. Heinz knew what he wanted and went after it."

"Including you," Carly said.

Astrid laughed softly. "Yes, including me. I was well loved."

Carly turned away for supplies.

"Someday," Astrid said. "Don't lose hope."

Carly shook her head and sighed heavily. "I have a feeling you mean Sam. He seems nice, but I'm not looking. I missed my chance for Prince Charming when I squandered it on Tyler's father. That was a mistake from the get-go."

Astrid sat up and reached for Carly's hand and locked on her eyes. "Don't lose hope."

"It's not that easy."

"You're not alone. There is always a second chance."

Chapter 16

A strid had always been a newspaper person. Alex and Ingrid claimed they got all the news they needed by reading on their phones. Astrid had a phone. It was even a smartphone, thanks to Alex's insistence. And she even knew how to send a text and get on the Internet. But it wasn't the same as pouring a second cup of coffee and unfolding a newspaper to leisurely look at whatever piqued her interest.

After her therapy session with Carly finished, Astrid took the elevator downstairs, rolled through the dining room into the adjoining bistro for coffee. Someone had assembled a tabletop tree since yesterday, bringing the total to seven. Astrid got lucky. A staff person was tidying up the bistro.

"Have you come for your newspaper coffee?" Maureen said.

Astrid nodded. Eight days at Sycamore Hills and already she had a recognizable habit. "When I break free of this contraption on wheels, I'll be able to pour my own coffee and carry it across the hall."

"Until then, it's my privilege to do it for you."

Astrid made a wide turn and headed to the library, where she chose a table near the window and across the room from the fireplace and tree. Compared to the towering trees of the lobby and parlor, this one looked ordinary. It was the ornaments that drew her attention, as they had for the last week. The entire set was cross-stitched little vignettes of the Christmas story, or symbols that had come to be associated with Christmas, all in tiny gold-rimmed round frames. There must be a history to how Sycamore Hills came to possess this collection. Perhaps it had been donated by one of the residents. Certainly it reflected years of dedicated work. Everyone had a story. Astrid would have to make a point to ask Penny about the ornaments.

Maureen set a steaming mug of coffee on the table. "Enjoy. You can give me the news highlights later."

Astrid smiled and picked up the mug to breathe in the aroma before testing the temperature against her lips. After a satisfying swallow, she smoothed the newspaper in front of her and began with the front page. This was a local paper that wouldn't take long to consume. Then she would move on to what she thought of as the big city paper.

She finished her coffee halfway through the second paper and leaned over to move the mug out of her way.

Her pants pocket rang. That's what her youngest grand-daughter said when a cell phone went off in someone's pocket. Astrid leaned to one side so she could release the phone from dark captivity. The screen announced Alex was calling.

"Alex! How are you?"

"I'm doing well, Mom. How about you?"

"Settling in."

"Therapy going well?"

"I can very nearly pick up a small marble with my toes."

Alex laughed. "A useful skill, no doubt."

"No doubt. How is France?"

"Complicated." Alex's jovial tone shifted. "I was supposed to fly home tomorrow, but this deal is taking longer than I anticipated."

Astrid moistened her lips and awaited explanation.

"Just a couple more days," Alex said. "It's still a week until Christmas. I have plenty of time to get home, and we'll all have Christmas together just like we planned."

"Of course we will," Astrid said. "You should see this place now. They take the holidays very seriously at Sycamore Hills. Trees and tinsel and garland everywhere."

"I haven't even seen the tree at my own house yet," Alex said. "The boys promised to put it up while I was gone."

"Then I'm sure they have."

"Have you heard from Ingrid?"

"Only briefly. That reminds me—do you recall what you did with the gold ornaments?"

"The ones from your grandmother?"

"Yes, those." What other gold ornaments would she be asking about? "I asked that we be sure they came with me here."

"I remember," Alex said. "I packed them up myself. I'm sorry I couldn't stay long enough to unpack the boxes, but they should be in one of them."

"I've unpacked everything," Astrid said, "and they weren't there."

"Are you sure you didn't miss a box?"

She was living in six hundred and twenty-three square feet and had only a small front closet and a larger one in the bedroom. It wasn't as if a box could have been set down someplace where she wouldn't easily see it.

"Are we sure we got everything off the truck?" Astrid said.

"I looked in the empty U-Haul myself. They'll turn up."

Astrid controlled her sigh so Alex wouldn't hear it. The ornaments wouldn't simply "turn up." She was quite sure they weren't in the apartment.

"So you're rebooked for the day after tomorrow?" she said.

"Right. I'll get in late, but I'll pop over the day after that."

"It will be good to see you." He would see for himself that the ornaments weren't there. Her stomach squeezed at the thought that three ornaments that survived the bombing of Würzburg and spent a year buried under rubble would now be lost to negligence.

"My meeting is about to start," Alex said. "I'll talk to you soon."

He clicked off, and Astrid's phone went dark. She dropped it into the scooter's bag and returned to perusing the big city newspaper. About the time she wished she had another half cup of coffee, the commotion began. Even in the library down the hall from the reception desk, it was hard to ignore the fact that something was happening—and had the potential to go wrong. Astrid closed the newspaper, folded it—she was never one to leave a mess—and arranged herself on the scooter to navigate toward the sound.

"Carly," a man said, his volume raised. "She's a physical therapist who works here. You must know her."

"I'm sorry, sir," the receptionist said. "I don't know the name."

"Well, look at a list or something," he said. "You must have an employee directory."

Astrid stayed behind the broad lobby Christmas tree and peered between its long branches laden in gold.

"There is no Carly on the list," the receptionist said. "I think I heard that the therapists are contracted through an agency, not employees."

"What's the name of the agency?"

"That's not information I have, but I can try to find out."

"You do that."

The young woman at the desk picked up a phone and pushed several buttons before dipping her head and lowering her voice. Astrid watched the man. He didn't look like the demanding sort, but he certainly acted the part. A flash of dark hair caught in her peripheral vision, and Astrid raised her head slightly to see Carly cautiously leaning over the railing at the top of the stairs. She should have been in the middle of a session, but the sound of the insistent man surely would have carried up the stairs to the therapy room. Blanched, Carly quickly withdrew.

The receptionist put the phone down. "I'm afraid I can't answer your question."

Because she hadn't gotten an answer, or because she'd been instructed not to give out the information? Astrid suspected the latter.

"Then just point me to wherever the physical therapists work," the man said, his tone abruptly becoming congenial. "I'm an old friend. I just want to say hello."

Astrid didn't believe that for a moment.

"If you'd like to leave a message," the receptionist said, "I'll give it to the therapy supervisor. She'll know whether someone named Carly is assigned to this location."

"I'm here now," he said. "Wouldn't it be easier if I just popped in and saved you the trouble?"

"That's not our policy, sir. No matter who comes in the building, we verify the reason for the safety of all our residents."

Behind Astrid, the elevator doors opened, and she looked over her shoulder. Carly emerged, glanced at Astrid, and turned to walk swiftly down the hall to an exit that would take her to the other side of the building. There was no parking lot over there, just a sidewalk that looped the building and a small area where people could take their dogs. The duffel hung from Carly's left shoulder, and as she walked she pulled it to the front and unzipped it partway to plunge her hand in.

It was no easy feat to turn the scooter around in small spaces, but Astrid managed and rolled off in the direction Carly had gone. This man was somehow the reason Carly began carrying a baseball bat. But even on wheels, Astrid couldn't catch up with Carly, who shoved open an exit door and was out of sight.

Astrid once again turned around. This time she rolled into

the lobby without taking refuge behind a Christmas tree. The man was gone.

She smiled at the receptionist. "My, what an insistent visitor."

"We don't get many like him, that's for sure."

"Did he leave a message, after all?"

"No. He just said he would contact Carly another way."

Astrid cocked her head. "May I say I think you handled the situation quite well?"

"Thank you. He did rattle me a little. He finally said he had to get to work himself."

Astrid pushed off again and crossed to the front door. She hadn't been outside since arriving at Sycamore Hills more than a week ago. Winter air blasted in when the doors parted, but Astrid had never been afraid of a little weather, and the sidewalk was dry. She rolled out far enough to be sure the doors would close and then steadied herself on a bench. Pulling up the collar on his brown bomber jacket, the man strode to the end of the curved driveway that came through the portico. For a moment, Astrid feared he would pace around the corner of the building, where there was more parking. Carly had exited the other side of the building, but if she went to her car and this man explored the parking lots, he might yet find her. Astrid would never be able to roll around fast enough to warn Carly.

The man paused at the corner, looked down the side of the building, and checked his watch. He turned toward a vehicle parked in front, a fancy SUV-type of car that Astrid never learned to tell apart from all the other SUV models. He opened the door and got behind the wheel. She would just stand there long enough to make sure he left.

The doors behind Astrid whooshed open.

"Goodness," Maureen said, "when they told me you'd gone

outside I couldn't believe it. It's freezing and you have no coat. Come back inside."

"A breath of fresh air never hurt anyone," Astrid said. The man's car started and he backed out of his parking spot.

"It's cold, and you have your foot to think of. You shouldn't be out here alone."

"Well, I wouldn't want to start a rumor that I'm thoroughly lacking in common sense." Astrid turned her scooter around, watching as the man left the parking lot and turned onto the road.

Now the question was where Carly had gone.

CHAPTER 17

Carly waited. She didn't go to her car. Truman knew her car all too well. A new car was rising on her convoluted priority list. She'd get a different car that he couldn't spot easily, and she'd have the windows tinted so no one could look in easily. The next job would have to be farther away, and she'd have to figure out what to do for Tyler.

At first Carly huddled in the chilly stairwell, sitting on a step beside the exit. When three employees came through, each one asking if she was all right, she ventured outside. With the duffel over her shoulder and her hand on the bat inside it, she stuck herself to the exterior wall and inched to the corner where she could get a good look at the front parking lot.

The SUV—the same one she'd seen the other day—eased into traffic on the road. The exit door had closed behind her, and she didn't have a badge that would open it, so she freshened her grip on the bat and followed the sidewalk that took her back to the front of the building. So far he hadn't circled back. It was the middle of the day. He should be at work.

But he knew where to find her. Again.

Carly took her phone from a pocket, debating whether to punch in a number. Just because he'd tracked her down didn't mean he knew where Tyler's new school was, and the school was strict about having authorizations on file for anyone allowed to pick up a child. They even required photos, which none of the other schools had done. For now, she wouldn't call the school. Instead her finger hovered over her mother's contact listing in her phone. Her mother had worked for the same company for the last twelve years—and they already had an alert and a physical description at the reception desk. Carly dropped her phone back in the bag. Eventually she'd tell her mother about today, but in the meantime Carly didn't need maternal advice. She knew what she had to do.

She went through the automatic front doors and fixed her intention on the wide public staircase, making sure her agency ID bag was plain to see in case anyone stopped her. At least she hadn't left a patient hanging when she made her escape. Now, though, her free hour was just about up. Only a few minutes were required for what she had in mind.

At the far end of the room, one of the other therapists worked with a man who had fallen and injured his rotator cuff. He glanced up only briefly, and Carly went to the corner of the room that functioned as a shared-space office. On one of the laptops the therapists used, she opened a new document and began typing. She didn't need a lot of time. She'd done this often enough that she only had to alter a few words in the letter imprinted in her brain.

Privilege to work.

Admire the patients.

Circumstances have shifted.

Two weeks.

Carly hit PRINT and walked over to the printer to receive the single sheet it spit out before anyone else saw it. There was nothing to do but give up and move on. The police weren't much help, and she certainly didn't want to endanger any of the residents of Sycamore Hills with the possibility that Truman would force his way past the front desk.

Patricia, who supervised all the therapists—physical, occupational, and speech and language—strode into the room. Carly folded the sheet into thirds and sat down at a desk and started flipping through a procedures guide. With the letter still in one hand, she shuffled several folders. She knew what she had to do, but every time she got nervous.

"Good morning," Patricia said, draping her coat over the back of a chair.

"Good morning," Carly said.

Patricia glanced at the desk where Carly sat. "I thought we discussed the necessity that you get your paperwork up-to-date on your own time if that's what it takes to keep up.

Carly removed her hands from the folders.

"I caught up over the weekend," Carly said.

"Good. A fresh start. It won't always take this long, now that you've learned our system."

Carly nodded. "I. . . I. . ." She swallowed hard.

"What is it, Carly?" Patricia stepped closer.

Carly thrust the letter toward her. "I'm sorry. I really hoped I would be able to stay much longer."

Patricia's forehead scrunched into three distinct rows as she unfolded the paper.

"A resignation?" Patricia said.

"Two weeks' notice." The words caught in Carly's throat, giving her a gravelly tone. Starting tonight, she would spend her evenings on the Internet looking for a job. Maybe she'd take a break from working as a physical therapist. Another type of work could make it harder for Truman to find her. She couldn't ask her mother to move to another county or even another state, but she and Tyler certainly could.

"I'm sure this is not necessary," Patricia said. "I run a tight ship, but that doesn't mean I don't value what everyone on the team brings."

"I appreciate that," Carly said. "I really do. It's not working out for. . .other reasons. It has nothing to do with you or Sycamore Hills."

"I don't know what you're talking about." Patricia opened a locker and stowed her purse. "You're a fine therapist with a lovely, gentle touch for the older population we serve here."

"I'm really sorry." Carly didn't know what else to say.

"Two weeks, it says here."

Carly nodded.

"I have a counterproposal." Patricia put the folded letter on the desk and slid it toward Carly. "Let's make sure the stress of the holidays isn't influencing your decision. I won't start the wheels moving on this just yet. In two weeks, the holidays will be behind us, and we'll talk again then."

No one had ever refused Carly's resignation before. Her last supervisor had told her to gather her things and go the same day. She stared at the paper on the desk, not wanting to pick it up but not wanting anyone else to see it, either.

"Two weeks," Patricia said. "The same two weeks you offered me. You have nothing to lose. If after we talk you still feel you should leave, I'll work with you for a short transition."

Carly ran her tongue over her dry lips. "All right."

"It's Christmas! Let's just enjoy the season without making life-altering decisions. Anything can happen in two weeks."

That was just it. Anything could happen in two weeks.

CHAPTER 18

After a week and a day at Sycamore Hills, Astrid had figured out the dining room. She knew what time to go down for a meal if she wanted to socialize with Betty's Brood, and what time to go if she preferred to sit by the window and linger in solitude. This was one of the lunchtimes when she wanted space to think. Betty's Brood had come and gone, and Astrid slid into a seat and ordered the tomato soup and a tuna sandwich—choices that wouldn't put the kitchen into chaos at a time when Sam would be trying to close up lunch and prepare for dinner.

Something was wrong with Carly. The baseball bat. Sneaking out a back exit. Tears when Astrid talked about Heinz.

Today wasn't a therapy day for Astrid. If she saw Carly at all, it would be an incidental encounter. But Astrid would be ready. There was more to the story than Heinz. The last of the lunch eaters straggled out. Astrid declined dessert—ice cream wasn't her favorite—and accepted a cup of coffee to top off her meal. The young woman who waited on her had figured out that Astrid liked a generous dose of milk in her coffee, though she would drink it black if she had to. She had done too many things in her life out of necessity to make a fuss about milk. Staring out the window and wondering what the back gardens, now crusted with snow, would be like in the spring, she lifted her coffee cup for a final swallow.

"Well, look who's closing down the joint once again."

Astrid pulled her gaze from the window and smiled at Sam.

"I order the simplest items when I come down late," she said. "But you may tell me at any time that I should come earlier."

Sam folded himself into a chair across the table. "I understand solitude. Not everyone likes a crowd every moment of the day."

"Yes, very true," Astrid said. Alex and Ingrid had been out of the house for ages, and Astrid had become quite accustomed to keeping her own hours, including eating when she felt like it or got in the mood for something in particular.

Sam pointed to a square table against a wall. "We have a suggestion box. You can be anonymous and tell us exactly what you think."

"Why would I not just tell you to your face?" Not that there was anything to remark on. She was still getting used to the freedom of eating without the trouble of cooking and cleaning up. She was likely to gain five pounds in her first month at this rate.

Sam laughed. "Some people like it that way. Maybe they think I'll put arsenic in their food if I don't like their opinions."

"Do you get many comments?"

"Thankfully, no."

Astrid pushed her empty coffee cup away. "I should get out of the way so your staff can do their jobs."

"You're not in the way," Sam said. "In fact, I'm glad I ran into you. I know you're new here, and I heard you didn't bring a car."

"True enough." Even if she had argued more firmly with Alex about hanging on to her reliable old car, she couldn't drive right now anyway.

"I'm in a choir for Christmas," Sam said. "In fact, I even have a solo."

"Congratulations! I'm sure it will be lovely."

"You could come hear me—on Christmas Eve. If you want to, I'd be happy to come fetch you."

"That would have been delightful," Astrid said, "but I will be with my children and their families."

Sam nodded. "That's nice for you. I just thought I would offer."

"Maybe Carly would like to go. You could at least ask."

Sam pushed air out of his lungs. "I try to ask Carly a lot of things, but she always looks distracted or like I'm disturbing her."

"I'm sorry."

"It's not your fault."

"Keep trying," Astrid said. "Something tells me Carly could really use someone on her side."

"I'll think about it." Sam stood up. "Time to transform this place into a dining wonder."

"What's on the menu tonight?"

"Pot roast for a hundred people."

Astrid laughed. "That's no small feat." She pushed her chair back and reached for her scooter.

"Don't forget you owe me some German recipes," Sam said, holding the scooter steady while Astrid got her knee situated on it.

"You'll be pleased to know that my cookbooks surfaced in the unpacking." She didn't need the cookbooks, both because she had prepared her favorite foods hundreds of times and because she no longer had the large, comfortable dining room that made cooking for groups rewarding. Finding the missing ornaments would have pleased her more than figuring out what to do with cookbooks in her shiny but compact kitchen. She should give them to Ingrid or to Gwen, Alex's wife.

"See you at dinner," Sam said. "I know you don't like ice cream, but maybe you'll have room for apple pie."

Astrid wagged her eyebrows and pushed off. Both her orthopedist and Carly were consistently vague about how much longer she would need the scooter, but Astrid was ready to skip the walker phase and exchange her wheels for a cane.

Several times a day now, the gold-strewn tree in the lobby reminded her of the missing ornaments. She could do nothing until Alex came home. Somebody must have gotten the boxes mixed up, and the one she wanted was in a storage unit to be sorted later. She hoped they were there and he was confused about what he'd done with them. This might be the first Christmas without the ornaments since the year she rescued them from the rubble. Astrid turned away from the tree and rolled to the elevator and pushed the UP button. Getting out on the second floor, she paused on the broad landing when she saw Betty's Brood were playing cards at the round table.

"Always room for one more," Betty said.

"Come sit next to me," Mae said.

Astrid shook her head. "I must go back to my apartment and practice picking up marbles with my toes."

The remark got the laughter she expected and Astrid resumed her course. At the door to the exercise and therapy room, she slowed and scanned as much of the room as she could see through the opening. Carly was wiping down some equipment and looked up.

"Hi," Carly said, sounding tentative.

"Don't worry," Astrid said. "I haven't gone dotty. We don't have an appointment today. I just wanted to see how you are."

Carly shrugged one shoulder. "All right."

Astrid bit back the temptation to comment that she had seen Carly avoiding the man in the lobby the previous day. Carly might tell her what that was about, but on her own terms. The duffel with the bat was once again against the wall behind a desk. In the meantime, though, Astrid could continue her story.

"Do you have any free time this afternoon?" The room was empty, and if there were any appointments during this hour, the therapists would have been at work.

"A few minutes," Carly said. "I have documenting to get done at some point today."

"I won't take up too much of your time." Astrid adjusted the angle of the scooter to enter the room. "I felt like I left off an important part of my story the other day."

"About Heinz?"

"Heinz and Peter," Astrid said.

"Who's Peter?" Carly tossed the towel she'd been using onto the corner of a desk.

"The star of another Christmas story." Astrid sat in a chair against the wall, and Carly angled another chair toward her. "I told you about Heinz."

"So awful for you! I can't imagine."

"Neither could I, but one carries on. I had Heinz's 1947 Plymouth, one suitcase with my clothes, a painting from my parents, and a box of family photos."

"The ones we looked at the other day?"

"Yes, that was some of them." Astrid didn't tell this story often, but Carly needed to hear it.

She had moved in with a girlfriend and worked in a department store. In the evenings, she went to classes of immigrants trying to learn English. One day at the store, her friend Elisabeth waited on a German man and called Astrid over to meet him. He had just graduated from Indiana Tech University and was hired by a company in Cleveland as an engineer. Elisabeth stepped away and gave Astrid the sale. Peter, his name was, bought a pair of leather gloves. By the time he left, Peter had both their names and phone number.

Two days later, he called and asked Astrid for a date. They went to dinner to get acquainted. Peter told her about his life in the German army, his escape, and how he came to be in the United States. After that Peter came to visit nearly every day. A month after they first met—on Thanksgiving—Peter slipped an engagement ring on Astrid's finger, and they planned to marry a couple of months later.

Yet Astrid was unsure. She twisted the ring around her finger, starting to pull it off and then pushing it back on. She lay awake at night wondering if she was on the brink of a big mistake. Could she really become engaged to a man she'd only just met? Of course, she had done this with Heinz, but did that mean it was right to do with Peter? She was still only nineteen. Confused, Astrid returned the ring to Peter.

The weeks passed and the season moved into Christmas—a time of making peace. Peter wrote to Astrid's parents asking for her hand in marriage, and they replied with their approval. Astrid's doubts thinned, and she put the ring back on her finger.

"He sounds persistent," Carly said.

Astrid smiled, her gaze drifting over Carly's shoulder as Peter's face filled her mind. "He was. And I'm so grateful. He gave me a second chance at love."

"So you married him?"

Astrid nodded. "It was Christmas that brought us back together. Christmas love and Christmas hope."

"That's a sweet story." Carly fiddled with her fingernails.

"Everyone has a story," Astrid said softly.

"But not every story has a sweet ending." Carly looked away.

"No." Astrid debated whether to continue telling this particular story. "But sometimes it helps to tell your story."

Carly squirmed in her chair.

"You don't have to say anything," Astrid said. "I tell my story so you can understand that I have known both great pain and great joy. There will be a new chapter for your story. I'm sure of it."

"Well, I'm not," Carly muttered. She stood up and replaced her chair in its spot against the wall. "Thanks for stopping by. I'd better get my desk work finished before my next appointment."

CHAPTER 19

It was too early in the morning for a phone call, yet the cell phone on Astrid's nightstand was ringing. She rolled over, realized that she was in peril of missing breakfast completely, and answered the phone.

"Ingrid!"

"Hi, Mom."

Astrid pushed herself upright in the bed. "What's wrong?"

"Ellie is pretty sick."

"I'm sorry to hear that."

"We've been to the doctor a couple of times."

"Antibiotics?"

"Yes. The liquid pink stuff that she hates."

"If she swallows enough it will do her good anyway."

Ingrid's sigh into the phone was heavy. "That's not all."

"What else?" Astrid snapped on the nightstand light to dispel the streaks of gray still hovering between stripes of daylight coming through the blinds.

"The doctor thinks that maybe we shouldn't travel for Christmas."

"Oh, no."

"I could just cry, Mom. In fact, I have."

"Oh, sweetheart, what a disappointment—for all of us." Astrid would never tell the rest of her grandchildren, but she did feel a particular affinity for Ellie.

"He thinks we might need a stronger antibiotic, but the main thing is that she needs rest."

"She could rest at Alex's house when we're together."

"She won't want to," Ingrid said. "Can you imagine me trying to convince her to stay in bed, or even on the couch with a movie, with everything else that goes on?"

"I see your point."

"Anyway, the doctor wants to see her again."

"When?"

"That depends on how the next few days go."

"I'm sure Ellie is as disappointed as the rest of us."

"She is. She keeps trying to prove she's not so sick, after all, but that only lasts about twenty minutes before she starts coughing up a lung."

"It does sound like she needs to stay home where she can rest without fuss."

"Her sister is beside herself."

"Of course she is." Astrid eyed the chair across the bedroom where she had placed the gifts she had ready for Christmas Day. Even if she could get them boxed up and to the post office today—which she couldn't—there was no guarantee mailed packages would arrive in time without paying dearly for overnight delivery. If any of Betty's Brood had a license and a car, they hadn't yet mentioned it. Astrid didn't even know where the post office was in this town, and she had already flattened and disposed of the moving cartons she'd unpacked.

"It's all a mess." Ingrid's voice sagged. "I am not the least bit prepared to make a nice Christmas here. We didn't even put up a tree."

"I'm sure whatever you're able to do will be lovely. Shall I talk with the girls and try to cheer them?"

"Ellie's sleeping—she was up half the night—and I put Ava on the bus half an hour ago."

"Later, then," Astrid said. "I can call in the afternoon, when Ava's home from school. How would that be?"

"I'm sure they'd both like to talk to you."

"Then we'll do it."

"Thanks, Mom. We have gifts for you, but. . ."

"No worries. We'll just call all our packages New Year's gifts, and everything will arrive right on time."

Astrid set the phone down and reached for the scooter. Ravenous, she was in no mood to skip breakfast. In her years of living alone, she'd often slept as long as she liked in the mornings, or she'd make coffee and take the newspaper back to bed to peruse. A geriatric population shouldn't be expected to conform to an early breakfast. The mental list of groceries she wanted to keep in the apartment grew steadily. How was it that she had moved into this apartment with a coffeemaker but without even a bag of ground coffee?

Astrid hustled—as much as a person in a brace riding a scooter could hustle—to make sure she got downstairs in enough time to at least ask for a couple slices of toast and some coffee. She didn't spot Betty and the others anywhere on her way down or while she sat in the dining room. Perhaps they'd gone back to their rooms to nap, as Astrid was tempted to do. To keep out of the way of the staff straightening the dining room at the end of the meal, she folded her toast into a napkin, set it in the basket attached to the scooter, and rolled into the bistro hoping to see Maureen.

"The library?" Maureen asked.

Astrid nodded.

"Coffee with lots of milk coming right up."

Astrid smiled and kept moving. She wondered how many people ever used the library or read the newspapers there. Not a soul had ever been in there at the same time she was. Settling into a chair, she unfolded the napkin. When Maureen entered, steam was visible from the cup.

"You spoil me," Astrid said. "How do you always manage to be in the bistro making coffee at the exact minute I want some?"

"It's a special gift that I can't divulge." Maureen waved over her shoulder and left Astrid to her papers.

She had finished the big city paper and had just opened the regional publication when her phone rang for the second time that morning.

"Mom, it's me, Alex."

"Good morning, Alex—or whatever time of day it is in France."

"Afternoon."

Alex sounded no more cheerful than Ingrid had an hour ago.

"Is your deal not working out?" Astrid asked.

"Everything is fine in that department. It's a good solid deal that everyone is happy with."

"Then why do you sound so disconsolate?"

"I'm afraid I have to delay coming home again."

"Oh?"

"Another employee from my team was in on the meetings, and she's found herself in some trouble."

"What sort of trouble?"

"She rented a bicycle to pedal through the countryside this afternoon, and a car hit her a few hours ago. Mom, she's in critical condition. I can't just leave her and get on a plane tonight."

"Of course not."

"I got hold of her husband and he was going to call her parents. I'm sure someone will want to fly over, but I don't know when that will be. And she needs surgery. Somebody has to be here, and for now I'm that somebody."

"I understand," Astrid said, leaning back in her chair and allowing her shoulders to droop.

"It could take a couple days for them to get here," Alex said.

"Finding flights at this time of year, making arrangements to be gone indefinitely. They have small children to think of. Maybe the grandparents will help. I just don't know what to predict. I might not make it home in time for Christmas Eve."

"You're a good soul, Alex." She might as well make the best of the situation. If Alex were the one in critical condition in another country, Astrid would like to think a coworker would stand by until the crisis passed.

"I'm sorry, Mom. I know there are things I promised to help with to get you settled in."

"No problem. These things can't be helped."

"Hopefully I won't completely miss Christmas Day."

"Hopefully. You still have a few days." Despite this response, Astrid's intuition suggested she must prepare herself for the possibility that she would be on her own at least for Christmas Eve. Alex's wife, Gwen, would still come for her on Christmas Day, she supposed. "I expect to speak to Ingrid later today. I'll let her know what happened."

"Thanks. Hopefully her trip will go smoothly."

Astrid didn't answer. It seemed premature to dash Alex's hopes. Gwen would need to know soon, though. If Ingrid's family of four weren't coming, it would change all the plans.

"You stay as long as you need to," Astrid said. "Of course your family wants you home, but you needn't rush on my account. I am safe and warm and eating well."

They said their good-byes, and Astrid dropped the phone back into the bag. Christmas was sure to be different this year. Ingrid's family made the eight-hour drive every year. The girls looked forward to a week with their grandmother and cousins. All the children disappeared into the wide-open finished basement of Astrid's house, and the grown-ups barely saw them until hunger drove one of them upstairs. Astrid had imagined they would do the same thing now that the traditional festivities had shifted to Alex's home, but it seemed that the whole season would be a series of adjustments.

"Okay, then," she said aloud to the empty room. "Christmas is still Christmas even if it looks a little different. We'll survive."

She had been through worse. All the Christmases during the war when Papa put forth his best effort, but the family still knew that they could end up in the bomb shelter. All the Christmases after the war, when her family was impoverished and separated, each of them just trying to find a way to survive. The first Christmas after losing Heinz, confused by also being the first Christmas with Peter. All the Christmases when it was just her and the children, an ocean away from her mama and papa and Harald and Uta.

It would be all right. After losing Heinz, she'd had a lovely life with Peter. She'd gotten the education she missed in Germany and raised two children she'd always wanted. Her own photo albums showed them every year hanging the gold ornaments. She had no regrets—only hope.

Chapter 20

Carly's mother had canceled her newspaper subscription long ago. Between television news and their computers and phones, they had all the news they needed. What they didn't have, however, was loose paper to stuff around gifts that might shake too hard. Carly headed to the library to find old newspapers that would soon enough be in the recycling bin anyway. And it wouldn't hurt to have some of the older magazines in the therapy room for patients to pass the time. She hadn't expected to find Astrid in there.

"Oh, hello," Carly said.

Astrid looked up, tears gleaming.

"Are you all right?" Carly crossed the room and pulled out a chair beside Astrid.

"Perfectly fine," Astrid said. "Although I find myself in need of a tissue."

Carly looked around the room, spotted a box of tissues, and got up to claim it. Astrid pulled one out and delicately wiped her nose.

"Are you sure you're all right?" Carly fixed her eyes on Astrid's face, wondering if Astrid had been having crying fits ever since moving to Sycamore Hills. The last thing Carly would say to her was *It will be all right*. She hated when people said that about situations that had nothing to do with them. She already knew that Astrid had been through enough hardship that the phrase would hardly be reassuring.

"I'll be fine." Astrid dabbed at her eyes with a second tissue. "I was just remembering the first Christmas with my husband."

"Oh." Carly sifted bits of information in her mind trying to discern whether she should know how long ago Astrid's second husband had passed away. For all she knew, it might have been only a few weeks ago. "Everyone grieves in different ways."

"Oh, I'm not grieving," Astrid said. "Not anymore."

"Something else happened?"

"Memories of a sweet life," Astrid said. "How fortunate I was to have two great loves. It's hard to believe that part of my life ended forty years ago."

Forty years?

Carly tilted her head. "Peter died forty years ago?"

Astrid nodded. "In February it will be forty years."

Carly sank back in her chair. "And you never married again?"

"No. I had opportunities, but Peter was the man I built a life with. Our children were—and are—great comfort."

Astrid never struck Carly as being as old as her chart said she was, so Carly was stumbling over the math. By the time Astrid was barely forty, she'd been widowed twice.

"I'm so grateful," Astrid said.

Grateful? To be widowed twice?

"It snowed the day we married," Astrid said. "Our witnesses were very late arriving. For a while I thought we would have to go out on the street and ask anyone we could find to be our witnesses. Whenever there's a snowstorm, I think of that day."

They were happy. Most young brides might have screamed at the sight of a mouse in the kitchen, but for Astrid it only reminded her of Wenkheim, the village where her family took refuge after Würzburg was bombed and the war ended. Though she could speak German with Peter, Astrid worked on her English every day. She listened to tapes over and over. She translated everything she read for the practice. And finally she was ready to enroll in an evening school offering high school classes.

She also worked for a bank as a bookkeeper and later as a teller. It took six years to earn a high school diploma, and once Astrid had that diploma in her hands, she entered university. Peter always encouraged her educational pursuits. Peter also went to evening classes. He worked on three different master's degrees—physics, mathematics, and operation research.

Eventually they had saved enough to purchase a home and make investments. Astrid stripped so much wallpaper that she became oblivious to the dripping dissolved paste, and if bits of wallpaper fell in her hair she left them there until she could clean up properly. Peter brought home gallons of paint and they freshened every room. Astrid's favorite room was the nursery. The baby was on the way, and sometimes Astrid just wanted to sit in the room where she would sing lullabies to her child.

Then came the job offer for Peter to work as an engineer on the Apollo space program—in Daytona Beach, Florida. The house was perfect, the baby was coming in six weeks, and they moved.

Astrid hadn't hesitated. The opportunity was Peter's dream. Of course they would go. Within a week, the movers had come to load the household goods, and the house was rented out. The baby came right on time. Alex.

Three years later, Ingrid arrived. Life was so leisurely in those days, enjoying the sunshine and the beach. Alex was an active toddler. He never walked but only ran, often falling facedown and ending up with scratches, bruises, and a swollen lip. Climbing on chairs to reach the cabinets caused him no distress, even though he fell more than once. If Astrid turned her back for a few seconds, she could never be sure what Alex would attempt. She traveled with the children to Germany to make sure they knew their family there. Harald, who had become a priest, showed Alex the bells in the church bell tower. Life was lovely.

Then the Apollo project ended, and all the missile specialists and engineers were laid off. The family moved to Philadelphia, where Peter worked as a civil service engineer. A few years later, he got sick.

During the war, Peter was in the German navy. He had been hospitalized in a military hospital in Greece with yellow jaundice for several months. His liver was badly damaged, although he never felt ill until all those years later. By that time he had interviewed for a dream job in Alexandria, Virginia. The evening he returned from his interviews, ebullient, seven times excruciating spasms gripped him. He passed out. The liver damage caught up with him with a vengeance. Astrid called an ambulance. The last time Alex and Ingrid saw their father was when Astrid smuggled them into his hospital room against the rules. Three days after the first pain, he died in the hospital.

Astrid sat in her kitchen, wondering what to do next. The phone ringing startled her, and for a moment she wanted only to make it stop. At the ninth ring, she picked it up.

A call from Virginia.

A voice full of enthusiasm to have Peter on their team.

When might they reach him?

Astrid let a long silence hang across the miles. No one could reach Peter now. He was in God's hands.

Astrid swallowed hard in the telling of all this.

"How awful for you," Carly said, her own eyes moist.

"No." Astrid shook her head. "We had twenty-one years together, and I never regretted a moment of it. I've been so blessed."

"Blessed?" Carly said. "You just told me about how your husband died."

"No," Astrid said, "I told you how he lived. How we both lived. How we raised our children to live."

"The war took so much from you." Carly pulled a tissue from the box. "In the end, it even took Peter."

"It also gave me Peter. The same dream for a better life that brought me here with Heinz also brought Peter. And it has been a better life."

Carly moistened her lips. "Even all these years. . .alone?"

Astrid shook her head. "I am never alone. God is always closer than we realize."

Carly looked at her lap.

"Think about it," Astrid said. "We all have stories, and it's a wonderful thing when our stories catch up with just the right person. It's the beauty of God Himself, showing Himself among us by pulling our stories into His great story of grace."

"I wish I could believe that."

"I wish that for you, too."

Carly blew out her breath. "I'd better get back upstairs. I have a patient."

CHAPTER 21

At home Astrid was accustomed to lunch out with a friend at least once a week. It was never anything fancy, just a chance to satisfy a craving or have a catch-up conversation away from the distractions that inevitably came up at home.

Astrid wanted to go out to eat.

Not because she didn't like Sam's menu, and not because she could identify a craving that the food of Sycamore Hills wouldn't meet. It was because she wanted to be at least a little bit nosy. Carly's face was more drawn each day and her posture more slumped.

When the posted lunch hours in the dining room began, Astrid instead went to the therapy and exercise room. She recognized the finishing-up movements of Carly, who laid a gentle hand on her patient's shoulder and handed her a photocopy of some suggested exercises, just as she had done for Astrid when their sessions ended. This time, though, Astrid wasn't there for therapy. She had deduced that the therapists avoided appointments at lunchtime so none of the residents would be anxious about missing a meal. She rolled in and waited for the fellow resident to gather her things and leave the room. Another therapist across the room similarly was finishing a session.

Carly looked up, a question in her features.

"I'm here to offer you a deal," Astrid said.

"A deal?" Carly said. "Have you got another therapist hidden away somewhere?"

Astrid smiled. "I would never do that to you."

"Glad to hear it."

"Do you get a lunch break?"

"Sort of. We usually catch up on documentation or make plans for sessions."

"I'd like to offer you an alternative, if you think you can squeeze it in."

"And this deal is?"

"Lunch. An actual lunch break involving food outside these walls. I'd love to treat you to lunch if you provide the transportation."

Carly narrowed her eyes. "I don't know. It's kind of wintry. Are you sure your physical therapist would approve of your going out?"

"I have a feeling she could be persuaded." Astrid winked. "Would there be anyone more safe for me to go out with? If you've got a car, I've got the cash. Let's go."

"Where?"

"You pick," Astrid said. "Someplace close and quick."

Carly slapped the manila folder she held against an open palm. "It might be nice to actually eat lunch."

"Indeed."

"You need a coat."

"I can just zip down the hall for it."

"Okay. I know a place with fast service. Let me get my things."

Astrid imagined Carly might don a jacket and scarf, and perhaps a purse. But once she was dressed for the cold outside air, she picked up that duffel and arranged its strap on her shoulder.

"Do we need all that?" Astrid said. "Just for a bite of lunch?"

"My purse is in it. I have to have my license to drive."

Astrid didn't argue the point further. Obviously Carly could have extracted her purse and left behind the bat and whatever else was in the bag.

Carly settled Astrid, coat on, in a chair in the lobby, nearest the doors, while she went to get her car from the back lot and bring it around to the portico. What was Carly afraid of that prodded her to carry a baseball bat? Fear was the only explanation Astrid could believe. But was it a justified fear? And would a baseball bat really solve it?

Astrid offered chitchat all the way to the restaurant, which was only a mile or so away from Sycamore Hills along the highway that wound its way through several towns in this part of the state. Carly assured her the place had good parking and she would have no trouble navigating her scooter inside. Once she had parked, Carly jumped out of her seat and scurried to the passenger side to assist Astrid. She pulled the scooter from the backseat, made sure Astrid had a good grip on it, and then reached back into the car for the duffel.

"Why don't you leave that?" Astrid said softly. "We'll eat, we'll talk, and we'll both feel better."

"I can't leave it," Carly said, her hand still on the open back door.

"Would I be intruding too much if I said I would like to understand why it's so important?"

"It's hard to explain." Carly's face twitched, her eyes shifting from Astrid to the duffel that was half out of the car.

"I'm a patient listener," Astrid said.

Carly sucked in her lips. Astrid waited and looked toward the restaurant entrance, only thirty feet away.

"I'll just put it under the table," Carly said. "It won't be in the way."

"Of course you must do whatever makes you comfortable." Astrid lifted her chin and eyed the bag that had seen better days.

Carly blew out her breath. "All right. You're probably right. I should just leave it. But I have to get my purse out."

Carly unzipped the bag, moved the bat into sight for a few seconds while she groped underneath it for her flat cross-body bag, and then slammed the back door.

"Let's eat," Carly said. "I'm suddenly ravenous."

"So am I." Astrid steered her scooter toward the entrance. Despite the cold, it felt good to be outdoors even if only for the time it took to get from the car to the restaurant. She felt stable on the scooter, but Carly was a little jumpy and kept a hand outstretched to grab a fistful of Astrid's coat as if that would keep Astrid from falling. Inside, they easily found seats at a small table in the middle of the restaurant.

"I've never been here," Astrid said. "Do you have a favorite menu item?"

"They make an incredible roast beef and Swiss on sourdough."

"That sounds delicious."

They ordered and settled in, each with a soft drink to occupy them while they waited for sandwiches. Carly held her cell phone in one hand.

"Thank you for coming out with me," Astrid said. "I haven't quite gotten used to the notion that I can't simply get in the car and go."

"You'll be weight-bearing soon," Carly said, "and from there it doesn't take long to get your gait back."

"Never mind the shop talk," Astrid said. "Tell me about your little boy."

"Tyler," Carly said, her lips pulled into a half smile. She set the phone on the table but still wrapped her fingers round it.

"Does he like his school?"

"He loves school. I've had to shift him around a little, but he adapts quickly and makes friends. The teachers only have great things to say about him."

"Sounds like my son," Astrid said. "He never goes anywhere

without making a friend. It was always that way. What does he like to play with?"

Carly laughed. "Trucks, trucks, and more trucks."

"That must make your Christmas shopping easy."

An odd hue passed through Carly's face. "I had a Tonka truck all picked out, and then I had to leave the store unexpectedly. When I went back later, it was gone and I had to choose another model."

"You can't go wrong with Tonka."

"That's my philosophy." Carly jiggled her straw around before sucking in a long draw of cola.

"This is nice," Astrid said. "Thank you for indulging an old lady."

"You're not an old lady."

Astrid grinned. "At least I haven't yet dyed my hair blue."

"I love your hair color. It's a lovely shade of silver." Carly pushed her phone a few inches toward the center of the table—within reach but no longer in her hand.

This was progress. Ordinary conversation felt good. Carly was relaxing. She might yet tell Astrid what was behind her fearful moments.

"What will you do for Christmas?" Carly asked.

Astrid shrugged both shoulders. "That's a bit up in the air right now. My son is delayed coming home from a business trip, and my daughter's little girl is too sick to travel."

"Oh, no."

"Something will work out," Astrid said. She caught Carly's gaze, which had been panning the surroundings more than settling at the table. "I understand Sam will sing a solo at his church's Christmas Eve service."

"Sam? The cook?"

"Yes, Sam, the cook. He's such a nice young man. I thought

he might have mentioned the service to you."

Carly flushed. "I haven't run into him the last couple of days. I didn't know he sang."

"One learns the most surprising things about others. A little conversation goes a long way." Astrid sipped her drink. "What about you? Any Christmas traditions?"

"Tyler is the center of attention. My mother is knitting him a sweater. He hung all the ornaments on the bottom branches of the tree."

Astrid laughed. "Take a photo. Someday you'll all enjoy looking back on times like that."

Their sandwiches arrived. The bread was wider and sliced thicker than what Astrid had imagined. She picked up her table knife to cut it into more manageable pieces. A man approached and stood behind Carly.

"Can we help you?" Astrid asked.

"Carly can."

Carly spun around. "What are you doing here?"

"I would think that was obvious," he said. "Picking up lunch."

"Truman, you can't be this close to me."

"Yet I am. What are you going to do about it?"

Astrid adopted her most firm and in-control tone. "Sir, Carly doesn't wish to entertain your overtures. Perhaps you can wait for your food at the pickup counter."

"I'll wait wherever I want to wait," Truman said. "They'll call my name."

"I'm calling the police," Carly said, reaching past her plate for the phone.

Truman's hand got there first. Astrid startled. The baseball bat made sense now.

"That phone is my personal property," Carly said. "Give it back."

"Wow, Carly," Truman said. "Something has hardened you since the time we worked together. Maybe you need some help, if you know what I mean."

"You're breaking the law. I have a restraining order." Carly's voice rose enough that diners around them turned to watch, the way people gawked at an accident along the highway. "Give me back my phone."

"All I ever wanted was to be your friend, and maybe see if we could be something more," Truman said. "There was no reason for you to get the police involved."

"Truman." Carly packed thick pleas into one word and gripped her purse in her lap.

He raised his eyebrows at her, unmoving.

Astrid was tempted to send her scooter rolling in his direction. She started to stand.

"Don't, Astrid," Carly said. "Don't get involved. I have it under control."

Astrid raised her hand to get the attention of a member of the wait staff. The young woman who had brought them their sandwiches a few minutes ago was frozen, and the gasps of several people around them were audible. No one moved in their direction.

Standing on one leg with the other on her chair, Astrid turned her attention back to Carly. As Carly stood, she let her purse fall on the table—but not before she had taken from it the thing that mattered most in the moment.

A knife.

CHAPTER 22

Astrid gripped the back of her chair to reset her balance. If she were able-bodied, she would have scooted around the table to grab Carly's arm. She even would have put herself between Carly and this man if such a risk was required to persuade Carly to abandon her ill-thought plan. But from the awkward angle of having her knee on her chair rather than on the scooter, there was little physical action Astrid could take. She couldn't even reach her cell phone in the quilted and embroidered bag hanging on the front of her scooter. Her eyes darted from Carly to Truman and on to the innocent diners looking up from their menus and meals. Several pushed away from their tables, as if to be ready for a swift getaway. Surely somebody was dialing 911. A toddler squirmed out of his booster seat in one of the booths against the wall and slid down to the floor, pointing at the knife Carly still flashed. The child's mother reached for him, but he dodged her and set off, pointing still. Another adult scooped him up, and he wailed as he was returned to his mother's arms and she fastened her hold on him.

The blade, Astrid judged, was seven or eight inches in length—plenty enough to do considerable damage. It was a German knife. Somewhere in the back of her mind, the brand name was buried under more-pertinent information.

"Carly," Astrid said, "we don't need the knife."

"Put my phone down and go away, Truman." Carly didn't flinch.

Two sets of diners abandoned their lunches, widening the circle of safety—for now. All it would take was for Carly or Truman to charge at the other, oblivious to furniture, and someone would get hurt.

Carly adjusted her grip on the black handle, never wavering as her shoulders rose and fell with heavy breath.

"Carly." Truman's voice lifted in false amusement. "You're going to get hurt."

"I bet you didn't even order any takeout," Carly snarled. "You came in here because you saw me come in."

"Does it really matter?"

"Carly," Astrid said, "put the knife down."

Astrid had no doubt that if Carly tried to use the knife, Truman would overcome her, and she might be the one who was wounded.

"Not until he leaves." Carly took a step forward and braced her feet.

Astrid swept the lunch crowd again. Why were there so many women and children and so few men? The only three men Astrid saw were nearly as old as she was and unlikely to try to tackle a man not yet thirty.

"Put it back in your purse," Astrid said. "We can try an outing another day. Let's go back to—"

"Don't say it," Carly said.

Astrid bit back her words. *Sycamore Hills.* Carly was right. If this man had any doubt about whether he had correctly identified Carly's place of employment, they shouldn't provide him with the confirmation under these circumstances.

Carly's eyes remained fixed on Truman. "Astrid, you should sit down. You'll be safer."

Safe from what? A rolling tussle of an unrestrained man with a grudge versus a frightened woman with a knife? Truman's hands were lost in the awkward angle of the pockets of his brown bomber jacket. The style hadn't changed much in the decades since Americans turned up in the village where Astrid's family had taken refuge. They were the conquering heroes, and the bombing had stopped at last. But their presence also signaled the final days of all five members of the family being together.

Astrid was a hair's width from just putting her injured foot on the floor against medical advice and limping toward Carly. Instead she adjusted the knee on the chair for better stability.

"Don't do something you'll regret," Astrid said.

"Oh, I'd never regret this."

Carly's eyes had gone steely.

"If you do this, you can't take it back," Astrid said softly.

"I'd only be protecting myself."

"Mama, the lady has a knife." A child pointed, without leaving the relative safety of the grip of her mother's hand.

"Come on, sweetie. We're leaving." Like others around her, the little girl's mother tossed money on the table for the half-eaten food and headed for the exit.

"Think of Tyler," Astrid said, her voice measured.

Carly's eyes flinched. "I am thinking of Tyler. Every minute of every day."

Truman sidled around the table, unperturbed. "If you would just let me talk to you, we could sort this out."

"You are not supposed to be this close to me."

He shrugged. It was a dare.

"Carly." Astrid's tone sharpened, taking a different tact. "Help me with my scooter and we'll go."

Carly's tongue circled her lips.

Truman helped himself to a recently vacated table. It was no coincidence that it was the one closest to Carly. Astrid didn't know how many feet away he was supposed to stay under the restraining order, but unquestionably this was too close. With great deliberation, he put Carly's phone on the table and picked up a menu.

A man sporting a white shirt and black necktie broke through the ring of gawkers.

"I understand we have a situation here," he said.

The tag on his shirt said his name was Gary, the manager.

"You can't wave a knife around in here," he said to Carly. "Whatever your private issue is, take it outside."

"He's violating a restraining order."

Gary sighed. "Those things aren't worth the paper they're printed on."

Carly's eyes hadn't left Truman.

Gary scanned the remaining customers. "Ladies and gentlemen, I apologize for this disruption of your meal. Of course there will be no charge if you decide to leave. Please do whatever you think best for your own safety."

"She's not going to hurt anyone." Truman spoke from the table where he pushed dishes of half-eaten food aside. "I know her. She's not capable of hurting someone."

Astrid looked from Truman to Carly. Even with both hands gripping the knife, Carly trembled.

"Maybe you ought to leave," Gary said to Truman.

"I haven't ordered yet," Truman said.

"Sir, you must leave. I can't have this going on at our busiest time of the day." Gary took a step toward Carly. "Let's just put the knife away."

Carly shook her head.

"Then perhaps you should gather your things and go. One of you has to leave. In fact, I must insist that both of you leave. This isn't the time or place for whatever is going on between the two of you."

"*He* has to leave." Carly spoke through gritted teeth. "And give me my phone back."

"I don't want anyone to get hurt."

Gary approached Carly. Astrid was relieved he had stepped in to help, but it was hard to predict how Carly or Truman would react.

"Nobody will get hurt," Carly said, "if he just leaves."

Had this man ever hurt Carly? The question tumbled around Astrid's mind as she searched for any other explanation for both the young woman's fright and her decision to carry a kitchen knife and a baseball bat wherever she went. So far Carly showed no inclination to accommodate Gary's request to put the knife down, and Truman had simply moved the used dishes to another table and perused a laminated menu.

"Sir," Gary said, "I'm exercising my right not to serve you today. It's best for everyone if you leave."

Truman turned a page in the menu.

Gary glanced toward several of the waitstaff who had congregated in one corner and shook his head. No one was to take Truman's order, but his firm directives toward Truman and Carly had accomplished nothing more than Astrid's pleas.

Bracing herself so the table would take most of her weight, Astrid hopped toward her scooter.

"Astrid, don't," Carly said. "You'll hurt yourself all over again."

If she did it would be worth it. Astrid continued to where Carly had parked the scooter out of the way. When she reached it and got situated, she rummaged for her cell phone in the bag.

It wasn't there.

She expelled breath. She had left the thing on the kitchen counter plugged in to charge. Surely by now someone had called the police. Surely. Astrid opened her wallet and took out bills representing five times the cost of their food and rolled back to the table to tuck them alongside a plate.

Half the lunchtime rush had come to their senses and stopped gawking, instead abandoning meals and leaving the restaurant. Others, she presumed, felt trapped by the fact that the "lady with the knife" was between them and the exit. Outside, two dozen faces pressed against the front window of the restaurant, and no doubt a larger crowd was amassing on the sidewalk.

"Carly," Astrid said, "please put the knife away. I'm ready to go, and you are my ride home."

"I can't leave right now," Carly said. "This is my chance."

Chance for what?

"Tyler will be waiting for you to come home this afternoon, just like you do every day."

"Cute kid," Truman quipped. "You should meet him. I've known him since he was a baby."

"Shut up," Carly said. "Leave my son out of this."

Truman turned another menu page.

"Carly," Astrid said, her breath a prayer for this despairing young woman.

For the first time, Carly's eyes wandered from Truman and met Astrid's gaze.

"I know you want to keep Tyler safe," Astrid said. "Let's keep everyone safe today."

"Hand me the knife," Gary said, covering Carly's hands with his. Her resistance faltered. "Sit down. I'll bring you a cup of coffee and you can collect yourself."

"I am not sitting down anywhere near him," Carly said.

"Wherever you'd like," Gary said.

"I don't need coffee."

"Something else, then." Gary eased the knife free of Carly's hands.

Both front doors opened wide, and two uniformed police officers entered.

"Over here," Gary shouted.

"Did you call for assistance?" an officer said.

Gary nodded. "I imagine you had several calls."

"That we did. Something about a woman with a knife."

Gary looked at his hands. "I have the knife now. The danger is past. But I believe you will find someone in violation of a restraining order."

"Is that so?"

"Yes!" Carly grabbed her purse, swiftly extracted the legal document, and pointed. "He's right there, clearly not far enough away."

The officer took the document, glanced at it, and said, "Are you Truman Gibbons?"

"It's him," Carly said.

"Please step back for your own safety," the officer said. "We'll just need to verify his identity. Routine procedure."

"So?" the second officer said. "Are you Truman Gibbons."

Truman closed his menu. "I am. But I assure you this is all a misunderstanding."

The first officer creased the order of protection along the lines it had formed while in Carly's purse. "Looks like we have grounds for an arrest."

The second officer moved to Truman's table. "Sir, have you ever been arrested before?"

"Of course not."

"Well, you're being arrested now." He unfastened a set of handcuffs. "Please stand up. I'll read you your rights and explain what happens next."

"What happens next," Carly shouted, "is that I don't ever have to see you again. And give me back my phone."

"He took your phone against your will?" an officer said.

"Yes." She pointed at it.

"Okay. We'll note there's an additional charge."

While one officer escorted Truman out of the building, the other asked questions of Carly, Astrid, Gary, and the surrounding straggling customers. Finally, he closed the small notebook.

"Have a good day," he said. "We'll be in touch if we need you."

Astrid rolled over to Carly and let the young woman fall into her arms.

CHAPTER 23

A strid had a *Q* and a *U* in her Scrabble rack. Betty's Brood had nabbed her with a game after lunch and she welcomed the distraction. Her boxes were unpacked; her laundry was finished and folded on the end of her bed, courtesy of the morning blue-smocked staff; she'd read all the papers after breakfast; and she'd never been one for daytime television. Well, maybe a little *General Hospital* now and then, just enough to stay caught up. Sooner or later she had to get past the settling-in phase of her new life and create some hooks for her days beyond mealtimes and physical therapy appointments.

It seemed she was positioned to do very well with a *Q* on a double-score square. She pursed her lips in thought, looking back and forth between her rack and the available options to connect to with the perfect word. Years had passed since she played Scrabble with any serious competition. Her grandchildren were only now becoming skilled enough to win without her intentionally passing over plays that would have given her triple-score victory. But Betty's Brood seemed sharp enough that she should pay attention. Quart. Quell. Queen. Quarry. Query. Quiz. Quetzal. If only she had a *Z*. Quetzal would have been especially noteworthy both because it included *Q* and *Z*, thus sure to produce a good score, and also because if she were challenged and Betty brought out the dictionary, Astrid would gladly describe a quetzal's brightly colored plumage. Alas, she had no *Z*. Her gloating would have to wait for a future game. But she could put down QUAR attached to descending *T* and clear most of the tiles out of her rack.

"We're going to have to watch out for this one," Mae said. "I can tell already she could be dangerous with the right letters."

Astrid laughed. "Years ago, when I first came to America, I played with friends to help me learn English and improve my vocabulary."

"What was your favorite word in those days?" Betty asked.

"Syrup," Astrid said. "I found that people weren't prepared for the *SY* combination at the beginning of a word."

"See?" Mae said. "Dangerous."

Little did they know Astrid was holding *quetzal* in her back pocket for future use.

A blue-smocked employee approached the table. Astrid was fairly certain this one was Jennifer, the caregiver who helped her during the tornado drill. There were so many names to learn. It was like being the new student in a school where everyone else had been together since kindergarten.

"There you are," Jennifer said, looking at Astrid.

"Oh?" Astrid glanced up as she chose new tiles to replace what she'd used.

"Your physical therapist is looking for you," Jennifer said. "I promised that if I saw you I'd let you know."

Astrid turned her wrist and checked her watch. "My appointment isn't for two hours."

Jennifer nodded. "One of her patients is gone already to be with family for Christmas, and another isn't feeling well enough for therapy. She thought you might not mind coming earlier. That way she'll be able to leave sooner. She still has shopping to do, apparently."

"Well, that seems like a reasonable request," Astrid said, returning her tiles facedown to the pool of options. "I shall have to prove my prowess another day."

"We are quaking in our boots," Mae said.

Astrid accepted help from Jennifer to get on her scooter and pushed off down the hall toward the therapy and exercise room.

She and Carly hadn't yet spoken about what happened in the restaurant the day before. Once she regained her composure enough to drive, Carly had been silent on the way back to Sycamore Hills. Astrid still didn't know how Carly knew Truman Gibbons or what had occurred to prompt her to seek a restraining order against him. The police officers were content to overlook witnesses mentioning the knife Carly had produced—at least for now. Astrid hated to think what might happen if Carly had to defend herself in court against a charge. She hadn't actually used the knife, a fact that encouraged Astrid.

Once they returned to Sycamore Hills, Carly still looked pale to Astrid, but she was concerned that she had missed a patient by now, and her supervisor wasn't going to be happy.

"Just tell her what happened," Astrid had said.

But Carly shook her head, and they parted in the hallway.

Astrid had gone to her apartment, where she sat in a chair that caught a shaft of afternoon sun and fingered the gold cross hanging on a thin chain around her neck. She only knew what she'd seen, not any of the circumstances surrounding the event. Never in all her years had she known anyone who took out a restraining order—though she suspected that several people she'd known ought to have done so.

On her way down to an early dinner—ravenous after having not a single bite of her roast beef and Swiss on sourdough—Astrid had peeked into the therapy and exercise room. Carly hadn't been there, and Astrid didn't know where else in the building she might be. Sometimes the therapists worked with residents in the privacy of their own apartments.

But this was too big to gloss over. She couldn't go in for a session of picking up marbles with her toes and stretching her arch over a rolling pin as if yesterday's outing had never happened. At the same time, she couldn't pry. If Carly didn't want to talk about it, Astrid would have to let it go and fervently pray for Carly, but she had to try to offer solace.

She wheeled into the therapy room. "Hello, Carly."

They were alone for the moment. Therapists seemed to come and go in a manner lacking structure to an onlooker. At the moment, it might be in their favor that they weren't sharing the room with listening ears.

"Thanks for coming early." Carly spread a clean sheet on a therapy table.

"Starting with heat?" Astrid said.

"You know the drill." Carly helped Astrid transfer to the table.

It took several attempts, but Astrid was persistent and finally caught Carly's gaze and held it. She moved one hand to cover Carly's while she wrapped her ankle and waited.

Carly stood still for a few moments before gasping for air. "I'm sorry about yesterday."

"Sorry? You? What on earth for?"

"I knew something like that could happen. I should never have put you at risk."

"My dear Carly, I'm sorry you have carried this weight all alone."

"You've been through so many terrible things." Tears glistened in Carly's eyes. "Truly horrific things. I can't compare my problems to what happened in Germany—and losing two husbands."

Astrid squeezed Carly's fingers. "No two people suffer in identical ways, and we must not discount any suffering. The greatest gift we can give each other is to see suffering and name it as real. Always in suffering we meet fear. Always in suffering we must raise our eyes from darkness to light that awaits. There we will find others who have known suffering. Even God knew the suffering of His own Son."

Carly nodded and wiped one eye with the back of a hand.

"Many people who hear my story," Astrid said, "wonder how I can still have faith in God."

"Honestly, it boggles my mind."

"The Nazis, the events that separated our family after the war, Heinz's senseless death, Peter's illness that we never knew could take him so quickly. My faith means everything. Everything. I've lived a rich life—and it's not over yet. And neither is yours. There is always hope for new life."

Carly shook her head slightly. "I think I've probably used up all my chances."

"Nonsense. God never runs out of chances."

Carly puffed her cheeks and blew out her breath. "At least there's only one more week in this year. I want it to be over."

Astrid nodded. "Some years are like that. But we never fully leave them behind. Instead they carry us forward."

Carly shrugged one shoulder. "Maybe."

"We're two days from Christmas Eve," Astrid said. "What will you do?"

"It's just the three of us since my aunt and uncle moved to Phoenix." Carly laughed. "Believe me, winter in the Midwest isn't on the list for people who live in Phoenix."

Astrid smiled. "No, I suppose not. It was the same when I lived in Florida and the snowbirds came down."

"We'll probably just stay in. Or I might take Tyler on a drive to see Christmas lights in the neighborhood."

"We used to do that," Astrid said. "Looking at lights won't take the entire evening. Why don't you come to a Christmas Eve service with me?"

"Church?"

"Yes, church. Sam's church, as a matter of fact."

"Sam the cook?"

"Yes, Sam the cook. It's an early service—five o'clock. There will be plenty of time to see the lights as well."

Astrid had only decided in that moment that she would like to go to Sam's church. Alex was stuck in France. Ingrid was tending poor Ellie. Her own excuses for not accepting Sam's invitation faded.

"Sam has a solo," Astrid said. "I know he would like to see our faces there."

"I barely know Sam. He seems nice, but. . ."

Carly rubbed her thumbs across her fingernails. A nervous habit, Astrid observed.

"I don't know him very well, either," Astrid said. "But I could use some wheels to get to church."

Carly laughed. "I'm a taxi?"

Astrid shook her head. "Uber. My grandchildren tell me that's the cool way to get a ride these days."

Carly's smile widened. "Well, I suppose it is."

"Christmas!" Astrid said. "Christ in the cradle. Christ, the hope of the world. There is nothing like the hope of Christmas."

Carly nodded slightly, Astrid was pleased to see. She'd hooked her. Now she just had to reel her in.

"Bring Tyler and your mother," Astrid said.

"I'm not sure my mother will want to."

"I would love to meet her."

"I don't know."

"It can't hurt to ask her," Astrid said, putting out a hand. "How will I get there if not for you? Give me your cell phone."

"My cell phone?"

"Yes. I want to give you my number."

Carly's eyes widened.

"Don't you know?" Astrid said. "No one writes down a phone number anymore. You just put it straight into someone's contact list."

"You are full of surprises!"

"I have grandchildren of a certain age. They keep me up-to-date. I even know how to read e-mail on my phone. Although I understand the cool kids don't e-mail. Everything is by text message."

Grinning, Carly rolled her eyes and handed her phone to Astrid. Astrid made sure they had each other's numbers and returned Carly's phone.

"I shall expect you day after tomorrow at a quarter past four," Astrid said. "I'll be waiting in the lobby beside the gold tree."

"The gold tree?"

"We'll have ourselves a merry golden Christmas."

CHAPTER 24

Two days later Astrid foundered. Christmas Eve. She should have been baking a cheesecake or frosting six dozen Christmas cookies, at the very least—preferably with a grandchild or two underfoot. Few of them were actually underfoot anymore. Several of them were capable of Christmas baking as long as she was nearby for questions, and the others were old enough to occupy themselves with a Christmas craft or a holiday movie. She should be anticipating a service in her own parish that would let out exactly at midnight, releasing the joy of Christmas Day upon the neighborhood.

Certainly she didn't lack for Christmas treats in a place like Sycamore Hills. Every time she turned around someone was encouraging her to eat or have something to drink. Goodies seemed to appear out of thin air as if they were a magician's trick, and Russell, the chaplain, had conducted a nondenominational service immediately after lunch.

These days Astrid had to allow twice as much time to prepare herself for an outing. Moving around the apartment still meant being obedient about the scooter. She suspected her ankle was ready for weight bearing, but her children were strict about medical advice, and she didn't want to have to be evasive even on the phone if one of them asked.

By three o'clock, Astrid had herself put together sufficiently to await Carly's arrival. As each quarter hour ticked by, she told herself that the likelihood Carly would cancel went down. Astrid sat in the recliner working a crossword puzzle she had snagged from one of the old papers in the library that morning. She worked in pen. She always had. It was so much more convenient than looking for a sharp pencil, and she rarely had to alter an answer.

A knock on the door surprised her.

"Coming," she called out as she reached for her scooter and hoped whoever was at the door had great patience for how long it might take her to get there. Opening the door inward while keeping the scooter out of its path was tricky business, but she'd had a couple of weeks to master the arrangement.

She opened the door and gasped.

"Alex!"

"Merry Christmas, Mom." Alex leaned in to embrace her.

"You didn't say you were coming," she said, rolling the scooter out of the way of the closing door.

"I wasn't sure I'd make it. I put myself on standby for every flight I could find, and one of them paid off."

"And your coworker?"

"Her family's there. It's Christmas in Paris for them. They'll fly home in a couple of days."

"It's so good to see you!"

"I haven't even been home yet," Alex said, opening a canvas shopping bag he held in one hand. "I found the ornaments."

"The gold ones?" Relief oozed through her.

"They got overlooked in the car when we unloaded, and then I left my car at the airport. They've been there all this time."

"Oh, Alex, that news does an old woman's heart good." She turned the scooter toward the table. "I want to see them."

Alex took the few steps required to cross the room and removed a small wooden box from the bag. It wasn't the original box that had sat in her father's office, but it was the only one Alex and Ingrid had ever known.

Astrid released the latch and opened the lid. Nestled in a mound of cushioning were the three ornaments still in the precise arrangement she had always used for packing them away.

"I can't tell you what this means," she said. "I was so afraid they were lost for good."

"I'm sorry I didn't remember they were there. I put that bag under a seat myself for safekeeping, and then I forgot what I'd done."

Astrid took the ornaments out of the box and laid them carefully on the table. "There's no place to hang them."

"I promise we'll fix that before next Christmas. A tabletop tree, perhaps."

Astrid nodded. "Perhaps."

"They mean something to all of us. My kids always love to see them."

"You should go home now," Astrid said. "Your family will be waiting."

"I just wanted you to see for yourself that they're fine." Alex kissed her cheek. "I'll be back for you first thing in the morning. We'll have all day."

A rap on the door made them both look toward the sound.

"Expecting someone else?" Alex said.

"I wasn't even expecting you." It was too early to be Carly, and Astrid had promised to meet her downstairs.

Alex shrugged and paced back to the door.

"Merry Christmas!" A quartet of happy voices shouted the greeting loudly enough for the entire second floor of Sycamore Hills to hear.

"Ellie? Ava?" Astrid's eyes went to her daughter's face. "I thought—"

"We all did," Ingrid said. "The doctor, me, even Ellie."

Ellie grinned. "I woke up this morning and felt better."

"Did you check with the doctor?" Astrid was overjoyed to see them all, but certainly she did not want to put her granddaughter at risk.

"Not exactly," Ingrid said.

"In fact, not at all," her husband said.

"And now we're here," Ellie said, "and nobody can do anything about it."

"You made some promises, young lady." Ingrid shook a finger at her child.

"I know, I know," Ellie said. "No running around. No staying up late. Drink lots of water. If I'm tired I should lie down, and if I feel sick I have to tell you immediately."

"Right."

Ellie reached toward the table. "You found the ornaments!"

"Your uncle Alex just brought them."

"I felt really sad that they might be lost."

"Me, too," Astrid said.

For a moment, all eyes were on the gold balls laid out on the table, and Astrid held the silence in her heart.

"Can we look around?" Ava said. "I love apartments."

Astrid laughed. Ava was six, and Astrid suspected she had never even been in an apartment.

"The bedroom is through that door," Astrid said.

Ingrid turned to Alex. "I didn't know you were coming in today. Mom said you didn't think you'd make it in time for Christmas."

"I wasn't too hopeful," Alex said, "but here I am."

"We should pack a bag and take Mom to your place tonight. Do you think Gwen would mind?"

"Of course not," Alex said, pulling out his phone. "I'll call and alert her, but there's plenty of space. I'll let her know the good news that you're here as well."

"I hope you brought a suitcase when you moved her in." Ingrid went to the front closet. "Here or in the bedroom?"

"The bedroom, I think," Alex said.

Astrid cleared her throat loudly. Both her children turned, puzzled.

"I have plans," she said.

"Plans?" they echoed simultaneously.

"People do make plans, you know."

"Of course," Ingrid said. "After all, we said we weren't coming. But we're here now and can be together like we are every year."

"In a few minutes, I need to be downstairs waiting for a friend. Together we'll go to the five o'clock service at a local church and hear another friend sing."

"Oh." Ingrid's brows pushed toward each other in that way that said she was befuddled.

From the bag strapped to the scooter, Astrid's phone rang. Alex reached in for it and handed it to her.

"Carly?"

"Yes, it's me. Thank you so much for inviting me, but I just don't think it's going to work out for me to go with you tonight."

"What's the matter, dear?"

"It's just. . .well, I don't usually. . .it just seems like too much."

"But without you, I don't have wheels." Astrid turned away from her children, whose faces had turned hopeful with the part of the conversation they were hearing.

"I know. I feel terrible about that part."

"I'll just have to persuade my children," Astrid said. "We can come pick you up, and then you won't be coming into a strange church by yourself."

Alex leaned in with one ear cocked toward his mother.

"Your children?" Carly said. "But you said they weren't coming."

"That's what they told me. We can leave right now," Astrid said.

"You are stubborn, you know that?" Carly said.

"So I've been told."

"Okay, then. I'll come. We'll come. All of us. Tyler hopes they'll sing, 'Away in a Manger' because he learned it at school."

"If it's not in the service, I would love to hear him sing it afterward."

"Okay. This is a little hard for me, but I'll come for you as we planned."

"Perfect."

Astrid ended the call and met Alex's eyes. He scratched his head right above the left ear. He'd been doing that so many years when he was confused that she wondered why he didn't have a bald spot on the side of his head.

"I was afraid you weren't settling in," Alex said.

"That makes two of us," Ingrid said.

"I haven't stopped being a grown-up just because the two of you grew up."

They both laughed.

"But Mom," Ingrid said, "what about our Christmas Eve?"

"Sam told me the service will be out by six."

"Sam?" Ingrid said.

"Come hear him sing and I'll introduce you."

"I don't know," Alex said. "I haven't even been home."

"I understand," Astrid said. "You can come back for me in the morning as you suggested."

"But we'll lose the whole evening together," Ingrid said. Her husband tapped her elbow, but she ignored him.

"Then you come to church," Astrid said. "Afterward I can ride with you to Alex's."

Ingrid grimaced. "The girls have been cooped up in the car all day."

"Then you should go on to Alex's, and I'll see you all in the morning."

"Christmas Eve without you?" Ingrid's face blanched.

Astrid paused to gather her thoughts.

"This is important," she said. "I love Christmas Eve because we welcome the hope of the world. And I know a young woman who needs the hope of the world this year. Give me these next two hours with her and I will happily come to Alex's tonight. I can Uber or something."

Alex laughed. "Uber? You don't know how to Uber."

"Or something, I said. I can always do things the old-fashioned way and arrange a taxi. Or you can wait here in the apartment. Put the television on and let the girls unwind."

Astrid held her own. She might let her children think they ran her life, but she was still capable of her own decisions. After all the cajoling leading up to Carly's agreement to go to church, Astrid wouldn't pull out. If she did, Carly would as well.

"Let the girls come with me now," Alex said to Ingrid. "My kids will be thrilled to see them, and then you can bring Mom later. Gwen isn't planning to serve dinner until eight anyway."

"There you go," Astrid said, "all worked out. You can come to church with me or make yourselves comfortable here."

"Girls!" Ingrid followed the sound of giggling coming from the bedroom.

"Someone find that suitcase," Astrid said. "I have just enough time to pack it."

In the end, Ingrid and her husband cited the grunginess of a last-minute, eight-hour drive as a reason to remain in the apartment. Ingrid had traveled in sweats, and Ava had spilled a soft drink on her a few hours ago. They could clean up at Alex's later. Astrid was waiting in the lobby beside the gold tree at promptly a quarter past four.

The drive to the church was brief. Inside, Tyler's eyes grew wide at the sight of a basket of candles.

"Remember," Carly said, "we don't touch the fire."

"I know, Mom. I'm not a dummy." Tyler rolled his eyes like a teenager. Above his head, mother and grandmother exchanged smiles. The three generations carried the same dimpled chin and wide-set green eyes.

They found seats that allowed Astrid to sit on the end with her scooter parked against the wall. Tyler asked to sit next to her. Carly and her mother studied the simple bulletin listing music, readings, and the title of a brief homily. At the center of the hour, the lights would be dimmed and the congregation would light candles and sing "Away in a Manger."

Tyler had indeed learned the song well, belting out the stanzas in great earnestness. In the glow of their candles, Astrid smiled at Carly, who beamed down on her own son singing of God's Son.

"What did the manger hold that night?" the pastor began. "Who was it the manger cradled?"

Tyler looked up at Astrid and loudly whispered, "It was the little Lord Jesus asleep in the hay."

Astrid managed to contain a gleeful laugh. Tyler had it right. It was the little Lord Jesus. She couldn't have asked for a better sermon for the listening ears of one young woman nearly devoid of hope.

The hope of the world.

The hope of the despairing.

The hope of all who seek God's abundant life.

Tyler laid his head in his mother's lap, and she gently stroked his head as she listened. Her expression wasn't one that suggested boredom. Quite the opposite. Carly had brought her weariness with her that night, ready to lay it down. Even with the lights lowered, Astrid could see the same glistening tears in Carly's eyes she'd seen before.

Sam, garbed in one of the deep blue robes with a gold collar that all the choir members wore, stepped out to sing:

"O holy night! The stars are brightly shining.
It is the night of the dear Savior's birth.
Long lay the world in sin and error pining
till he appeared and the soul felt its worth.
A thrill of hope, the weary world rejoices,
for yonder breaks a new and glorious morn.
Fall on your knees, oh hear the angel voices,
oh night divine, oh night when Christ was born."

Sam's voice was full, robust, and heartfelt.
"A thrill of hope, the weary world rejoices."
Beside her mother and with her son's sleepy head in her lap, Carly was transfixed.
"For yonder breaks a new and glorious morn."
Tyler was right. It was the little Lord Jesus in the manger. It was divine hope for weary souls.

"Truly He taught us to love one another.
His law is love and His gospel is peace.
Chains shall He break for the slave is our brother,
and in His name all oppression shall cease.
Sweet hymns of joy in grateful chorus raise we,
let all within us praise His holy name.
Fall on your knees, oh hear the angel voices,
oh night divine, oh night when Christ as born."

Truly He taught us to love one another. . . Sweet hymns of joy in grateful chorus raise we.
Carly's fingers stilled for a moment on her son's head before reaching for Astrid's hand.

Tomorrow a new and glorious morn would break for this young woman who opened her heart to the hope of the world. To joy. To forgiveness. To the redemption that comes with a second chance for love and life.

All through her childhood Astrid remembered the wondrous Christmases of her father's doing. As a young woman in a new country, she remembered the Christmas that brought her back to Peter. Now, in this late season of life, with a little boy sure of the little Lord Jesus and his mother opening her eyes to the hope of the world, this was the golden Christmas Astrid didn't want to forget.

CHRISTMAS IN BLUE

CHAPTER 1

The child never practiced. Angela didn't have to ask him or his mother to know this. She hadn't asked a piano student in years. The weekly practice forms she'd once used only got lost or crumpled. A child who opened the book to the correct page during the lesson might have practiced once or twice. A child who turned down the corner of the page at least intended to practice every day. A child who showed improvement over last week's lesson had actually practiced for thirty minutes at least four days out of the last seven.

Brian Bergstrom had done none of these things and rarely did, which was too bad because he had more aptitude for music than any of the other forty students who traipsed in and out of Angela's home in the space of a week. They came in the after-school hours or the early evening or Saturday morning. A few who were homeschooled came on Tuesday or Thursday mornings. As much as possible, Angela scheduled thirty-minute lessons back-to-back so that they did not truncate her days more than necessary. A few advanced students warranted an hour a week. Often this meant she ate her supper at eight thirty, but she had kept these hours for so many years that they did not strike her as odd.

Angela rescued Brian from his fumbling and pressed open the book to a pristine page, the piece she had assigned him two weeks ago. He stared at the page, arranged his fingers around middle C, and hummed the tune of the top line quite accurately. Probably he would break out with words soon, if not during this lesson, which was nearly over, then certainly when they resumed after the holidays. He was quite clever with spontaneous rhymes. He had been even when he was five. Some weeks Angela covertly created lags in her instruction to allow time to see what he might come up with. Brian's mother insisted on the piano lessons, and student and teacher placated her while also maintaining a wordless understanding that the instrument he preferred to play was a saxophone. In another nine months, he'd be old enough to join both the school band and the school chorus and, as he liked to point out, he would already know how to read music. She shouldn't take it personally, he'd once told Angela, that the piano was just not his thing. Periodically, when he did especially well despite his lack of practice, she raised her eyebrows at him. Someday he would be glad he could play the piano. No one with a musical bent ever regretted learning the piano, especially someone who did not yet know he would grow up to be a composer.

So they had an understanding of sorts. At least this was the last lesson before the Christmas break—for both of them. Angela had ten days off before Christmas and another ten days after, when she'd be free from students. Most years she organized a Christmas recital just before the break. Martin, the pastor at Main Street Church, where she was the organist and choir director, let her use the grand piano in the sanctuary for winter and spring recitals, and there was plenty of space for parents and siblings.

Angela just couldn't manage it. Not this year. She didn't have a festive cell in her body this year.

No doubt families would now be expecting great strides by the time of the spring recital. Angela wasn't sure she could manage that event, either, but she had time to decide. It wouldn't be in May as it usually was. She was sure of that much. Perhaps the last week of April.

Instead of the Christmas recital, she required every student to play a polished piece for a parent. Brian's mother, Liz, had just settled herself on the deep red love seat in the small music room Angela used for lessons on an upright grand. Angela eyed Brian. Without lifting his head, he looked at her out of the sides of his eyes through brown hair hanging well past his eyebrows. It was a wonder he saw anything. Angela turned the page back to a selection she was more sure he had mastered, and his shoulders eased down in relief. Then she went and sat on the sofa next to his mother.

Brian muddled through. It was a simple two-part Bach invention in C, the first one that most students learned. For the most part Brian had the notes right, though he played them too slowly. But his performance pleased his mother, and at this time and in this place, that is what mattered.

Liz Bergstrom beamed. "Not a note wrong," she said when Brian had finished.

"That's right," Angela said.

Liz crooked a finger at her son, and he slid off the piano bench in relief. His mother whispered in his ear before reaching into an oversized handbag and putting a package in his hands.

He took a few steps toward Angela. "Mrs. Carter, this is for you. Thank you for my lessons."

Angela suffered through this awkward moment with every student. Not every student, precisely. Some families opted out of the annual offering, and some extroverted children presented gifts with enough enthusiasm to blow Angela over.

"Thank you, Brian," Angela said, standing up. "It's lovely of you to think of me. Please be sure to take one of the gifts on your way out."

His head bobbed. She still couldn't get a good look at his eyes. Surely before he returned in three weeks his mother would insist he have a haircut. Maybe he'd get a comb in his stocking as a hint. He retrieved his jacket from the freestanding brass coatrack at the entrance to the room. The basket at the base of the rack had once held dozens of identical six-piece boxes of fudge from Spruce Valley's candy store, gift-wrapped in a variety of foil papers. She always prepared more gifts than the number of students she had, wanting every child to have a sense of choice. Brian, the last student having his last lesson of the year, still had four boxes to choose from. While he made his selection, Angela exchanged Christmas well wishes with his mother.

She walked them into the hall, a smile on her face, closed the front door behind them, and immediately dismissed the smile. From the kitchen, looking mournfully at her over the doggy gate, Blitzen's brown eyes begged for his freedom, and she padded toward him to grant his wish. Then, Brian's gift still in her hand, she returned to the music room. The gift array seldom varied from year to year. She blew out her breath and reached down to scratch Blitzen's neck. She didn't have to reach far. He was a big dog and she was a small woman.

"What do you think, my friend?" She talked to the yellow shaggy mutt as if she'd always had a dog in the house, when in truth Blitzen had only come to her seven months before.

In May.

Another month to dread.

"We might as well see what it is." Angela tore the paper off Brian's gift—or rather his mother's. She couldn't imagine Brian had any knowledge of what the package contained, or even curiosity. She based this opinion on the steady stream of eleven-year-old boys who came and went through her home over the last twenty-five years. Of course there were exceptions. She just didn't think Brian was one of them.

It was a small Christmas-themed notepad, useful enough for the next couple of weeks, she supposed. Grocery lists. To-do reminders. She might even inventory the freezer, to make sure she used up forgotten items, or start making lists of music to assign. After Christmas, of course, the seasonal art would look silly and she'd stick the pad in a bedside drawer. She might as well use it now.

Blitzen nuzzled her thigh and she squatted to return the affection. "We'll get through this, buddy. I know you understand. You're the only one who does."

He licked her face and she laughed, a sound she rarely made these days. She sat in the red sofa and patted her lap. So what if he was a seventy-pound sprawl? She didn't need to get up. Stroking his head the way he liked it, she took stock of the items that had amassed in the last couple of weeks. It was the same stuff every year. Santa mugs filled with candy canes. Canisters of homemade hot chocolate mix. Starbucks cards she'd never use—not because she didn't like coffee but because she rarely made the seven-mile drive to the nearest Starbucks. Enough cookies for a bake sale wrapped in various colors of cellophane and tied with ribbons. Garish ornaments that would never hang on her tasteful Victorian tree in the bay window—which she hadn't even put up this year. The odd handmade scarf in a color outside a palette she would ever don.

Spruce Valley was small, with distinct but overlapping social circles. Re-gifting was next to impossible, even if she waited a year, though she might be able to give away the Starbucks cards if she took them out of the envelopes. She might use the hot chocolate mix, though she never found it a bother to make hot cocoa on the stove. At least the mix would keep. She had no appetite for the cookies. The rest she'd have to box up and leave in the trunk of her car and hope she'd remember it was there the next time she drove to one of the surrounding towns large enough to at least have a thrift store where residents of Spruce Valley were unlikely to discover their items.

CHAPTER 2

W ho called a committee meeting on a Friday evening? Angela was not much inclined to attend, but she'd given her word, and when Rowena Pickwell called a few hours ago to remind her, she'd given her word a second time. It had something to do with Spruce Valley's traditional Christmas celebration. Angela had been helping for years, doing odd jobs behind the scenes, running errands, making sure the hot chocolate supply was uninterrupted, answering questions for people who visited for the occasion, staffing the first-aid booth. They might just want her to organize a children's choir from some of the families at church. She'd always done whatever Carole asked her to do.

Carole.

She pulled Blitzen's face up to look into his eyes. "I can't believe she's gone."

His jowls hung loose beneath huge sagging eyes. The only reason she had Blitzen was because Carole was gone. Maybe she should have said no to the committee this year right from the start. The closer the date got to Christmas, the less inclined she felt to do anything associated with Christmas. She couldn't beg off of Christmas music at the church. She was the organist and choir director, both positions that were impossible to find substitutes for at Christmastime. She would just have to soldier on through her duties. But why had she agreed to help the committee for A Christmas to Remember? It just seemed easier to agree to do something than to put up with all the pity looks and whispering that would come if she declined. The whole town knew how close she and Carole had been. As it was, the twenty-seven families represented by her forty piano students were probably speculating among themselves about why she had done away with the winter recital for the first time any of them could remember.

Ten days.

Since going to bed and waking on the other side of Christmas was not an option, she nudged Blitzen off her lap and padded to the closet in the front hall. The forecast didn't include a lot of snow, but temperatures would have dropped with the arrival of darkness. Angela selected her warmest coat with a hat and gloves.

"Let's check your water bowl, shall we?"

She walked into the kitchen. Blitzen sat in the hall. Angela grimaced.

"I know. You've got me figured out. But this is the way it has to be." She thumped her thigh. "Come on."

He stared, forlorn.

Angela sighed and reached into a zip-top bag on the counter. Blitzen stood on all fours. She threw the doggy treats well into the kitchen, and he chased them. It felt dishonest, but sometimes she had to do what she had to do. She opened the back door, dreading the frigid temperatures. At the last minute she remembered the water bowl and retraced a few steps to make sure it wasn't empty.

The house phone rang.

That's when everything began to unravel.

She picked it up and said hello just as she saw Blitzen nudge the door open wider and shoot out. Even after seven months with a dog, she made novice mistakes. She knew Blitzen had a tendency to bolt. Even when he had been Carole's dog, she knew this about him. Even the professional dog trainer had not successfully conditioned the behavior out of him. Not even with the best doggy treats.

The voice on the phone was already speaking in response to Angela's own weak habit of not checking caller ID before picking up the phone. She was not an unfriendly person. In fact she had only acquiesced to the caller ID feature a couple of years ago because the telephone company assured her it would be less expensive to choose a bundle that included it than to leave it out. Carole always teased her for not using it once she had it.

"Just glance at the phone," Carole used to say. "Don't pick it up if it's not a good time."

Angela always looked at it a fraction of a second too late, when the phone was already on the way to her face and her mouth was already forming a greeting.

And when Lea Sabatelli was on the other end of the conversation, there was no graceful way of backing out of it. Lea's soprano voice was the blessing of an angel in the church choir. In her presence the rest of the sopranos lost their timidity and believed in themselves, but it was Lea who soared to the highest notes at full volume and on perfect pitch when others dropped out. Angela was grateful to have her. But on the telephone? It was as if Lea fell into her favorite comfy chair with a plate of warm gooey chocolate chip cookies and a tall glass of milk. She was never in a hurry to get off the phone.

Lea thought this had been an exquisite day. She loved winter. She was getting *so* excited about flying to California after Christmas for the birth of her first grandchild.

Her speech utterly dripped with exclamation points.

Angela murmured soft affirmations as she stood in the frame of the open back door and scanned the yard for Blitzen. He had a way of getting out that she never understood. He was a big dog. How did he squeeze under the fence? Before much longer, she'd be out of oversized clay pots and miscellaneous items to put along the fence to discourage his efforts. Spring yard work might mean more intentional dog-proofing. He never wandered far. The thrill was in the escape. Then he'd turn up in the front yard or nosing around the neighbor's yard. Angela stepped out to the patio, unsure if she would lose the phone's signal if she went more than a few steps.

"It sounds like a lovely time of year for you." She managed to squeeze the words in while Lea stopped for breath. Or maybe she was wiping chocolate off her mouth with a napkin. "Did you have a question?"

"Oh. Right. I just wanted to double-check the rehearsal schedule."

"We're in good shape." Angela dared two more steps away from the door. By this time she thought there was a good chance Blitzen had left the yard. She wanted to call his name but couldn't quite bring herself to be that rude to Lea. "We'll have our usual rehearsal next Wednesday and run through all the Christmas Eve music a couple of times, and we'll be all set."

"If I circle a few measures that I'm not sure I'm singing correctly, could we go over those a few times?"

"Yes, of course."

"Well, then, I guess I'll see you on Sunday for church."

"I'll be there!"

Lea chuckled and hung up.

Angela cupped her hands around her mouth and bellowed. "Blitzen!"

The ground was damp enough to show recent dog prints illumined by safety lights. Blitzen had a favorite spot behind the garage, under some old paneling covered by a blue tarp. She ought to have gotten rid of it years ago. Until she had Blitzen, it was never a problem. With her hands on her knees, she peered into the hollow space created by the angle at which the panels were stacked.

No Blitzen. She looked at the tracks again. He'd been there, but the tracks deteriorated into muddy circles that she did not care to add to.

"Blitzen!"

The gate creaked.

Nora Neesen, her neighbor, appeared—with Blitzen. "Looking for something?"

"Thank you!" Angela said. "I left the door open for just a second when the phone rang, and he was out of there."

"You have to be careful with a pet. It's a big responsibility."

Angela made no pretense of smiling. She wasn't in the mood for one of Nora's lectures. Nora acted as if she were the only adult in the entire Spruce Valley. The maturation of the rest of the population stalled somewhere around eight years old.

"In any event, thank you for bringing him safely back to me," Angela said.

"You'll want to clean up his feet," Nora said, "before he tracks mud all through your house."

"Yes, I know."

"An old towel works well."

"Good idea." Angela gripped Blitzen's collar and tugged him in the direction of her house. He went willingly, almost triumphantly, as if he knew that he had successfully kept her from going wherever it was she was going when she pulled her warm coat from the closet.

Back in the kitchen, she shook a finger at the dog. "Stay right there while I get a towel."

She managed to get his paws cleaned up and then sponged off a spot on her coat. Ducking into the powder room, she examined the image in the mirror to determine if she remained presentable overall.

The gate was in place. The water bowl was full. Blitzen had

been fed two hours ago and was cordoned off in the kitchen. She had her purse and keys, hat and gloves. The meeting shouldn't last long—she'd probably missed the beginning by now—and she could come back home to enjoy the evening with Blitzen. Maybe she'd light the logs in the living room fireplace and find something to read. Perhaps a mystery novel—something that had nothing to do with Christmas.

It was a good thing the kitchen had no windows on the side of the house facing the garage because Blitzen would have set his sad face on a sill and done his best to shame her into coming back. She had a stack of music that she'd been driving around with for three days. This was the night she would remember to put it on the organ bench. Then she'd go to the meeting room and, for Carole's sake, agree to whatever it was the committee wanted her to do. Who was in charge this year, anyway? Rowena Pickwell had called the meeting. It must be her.

CHAPTER 3

Angela was a good twenty-three minutes late by the time she slipped into the room that used to be the church's library until somebody decided that nobody ever checked out a book anyway, and they needed the meeting space more than they needed piles of old donated books and no librarian. It wouldn't have been Rowena Pickwell who did that. She wasn't a member of Main Street Church. Her people were Methodists on the other side of town. If you showed the least bit of interest, she would expound on family lore about her great-great-grandfather laying the cornerstone of the Methodist church after having chiseled the date in it himself. The ironic thing was that after he died, there was no one to chisel his gravestone. For two years, it was unmarked limestone set in the ground above him, the only clue to his identity the proximity to the wife and daughter who had preceded him in death.

Rowena was a familiar figure at Main Street Church because for the last fifteen years she had chaired the town's committee for special events. The church's prominent location in relation to so many quaint shops that drew visitors made it difficult to imagine an event that didn't include it. There were Memorial Day, Independence Day, and Labor Day, of course. Every community across the country observed those days in some manner. But on Spruce Valley's Founders' Day and Spruce Valley's A Christmas to Remember, Rowena demanded perfection.

Angela glanced around. She didn't come in this room much. Its beige walls, built-in whiteboard, wide table, and chairs on wheels looked very much like a corporate meeting space. When she slid into one of the chairs, it rolled farther than she intended. The other heads around the table turned toward her.

"Good evening." Angela shirked out of her coat. "Sorry to be late. The phone rang. The dog got out. Well, I'm sure you know how these things happen even when you have the best intentions."

Four sets of eyes stared at her.

"I hope I haven't missed too much."

Rowena looked at Angela over her narrow black-rimmed reading glasses. Surely she got new glasses periodically, but they were always the same. Angela had a similar pair, which she used while she gave lessons and never remembered to put in her purse when she left the house. Ellen Schuman was Rowena's part-time assistant. She took notes at meetings so Rowena wouldn't have to. Nan Tarrington twiddled a pen between her fingers, but the pad of lined paper in front of her was unspoiled. Jasmine Tewell was dipping a tea bag in hot water with pronounced deliberation. Earl Grey, not jasmine, lest anyone was tempted to ask about Jasmine the person drinking jasmine the tea. Nan and Jasmine's husbands were known for their financial generosity to Spruce Valley's town budget, especially for underwriting events such as A Christmas to Remember. In Nan's case, the generosity also extended to Main Street Church. Rowena had recruited Jasmine from among the Methodists. It was never quite clear to Angela if Nan and Jasmine wanted to be on these committees or if their participation with some of the hands-on work was some sort of package deal that came with the checks their husbands wrote.

She shook off this pointless speculating. A Christmas to Remember was only eight days away. Rowena and her committee must have most of the planning buttoned down by now.

"How would you like me to contribute?" Angela said. "A few

of the children to sing from the sleigh as they did last year? I'm sure that wouldn't be a problem." She could get some of the older children from Main Street Church, and if they stuck to the first stanzas of several well-known carols, they wouldn't have to fuss with hymnals or lights to read by. Everyone would know the words. They wouldn't even have to rehearse. Angela could go home, send a few e-mails, have a few quiet days with Blitzen, show up for an hour on December 23, get through Christmas Eve services, and retreat once again into solitude until her lessons schedule began in the new year.

"Perhaps we should catch you up on what we have already discussed." Rowena moved her glasses a smidgen down her nose.

"That's not necessary," Angela said. "I don't want to take up everybody's time. I'll read the minutes later."

Rowena cleared her throat. "It was rather an important discussion."

"I'm sure you got right down to business. I apologize if I caused any delay at all."

It was possible that, at a subconscious level, she'd left that back door ajar when she answered the phone. She might even have hoped Blitzen would bolt, postponing her own departure for this particular meeting.

Carole used to love this meeting. Her face lit up weeks in advance. She had binders of cryptic notes—more ideas than she could use in a lifetime, she used to say.

No one expected her lifetime to be as short as it was.

For seven long months Angela had been walking around the empty space in her life that Carole ought to be filling. It only started with Blitzen, whose name was a daily reminder that Carole loved these meetings in the weeks leading up to Christmas. Sometimes she grabbed Angela by the wrist and made her get in the car to attend one of the meetings, and Angela had to admit she always came out feeling more excited about A Christmas to Remember. She could think back over each of the last fifteen years, since Rowena had attached the title to the event, and describe what she remembered from each year. Every memory involved Carole.

The surprise she had in store for the whole town that year. Even Angela wasn't allowed to know in advance.

The irresistible items she had amassed in her basement to sell in her seasonal Yule-Tidings Shoppe.

The handcrafted and personalized Christmas cards made by a pastor's wife in Illinois whom she discovered on Facebook.

Hundreds of gift bags for the children to pass out while the sleigh progressed down Main Street—and she filled them with practically no budget. All it took was an outgoing personality and people would donate all kinds of freebies.

A new design for the lights on the tallest spruce in town, at the north end of Main Street. It took days to string them, and all the while people guessed and guessed what they might form.

It was memorable every year.

"Go ahead, Ellen," Rowena said.

"Oh, no, no, no," Angela said. "Really, I'll just get up to speed with the minutes."

"It's important you get up to speed now."

Something hot passed through Angela's midsection.

Ellen cleared her throat. "Members present: Rowena Pickwell, committee chair; Ellen Schuman, secretary; Nan Tarrington; Jasmine Tewell. Absent: Angela Carter, guest member."

Ellen picked up her pen and made a note in the margin. "Tardy: Angela Carter, guest member. The meeting began promptly at six thirty with a reading of the minutes of the previous meeting, which were brief. In attendance at that meeting were Rowena Pickwell, committee chair; Ellen Schuman, secretary; and Nan Tarrington. Jasmine Tewell was absent due to unexpected out-of-town guests. At the beginning of the meeting, Rowena Pickwell entertained nominations to expand the number of members of the committee and make the work lighter. Everyone present agreed this would be a wise course of action. However, Nan received a telephone call informing her that her daughter had become very ill and she was needed at home. As her departure would only leave two members present, the meeting was disbanded."

Angela turned her head to one side and scratched at the base of her neck before raising a questioning finger. "I don't believe I heard the date of that meeting."

Ellen consulted her notes. "Six weeks ago. The first week of November."

Angela stretched an uncertain smile. With the right to-do list, a great deal of organizing could be done without meeting. Tonight's agenda was probably meant to put on the finishing touches.

"Shall I continue?" Ellen said.

"Please," Rowena said. "Skip to tonight's minutes."

Nan flipped her pen. Jasmine dunked her tea bag. Angela didn't like the way this was going.

Ellen found her place again. "We took a moment of silence to show our respect for Carole Freedholm and express our gratitude for the many years that she was at the helm of A Christmas to Remember and before that the many Christmas festivals that were held under other titles for the enjoyment of town residents and their guests. Her exuberance sets an inspiring standard for anyone who takes her place in planning this year's event and other events going forward."

Angela shuffled her feet under the table. *Anyone who takes her place?* Didn't they have someone taking her place? Isn't that why this committee was meeting?

"Please continue," Rowena said.

"After the moment of silence, it was noted that Angela Carter had not yet arrived. This was unfortunate. However, it was felt best to move forward with the evening's goal, which was to appoint an individual to fulfill the role that Carole Freedholm so ably filled for so many years. The traditional date for A Christmas to Remember is eight days away, so we can all appreciate that there is not a moment to spare at this point. It is hoped that ample supplies will be on hand to make this year's event as memorable as it has been every year. It was suggested that the best way to honor Carole's enthusiasm for A Christmas to Remember is to appoint someone who knew her well to take on the primary responsibilities. The name of Angela Carter was put forward to ensure that this year's event meets the expectations that Carole herself would have aspired to. In addition, the members present resolved to express gratitude for the quality of work that we are sure Angela will bring to the task. Both the nomination and the resolution passed unanimously."

Angela felt like she might have to reach out and shove her eyeballs back into her head.

"I really did mean to be on time," she said. "The dog got loose—Carole's dog."

Rowena waved a hand. "This is not some sort of punishment for tardiness. We're trying to honor Carole by asking the person who knew her best."

"I'm already quite busy with the music right here at the church, and there are only eight days till the festival. I had assumed the plans were. . .more developed. I would be happy to organize the children for that night."

Not happy, but resigned to that one task. What they were suggesting was beyond the realm of reason.

"I understand you helped to clear out Carole's house when it was rented," Rowena said.

"Yes," Angela said. "Her personal items."

"And her Christmas things?"

"We brought them here to the church to store."

"See? You already know more than we do. And the man who owns the sleigh?"

"Simon Masters," Angela said, her voice weakening. "But you all know him."

"We know you'll do your very best." Rowena removed her reading glasses, folded them, and put them in their case. "I'm sure all of us are willing to take an hour's shift here and there on the night of the festival, just as we always do. Just let us know where you want us."

Angela's jaw went slack. The last thing she wanted to do in her grief was try to match what Carole had done in her joy.

Once Rowena stood up, so did the others.

"You can lock up, can't you?" Nan said.

Somewhere in the middle of her sigh, Angela managed to nod.

CHAPTER 4

A ngela's plan for a quiet just-get-through-it Christmas was already ruined. What in the world were those women thinking? And how long had they been colluding to bring it about? It was hard to believe that this altruistic plot to honor Carole by plopping A Christmas to Remember in the lap of her best friend had occurred to them in the twenty-three minutes they'd been waiting for Angela to arrive.

From her queen-sized bed, Angela stared down at Blitzen in his doggy bed on the floor. She swung one arm down and he raised his head to lick her fingers.

"What have we gotten ourselves into?"

All she'd wanted was a peaceful Saturday. Light the fire. Sit with the dog by her feet, although he was more likely to be *on* her feet. Perhaps she'd write a few notes to old friends. Read that book. Nap. Most of all, she'd stay out of the stores. Even in a town of ten thousand people, it would be a busy week in the shops. She could almost smell the pot of soup she'd planned to simmer for half the day, and the bread that would rise in the warm kitchen.

Gone. All of it. Now she had only eight days, and she couldn't indulge herself even for an hour.

Irate, she threw back the quilts, startling Blitzen. Regardless of whether she had any appetite—and she didn't—he deserved to be fed. Carole had given him only the highest quality of food since he was a puppy, and Angela continued the diet. Pulling on her terry-cloth robe and finding slippers before she walked down the stairs and through the house, she sighed every second breath. She deluded herself that if she leaned far enough out the back door she'd be able to see if the gate had come unlatched, but Blitzen darted out and she had more cataclysmic things on her mind just then.

What would happen if she called Rowena Pickwell and said she just couldn't do this? An e-mail would be better. She could avoid the doubt and shame that would come from saying something Rowena wouldn't want to hear in a manner that would allow for immediate rebuttal.

Blitzen was at the back door already, and she let him in. She prepared several days of food for Blitzen at a time, so all she had to do was reach into the freezer and remove a dish and set it on the floor. He knew the motion and skittered to a stop at the end of the kitchen counter where she always set the dish. Next she filled his water bowl. Then, still sighing with such regularity that she began to wonder if her brain was getting enough oxygen, she set up the coffeemaker. She was going to need a lot of coffee today.

While it perked, she reconsidered the question of food. She picked up a banana, a frequent favorite for a quick breakfast. Not today. She put it back in the basket on the counter and opened a cabinet door to inspect the interior. Nothing there. Nothing in the fridge. Nothing. She didn't want to eat, and she didn't want to organize A Christmas to Remember. All she'd remember about the Christmas event was that it was foisted upon her.

She could send an e-mail and then leave town. Her sister was always saying she should come visit.

She smacked the counter. The church choir. She couldn't leave town, not this weekend, nor next. Church organists and choir directors never got Christmas off. In the summer, no one would notice if the choir didn't sing. She could go away on Youth

Sunday, and one of her competent high school students could play the piano.

None of that helped her now.

It took approximately three minutes for Blitzen to finish his meal and slop some water around. Even the coffee wasn't ready that fast.

"We'll go for a walk," she said. "I'll take the coffee in one of those thermal cups somebody gave me."

That was last year. If not for the fact that it was red and green, the thermal cup would have risen far above the usual gift fare from her piano students. Right now, no one would think twice about seeing her walking with it, and she would feel only slightly silly. Carole would have liked it. She had liked it, in fact. Angela had tried to re-gift it to her, but Carole insisted she take it back. She should keep it for at least one full Christmas season before she decided what to do with it.

Angela dressed quickly in jeans and a sweater, put on a warm jacket, poured steaming coffee into the cup, secured the lid, and put the leash on Blitzen. At the last minute, she dashed upstairs for the Christmas-themed notepad Brian had given her yesterday. It was small enough to fit in a pocket with a pen, and she started out with the theory that sometimes the best ideas came to people when they were out and about. The Main Street shops were still off-limits, but there were plenty of open spaces to walk in the other direction, where the brick buildings so iconic to American small towns of the era gave way first to homes like hers, residences to people who worked in town but lived a little ways out of town, and then fairly quickly to farms where pedestrians could lift their eyes to the horizon and see the red barns and silos two or three farms off and walk without too much interference from automobile traffic.

Blitzen tugged Angela along at a good clip. Every now and

then, she got a break when he stopped to sniff around and do his business. Once she made him stop long enough for her to lean against a fence post and start making a random list as thoughts came to her, trying to think as Carole would have thought. She could never be as creative as Carole was, especially with only eight days. But if she could just get the basics in place, that's all that mattered. If the committee had expectations for grandeur, then one of them should have stepped up instead of being so audibly relieved as they left last night.

Sometimes people who visited Spruce Valley wondered what caused people to move there. There weren't as many working farms as there used to be. The shops were quaint, but was it really possible to earn a living? There wasn't any real industry—no factories, no hospital, no military base to provide employment. It was a valid question. A lot of young people left for college and never lived in Spruce Valley again, yet they expected it to be there for the holidays.

Quite a few craftspeople supplied the shops that catered to tourists, whether passing through or visiting for a few days with friends or relatives. Quilts, woodworking, small furniture, toys, one-of-a-kind sweaters, blown glass—that sort of thing. People lived simply. Gradually, over the years, people with more ties to the nearest city were willing to accept longer commutes if it meant they could enjoy a country-style living on the weekends and their children could grow up knowing that food came from the ground and not just a box in the grocery store. Angela had come for a similar reason without the commute.

She'd been married then. Newly wed. Dan had spent two years working in a downtown law firm, which was more than enough for him to know he didn't want to spend a lifetime doing that. They'd bought the house, and he'd leased a storefront on Main Street, with the thought that he'd buy that property eventually as well, and hung his shingle: DAN CARTER, ATTORNEY. He was not even ostentatious enough to use *Daniel* or a middle initial. He was just Dan.

She met Carole, old enough to be an older sister but not quite of another generation, and settled in. Back then the dog underfoot was Dasher. Then Donner. Then Comet. Then Prancer. Sometimes two or three of the dogs overlapped in the years they romped through Carole's home. And finally came Blitzen, who was only three and should live quite a few more years.

Nine months.

When you're twenty-six and your husband is twenty-eight, you're debating whether it's worthwhile to strip the old wallpaper yourself or hire someone, and you wonder if the pipes in the old house are going to be trouble in the winter. In the back of your mind is the idea that maybe you should decide which of the upstairs bedrooms will be the nursery.

You don't imagine yourself a widow before you reach your second wedding anniversary. You don't imagine that in this peaceful little town a twenty-year-old with too much to drink will strike your husband on the sidewalk before wrapping his father's brand-new SUV around the streetlight.

You just don't.

Everyone supposed she would leave town. She'd thought about it. Her younger sister urged her to move back "home," to the city. Even after just nine months, this was home. Dan had been happy here. Angela held on to that as hard as she could, and when it threatened to slip from her grasp, she held on to Carole as hard as she could. Carole had seen the black scaly oozing inside of Angela's grief twenty-five years ago and never once turned away. Now Carole was gone almost as suddenly. She was only in her late sixties, but cancer plays no favorites. Diagnosis to death in the space of a month. The vacancy Carole left was like the emptiness that racked Angela when she was thirteen and her mother died suddenly. No one knew where her father was. He'd been gone for years. She and her sister ended up in a hastily arranged foster assignment with a neighbor who took pity.

Carole ran the Yule-Tidings Shoppe from September through the clearance sales in January. In between she stored some things in her home and others in a basement room at the church. All year long she gathered new goodies, while renting out the store space to others with seasonal goods—Valentines, Easter, summer, back-to-school, Halloween, Thanksgiving. It was a narrow space that didn't take much to convert between seasons. For the time being, the rental fees on the storefront and Carole's house went into an estate account. The storefront stood empty now. Eventually someone would want the Christmas business. It was an obvious opportunity, but no one wanted to be the vulture who circled the property the very first Christmas Carole was gone. Buford, who ran a diner on Main Street, sold some Christmas items on a rack in the front of his restaurant, but the inventory was fairly basic. He had none of the sorts of surprises that made people laugh, the way Carole always did. Angela couldn't imagine it was possible that another soul on the face of the earth could love Christmas as much as Carole had. The Yule-Tidings Shoppe and A Christmas to Remember—it all rolled into one gigantic festive holiday snowball for Carole.

Carole had put her affairs in order. After a brief respectful period of time, a Realtor contacted Angela about both the house and the storefront. The storefront was to be rented as always, with the exception that now it could be offered at Christmastime as well. The house could be rented as furnished as soon as Carole's personal effects were removed until such time as her heir could be located and he found it convenient to make more permanent arrangements.

Angela tugged on the leash. "Come on, buddy. I don't like this any more than you do, but we're going to do it because we loved her. Not for anyone else, just for her."

When she'd helped to clear personal items out of the house, Angela had taken one box of assorted items back to her own home. She had a feeling it was just the kind of collection where Carole would leave odd bits that could come in handy later—perhaps in the next eight days. By the time she got home from the walk, Angela was ready for another cup of coffee. At the kitchen table, Blitzen sat on her feet, and she outlined a just-the-basics approach to making some progress before the day was over.

Chapter 5

The list wasn't complicated. Angela was determined to keep it that way, though she'd left space to add obvious elements that had not yet occurred to her. After twenty-five years of traipsing after Carole, readying for Christmas festivals in Spruce Valley, she shouldn't even need a written list, but she'd feel better if she could check off the items as they were accomplished. The box she'd pulled from the closet, one of Carole's last boxes, had not given her the head start she'd hoped for. Instead it had made her weep. Only a little. She couldn't let herself get started doing that or she'd spend the next eight days crying instead of honoring Carole. *Honoring.* That was Rowena's word, and Angela wasn't sure it fit her, but she would at least try it on.

Her strategy was this: drive into town, which was about three miles, and park near the spot the sleigh usually began and walk the route. She wouldn't rush. Some of the shops had put up a few of their own decorations, but part of Spruce Valley's tradition was the anticipation that came from waiting until closer to Christmas and watching the lights and garlands go up, starting from the very place where she would begin her walk today and culminating on the tallest spruce in town at the north end of Main Street. Her task this morning was to see with Christmas eyes the fresh delight, to remember with Christmas eyes the details that made the scene magical, to hear with Christmas ears the sounds of the season and tilt her head in the directions they came from, perhaps even to breathe in the scents of Christmas. Her list would not be on a small pad jammed in a coat pocket. She would place the legal pad in front of her, with a blue roller-point pen in a firm grip. Dan had hooked her on using yellow narrow-ruled legal pads for practically everything, and a quarter of a century later, she maintained the same habit.

The day had more of a wintry bite to it than she expected. She had forgotten a hat when she went out earlier with Blitzen. This time she layered a scarf under her jacket and made sure she had both hat and gloves. The doggy gate was up, and the doggy had water.

"I'll see you later, buddy." She pulled up the zipper on her jacket. "Oh, don't look at me like that."

Blitzen padded toward her, sadder with every step, until he could rub his head against her thigh.

"You had a nice long walk this morning. Wouldn't you like to have a nice long nap? I know I would."

He lifted his eyes.

"Now that's not fair. Not fair at all."

His tail began to wag. He knew when he broke down her resolve.

"You'll have to be on the leash. I mean it. The whole time. And it will be a short leash, because we'll be on Main Street and I'll be concentrating on other things." She blew out her breath. "You know, before I had you, I just talked to whatever appliance was beeping at me. I guess you're quite the upgrade."

Angela took the leash off its hook, double-checked she had her wallet, picked up the legal pad and pen, and said, "Let's go."

Blitzen raced toward the back door. Angela decided she'd better leash him even just for the few yards to the garage to get him loaded into the back of the car.

If the length of time it took to find a parking spot meant anything, the last full weekend before Christmas was bringing robust retail sales. Angela found a spot on a side street two blocks off of Main Street and three blocks farther down than she was aiming for. Blitzen was agitated, ready for release. Angela calculated her movements carefully, opening the back of the car and getting a firm grip on the leash in one swift motion. Blitzen bounded to the ground.

She'd already forgotten the legal pad and opened the passenger door to grab it. The horse-drawn sleigh was one of the most memorable images of A Christmas to Remember. The sleigh was hitched to a team of matching horses with long manes—at least it seemed to Angela they were matching. She'd have to check. Perhaps it was only serendipitous some years. It can't have been the same pair for twenty-five years. While most people remembered the sleigh and the horses, the truth was that most years the sleigh was on wheels because more often than not the town didn't have enough snow in December for the runners of a sleigh to glide through. In fact, because Angela had seen the sleigh in broad daylight with Carole, she knew it was an old hay wagon with two axles painted a bright red. If there was enough snow, the owner jacked the axles up and put the wheels down on a pair of silver runners for a lovely effect.

Simon Masters had the sleigh-wagon. Were the horses also his? Who decided whether they would use the wheels or the runners? Angela wrote these questions on her legal pad, supposing that Simon could easily answer them.

The children came next to mind. She could still do what she originally thought the committee had intended for her and round up some of the children from the church, or perhaps some of her piano students or their older siblings, to sing a few carols from the sleigh. In her mind's picture, as many children as would like to would chase the sleigh as it progressed up Main Street. If there was snow, they clomped along in boots rather than tennis shoes. As the children ran, many of the shop owners offered goody bags. Angela debated about reminding shop owners. Was it really her responsibility to stir up enthusiasm?

The sleigh would pass Main Street Church, which was midway along the route. Angela made a note to be sure the Ladies Aid Society was ready with their baked goods fund-raiser and that the trustees would hang the bright red wreaths on the double front doors of the church with the welcome sign announcing the time of the Christmas Eve services.

Angela didn't have the slightest idea how to get the lights and garlands hung. She jotted down several names of people who might know how that happened, drawing a box around them to remind herself that she couldn't let that task go much longer.

At the north end of Main Street, the pinnacle moment came when the lights on the tall spruce came on and the whole town gasped at the same moment.

Well, that's what happened when Carole was in charge. Carole spent weeks planning mathematical arrangements of lights around the tree in a secret design. Only two other people would know the design they would create, and that was only of necessity. Somebody had to climb those ladders and string those lights. For three days, people stood and watched, speculating what might emerge. Angela would have no surprise pattern to offer this year. She would make a few calls, hire the usual crew, whoever that was, and be done with it. Straight lines up and down would have to do. The lines wouldn't even have to be straight, and if some of the lights didn't blink with the rest, so be it. She only had eight days. If they wanted creativity, they should have asked someone else. It might not even be realistic to do anything at all with the spruce.

CHAPTER 6

S lowly, throughout the day, the wind picked up and the temperature dropped steadily. Even with the extra layer of the scarf under her jacket, Angela started to feel like a human Popsicle. If it were not for Blitzen, she might have broken her resolve and ducked into one of the shops for a few minutes to warm up. It wasn't that Spruce Valley never had cold days or snow in December. It was just that so often they didn't. Where was a person to park her expectations? Angela hadn't even worn her boots for their furry warmth. The church was probably unlocked for the rehearsal of the children's Christmas play the next morning, but if Angela went inside with the dog she risked distracting the children—for which she would be rewarded with a scowl from the program's director. She'd also risk getting sucked into final decoration around the building. It was no place for Blitzen. He did all right left on his own at home in the kitchen, but he was too curious and enthusiastic to be off a short leash in an unfamiliar place.

So Angela waved at the two trustees hanging the red wreaths on the doors—something to check off her list—clapped her hands together seeking warmth, and tugged her hat down farther around her face.

"How about a hot chocolate?"

Angela had pulled her hat so far down that now she couldn't turn her head and lift her eyes. Blitzen's movement required her to twist her entire torso while she again adjusted her hat.

"Hello, Buford."

He gestured toward his diner across the street and down a

little way. "I was just heading back. You look like you could use some warmth."

"I could!"

"It would be against code to have the dog inside, but if you just duck in closer to the door, you'll at least get out of the wind for a few minutes."

"Thank you, I think I will, if you don't mind."

They crossed the street together and walked a couple of blocks. It was nice of Buford to offer hot chocolate. While she waited, she gave Blitzen more length on the leash and reviewed her notes so far. She just hoped he didn't get waylaid by customers inside. A few people stopped to give Blitzen some attention, which got his tail going at top speed.

Just as Angela thought of setting an outer limit to how long she would wait for him, Buford returned.

"I heard you're taking over A Christmas to Remember." He handed her a large Styrofoam cup with a lid.

Steam rising through the small sipping hole was a good sign. "I don't know if 'taking over' is the best way to put it," Angela said.

"That's what the scuttlebutt is."

"Oh? Has word gotten around already?" Angela took a test sip.

Buford folded his arms across his chest. "I only heard three or four days ago. Folks seem to think it's a good idea."

"Three or four days?" How could anyone hear three or four days ago when Angela had heard barely eighteen hours ago?

Buford nodded. "You've got some pretty big shoes to fill. Carole sure had it down to a science."

Angela swallowed more hot chocolate, waiting to see if Buford would toss any more clichés at her. Shoes and science aside, she'd stick to her legal pad. She wasn't sure if she liked or disliked other people mentioning Carole at this time of year. Lots of people liked Carole, or even felt true affection for her.

But somehow they managed to be lighthearted at the time of year when Carole's absence was most pronounced. She was an empty spot for someone to take over. Buford took over selling Christmas wrapping papers. Angela took over A Christmas to Remember—a decision that half the town seemed to know about before it was suggested to her. Maybe she would send that e-mail after all, politely but firmly declining.

If she did, she'd have to put up with endless questions about why she had said no. Dropping out at the last minute as she did, she'd be the reason Spruce Valley didn't have A Christmas to Remember. The Christmas they'd remember would be the Christmas she'd ruined.

None of them knew what Angela was going through. How could they?

"I'd better get going," Angela said, tucking her legal pad under her arm and adjusting her hat before tightening Blitzen's leash. "Thanks for the hot chocolate."

"Anytime," Buford said. "And if you need Christmas cards or paper, stop by and see me."

Blitzen tugged at the leash. Angela tugged him in the opposite direction. On her pad, she was keeping a count of how many streetlamps she saw that would need garlands and lights, as well as making a list of the shops to make sure she didn't omit any in her planning. Perhaps when she got into Carole's Christmas things at the church—tomorrow after the service, without Blitzen in tow—she might discover a planning guide. If not, at least she'd have her own notes to go by. Two blocks down she paused and looked in the direction she'd come from to double-check her notes.

"Well, hello, Angela."

She looked up to see her neighbor's face above an armful of packages. "Nora, hello."

"What brings you into town?"

"Just a bit of planning."

"I heard the news. I think it's fabulous."

"Thank you for your confidence."

"Did you see that young man who just came out of the quilt shop?"

Angela raised her eyebrows. "I'm afraid not."

"You must have seen him. He was just a second or two ahead of me."

"I suppose I wasn't looking in the right direction at the right time."

"I suppose. He's a curious young man. A peculiar accent, not quite British but something like that."

Angela shrugged. "Can't help you."

"Very good looking, too."

He could be eligible bachelor of the year in three countries, and it wouldn't change the fact that Angela hadn't seen him.

"Maybe you'll spot him again another time." Angela turned to continue toward the pinnacle spruce, wondering who might know how tall it was if the information didn't turn up in Carole's notes. Somebody who helped string lights or take them down must know. And they must have used something more than ladders. Scaffolding? Whose, and how much? Despite her determination to keep things simple, every detail that came to her mind made this task more complex. She was starting to appreciate the financial contributions to the event.

Once she had walked the entire route the sleigh would take, she diverted to a side street and let Blitzen have more leash and more speed. It was still early afternoon. She could drive out to Simon Masters's farm and see about the sleigh and horses. Once she got to her car and Blitzen was situated, she used her cell phone to track down the Masters's phone number and called ahead. Simon was standing outside the new barn, painted a classic red, wiping oil off his hands when she arrived.

She let her door fall shut behind her. "Okay if I let my dog out—on a leash?"

He turned his hands up and shrugged. "If you're sure he won't run off, you don't have to use the leash on my account."

Angela scanned the environs, fairly sure that Blitzen would stay nearby or come when she called. Just in case, she patted her leg, and when he dutifully stood right beside her, she dropped a few of the doggy treats she always kept in the back of the car. She transferred a small supply to her jacket pocket.

"So I heard you're in charge of A Christmas to Remember," Simon said.

Angela gave a nervous laugh. "I'm trying not to turn it into A Christmas to Forget." Blitzen sniffed the ground for a few feet and then began trotting in a wide circle.

Simon waved a hand. "Nah. The thing about Christmas is, it'll always come around again, and by then nobody much cares about last year."

"I hope you're right, but just in case, I'm trying to get things sort of right," Angela said. "So you have the sleigh. Do we also use your horses?"

"I've got a pair we've been using for a few years, mostly because folks think they look nice together. They're getting a little old, but they can still do the job."

"And the sleigh? Wagon? Not sure what the proper term is."

Simon laughed. "She's a creature all her own, that's for sure. We keep her in the old barn with some other odds and ends." He led the way.

Angela followed, keeping an eye out for Blitzen and suspecting he had cornered a rabbit. She grimaced slightly at the thought that she might be responsible for his goods.

Simon opened creaking doors that made Angela jump out of

the way lest they leave their hinges.

"The wagon's built heavy," Simon said. "It might take both of us to heave it out of there."

"What can I do?" Angela glanced again at the barn doors but moved toward them.

"I'll squeeze around to the back and push. Once it starts rolling, just try to steer a little and don't let it run away."

"Okay." Angela swallowed. If the wagon was "built heavy" as Simon said, she might not be the best defense against a runaway. She braced herself.

"Just grab the shaft," Simon said, beginning to push. "You'll be fine."

Angela gripped the wooden protrusion with gloved hands. Blitzen came close to inspect. The old wagon creaked forward.

"Blitzen! Out of the way!" Angela waved away the dog and quickly resumed steering. By now the wagon was halfway out of the ramshackle barn. It was a simple wooden bed on rubber tires. Angela glanced around for the add-on pieces that would transform it into a sleigh—painted wooden slides cut along a curved template and runners, if there should be snow.

A snap made her freeze. Blitzen?

It wasn't his doing. He was safely and obediently behind her.

"Simon?" she said. "Are you all right?"

He popped up from the back end of the wagon. "Axle cracked."

"That doesn't sound good."

He brushed his hands against his jeans. "It's not."

Angela's shoulders sank. "Can it be fixed?"

"I wouldn't want to promise. At least not in time. I'd have to special order the axle, and frankly, I'm not sure the wagon is worth the bother."

Angela pulled her hat and gloves off and ran her hands through her hair. Suddenly being cold was not her biggest problem.

Chapter 7

Angela closed the organist's oversized edition of the hymnal and centered it in the rack in front of her. The final Sunday service before Christmas Eve was complete. On one side of the hymnal were copies of the prelude, offertory, and postlude music she'd selected for next Sunday morning and for the late-night Christmas Eve service on the same day. She knew the pieces well, having used them many times over the years and practiced them in recent weeks. On the other side of the hymnal were the choir pieces for next Sunday. Wednesday would bring the final choir practice. They would sing as usual in the morning, as well as several pieces during the candlelight service. If she hadn't had A Christmas to Remember dropped in her lap two days ago, she could have gone on autopilot at this point, punctuating the final week before Christmas only with that one last choir practice.

That had been the plan. It was all out the window now. Angela's yellow legal pad got filled in more and more. When she left her house the day before, she was determined to keep her notes to one page. Or two, maximum. Since then she'd scribbled on the pages so much that twice she had started over with fresh effort to keep her notes orderly and legible.

The demise of the sleigh wagon was unfortunate. She had no clear solution to that dilemma, and frankly, she wasn't sure how hard she would even try. If she planted the information in the ears of the right shopkeepers along Main Street, by the night of the event everyone in town would know that the axle had broken and no one could blame her for not waving a magic wand and coming up with another one, especially if there was no snow. Or maybe it would be better to say nothing in advance and avoid having people bend her ear about it.

The more pressing issue of the day was the matter of the decorating options. When they cleaned out Carole's house last spring, Christmas items were boxed up without any particular system beyond what space there was in a box for the item in a person's hand. Even Angela had woefully underestimated how much Carole had at home, and there was more at the church. But everyone involved in boxing things up agreed it made sense to wait until after this Christmas for final sorting. They would have to get everything out again anyway. At the time, Angela nodded, barely registering the group decisions. Certainly she hadn't imagined this day, when *she* would be the one going through those boxes. That could take days she didn't have, unless they were more organized than she remembered.

For now she just needed help getting them out of the awkward storage room in the basement, where the property committee stuck old paint cans, ladders tall enough to change the light bulbs in the sanctuary, and file cabinets of old membership records.

She felt the presence of someone behind her and swiveled on her bench.

"Hello, Brian."

"My grandpa said he's ready to go to the basement. I'm going to help him get everything out. He said I should ask you what to do with it."

Brian's grandfather had a pickup truck that could carry far more boxes than her small SUV, but she didn't want any more of the boxes in her house than necessary, especially when they'd have to be lugged back to Main Street anyway.

"Let's just put them out in the big youth room," she said. The youth activities were suspended for the Christmas break.

No one would be inconvenienced if Angela borrowed the space. She could run down the street to Buford's Diner to pick up a sandwich and come back to sort the boxes.

"I'll tell Grandpa."

"Thank you. I'll be right down to help."

Brian hesitated.

"Brian?"

"Do you give organ lessons?"

She couldn't help but soften. "Where would you practice?"

"My grandma has an organ. It's not as big as this one. More of a starter organ."

Angela smiled. "Let's get through Christmas first. Then perhaps we'll talk about it in the new year."

Brian grinned and skedaddled.

Angela slid off the bench, slipped out of her organ shoes, and found her comfortable brown flats in the same spot where she'd been leaving street shoes during services for two decades. Clusters of murmuring conversation spattered the sanctuary as the last of the morning worshippers moseyed toward the foyer with its array of coffee, muffins, and fruit. The laugh Angela heard as she debated grabbing a cup of coffee before going downstairs to survey the Christmas boxes was Lea Sabatelli's. Even when she spoke, she emitted the lilt of a song, and when she spoke of the impending arrival of her first grandchild, she might have been one of the Christmas angels heralding joy to the world. New Year's Eve would find her winging west to California just in time for her daughter's due date, to greet her grandson. In a few weeks, when she tore herself away from her daughter's home to return to Spruce Valley, her phone would be full of photos of newborn snugglies and smiles.

Angela decided on the coffee. She might be here all afternoon. It couldn't hurt to bolster for the task. Her favorite squat white cup was available, and she arranged it under the spigot of the ubiquitous forty-cup coffee urn that every church seemed to have in triplicate, double-checking she was not getting decaf by mistake.

"Mrs. Carter! Mrs. Carter!"

It was not often she heard Brian Bergstrom's voice at this level, especially in the church foyer.

"Grandpa says you'd better come right down."

"Yes, I was just going to bring some coffee with me."

"Right now, he said to tell you."

Angela shut off the spigot and set the mug aside. Brian was already shooting through the coffee minglers at a faster speed than Angela would be able to match. Two people who seemed to want her attention had to settle for a smile and the touch of an elbow that might pass for a promise to connect later. The farther she got from the coffeepots and muffins, the thinner the crowd became. Nevertheless, by the time she got to the top of the stairs leading downward, Brian was out of sight. She readjusted her grip on her purse and scampered down the steps. As soon as she turned the corner at the bottom, she gasped.

Allen Bergstrom plopped a soggy cardboard box against the wall in the large room, where it nearly splatted open alongside another that had.

"What happened?" Angela shoved her purse onto a counter and tried to keep her jaw from dropping.

"Water leak," Allen said.

"These are Christmas boxes?" Angela approached the one that had helplessly spilled its guts.

"Yep."

She shrugged, squinting at disintegrating silk garland. "There are so many boxes. We were going to sort them anyway."

Brian backed into the room dragging another box longer than

he was tall. Trying to hold its sides together was as impossible as putting the fall leaves back on a tree after they'd dropped into an unexpected early snow.

"Maybe you should just let that be," Allen said to his grandson.

"It's a mess in there, Grandpa," Brian said.

"I know." Allen turned to Angela. "You should probably come have a look."

"At what?" Angela's stomach soured.

"Just come."

She followed Allen and Brian to the other end of the large room and into the storage space, stopping just inside the open door and wrinkling her nose at the stench of mildew.

"Allen," she said.

"Like I said, water leak."

"A rather big one, by my guess."

"You wouldn't be wrong."

Angela glanced around the room. Stacks of cardboard boxes that she had arranged herself a few months ago now weighed down on one another in lopsided bulges. At the base of each tower, what had once been cardboard was long compromised, as water wicked through the fibers from one carton to another. She made herself take another step in. Crates hammered together from wooden pallets scavenged from behind the hardware store lined one wall, sheltering Mary and Joseph and the baby Jesus with the shepherds and the barn animal figures, and behind them an impressive set of life-sized carved carolers that Carole had surprised the town with fifteen years ago. Angela could hardly imagine the street corners without these adornments of the season.

"This must have been going for weeks," she said.

Allen nodded. "We had that cold snap a couple of months back."

"I remember. Everyone said how unusual it was to be so cold so early."

"Took us all by surprise." Allen gestured toward a closet across the room. "There are pipes in there."

"But the path is blocked," Angela said.

"I'll get some help, and we'll move everything," Allen said. "Probably tomorrow. My guess is once we get that door open we'll find our damaged pipe."

Angela slowly moistened her lips and tried to make her vision focus on the boxes she had stacked. Carole's things. Carole's Christmas things. As much as Angela resented the manner in which A Christmas to Remember was thrust upon her, and as much as she dreaded a final sorting of Carole's belongings, losing them to these circumstances was a stab in the gut.

"The Nativity?" she said.

Allen shook his head.

"The carved carolers?"

"A little green around the gills, if you get my drift."

So many of the traditional pieces were wooden. That was part of the charm of A Christmas to Remember—and the reason nothing would have survived water damage.

"Nothing is salvageable," she muttered.

"I'm afraid not," Allen said. "Even the boxes on top have been damp long enough to be growing a good grunge by now."

Angela winced. "What about lights? Were there lights?"

Allen scratched the back of his head. "I doubt you'd want to have to clean them up only to discover they wouldn't work, after all."

She sighed. He was right. She only had a few days.

"You have lights, don't you, Grandpa?" Brian said. "The ones in your attic."

Allen chuckled. "The ones your grandma has been threatening to throw out an attic window?"

Brian nodded.

Allen looked at Angela. "They're about twenty years old, but Brian and I plugged them in just the other day. I know they work. You're welcome to them."

"How many?"

"I never counted."

"Lots," Brian said. "Lots and lots."

Angela considered the boy's expectant wide brown eyes.

"I guess we could at least look at them," she said, "and see if we think they're enough."

"Grandpa knows how to put them up," Brian said. "He always helped Miss Freedholm. Every year. He has all the right ladders and everything."

"That's right. He did." Angela looked at Allen. "I hope you'll help me, too."

"I'd be glad to," Allen said. "I have to warn you. If you reject the lights, Millie won't want to take them back. Once they're out of the attic, that's it."

"I want to help put them up," Brian said.

"Sure, buddy." Allen tousled the boy's hair. He nodded at Angela. "We'll bring the lights by as soon as we get them down and untangled."

"Thank you."

An undetermined number of lights and a couple of old horses. Not exactly the progress Angela had hoped for that weekend. No sleigh, makeshift or otherwise. No outdoor garlands. No Nativity figures. No carved and painted holiday carolers with cherry cheeks and mittened hands holding their hymnals to spread good news among the street corners.

CHAPTER 8

The afternoon turned sharply toward darkness. It was barely four o'clock when Angela drew living room curtains closed, wondering why she'd bothered to open them after church. The day hadn't been bright in any manner, so all she'd let in was dreary gray. The daylight hours came and went so quickly in the week before Christmas that it hardly seemed worth the bother to go through the motions of welcoming the day only to close the curtains on it before she'd even had her supper. Four more days. Every year she watched the calendar. Once it got past December 21, the days would begin lengthening again.

This year she wanted to be on the other side of Christmas as well.

After walking Blitzen, she was in soft jeans and an old sweatshirt. Thick socks slid slightly on the polished wood floor as Angela crossed to her favorite overstuffed side chair and picked up her yellow legal pad. Blitzen circled a couple of times before centering his weight on her feet and settling in.

Nothing on the yellow pad made sense anymore. Angela chewed on the end of her pen trying not to fling the whole mess against a wall. She'd used two whole days of her eight and had almost nothing to show for it. Was she supposed to string lights around a pair of horses and march them down Main Street? Children singing "Away in a Manger" might redeem the pathetic scene.

Angela flipped to a fresh sheet of paper. Given the revelations of the last two days, she needed a fresh angle on her planning.

Blitzen's head popped up.

"What is it?" Angela's gaze followed the dog's. She heard steps on the porch.

Blitzen's barking frenzy started in the same instant as the pounding on the front door. Angela tossed her pad aside, grabbed Blitzen's collar, and opened the front door.

"Brian!"

His chest heaved.

"Brian, what's wrong?"

He gulped air and said, "Grandma sent me. I'm staying with them. My parents are away overnight at my dad's company Christmas party, and Grandma doesn't drive at night, especially if she's nervous. It's her eyes."

"Does she need to go somewhere?" Allen and Millie Bergstrom were only in their sixties, but Millie was planning to have cataract surgery in the new year. Allen was an able driver, though.

"To the hospital," Brian said. "You're the closest person we could think of that I could run to."

"Hospital?"

"Grandpa and I were getting the lights, just like we said we would. There's no rail on the attic stairs."

Angela's heart lurched. "Did he fall?"

Brian nodded. "He says he's all right, but Grandma doesn't think so. He can't even stand up."

Angela blew out her breath, hoping that what Allen really needed wasn't an ambulance.

"Come inside," she said. "Let me find my shoes and get my keys."

As Brian stepped inside, Blitzen began a fresh round of barking, and Angela looked past him to see Nora from next door.

"Blitzen, shush," Angela said.

"I couldn't help noticing the commotion," Nora said, coming up the porch steps. "Your dog seems easily excitable. Are you sure you don't want the name of my friend who is a dog trainer?"

This was not the time to debate the realities of canine behavior. Angela tried to remember where she'd kicked off her shoes.

Nora eyed Brian.

"This is one of my students," Angela said. "I'm going to run over to see his grandparents."

"You won't leave the dog barking the whole time, will you?"

For a moment Angela imagined releasing her grip on Blitzen's collar. His tail wagging rapidly, his size, and his enthusiasm in greeting guests were more threat than evil intent. But the front door was still standing wide open.

"He'll be in the kitchen as usual," Angela said.

"My grandma said to ask you to hurry," Brian said.

"Yes," Angela said, her free hand on the heavy front door. "Have a nice evening, Nora. Perhaps we'll catch each other tomorrow."

She closed the door and released Blitzen. "I think my wallet is upstairs," she said to Brian. "I'll be right back. Why don't you use the phone in the kitchen and call your grandmother to let her know we're on our way."

Having donned appropriate footwear and double-checked her purse for her driving glasses, Angela raced back down the stairs, pulled a warm jacket from the closet, and headed toward the kitchen. Blitzen was at her heels, ever hopeful.

Brian hung up the phone. "I told her."

"Good."

"She said she got him down the stairs to the kitchen. She thinks it's broken."

"What's broken?"

"Can a person's back break?"

"There are a lot of bones in the back." Angela drew a measured breath and latched the gate that would confine Blitzen. A back injury was nothing to take lightly. She might have to quietly insist that Millie call an ambulance, after all.

She let Brian go ahead of her out the back door before tossing doggy treats across the room to keep Blitzen from begging to come along.

"It's been quite a day, hasn't it?" Angela pressed the button on her key fob to unlock all the doors of her car. "Give me a second. I'll have to clear off the seat for you."

Brian waited patiently while she gathered up the odds and ends of music that seemed to follow her everywhere and tossed the stack into the backseat. Reaching for his seat belt, he offered a sluggish smile.

"You're worried," she said as she started the car.

He looked at his hands in his lap.

"You did well. You did just what your grandmother needed you to do. We're going to get your grandpa the help he needs."

"Thank you."

His voice was faint, but he was a quiet child. Who knew? Maybe he would someday find his musical voice in a saxophone or an organ.

She put the car in gear and backed out of the driveway. "You'll have to remind me of the way."

He pointed, and she turned in the direction of his finger. In a distant part of her mind, memories tumbled into place. She'd been to the elder Bergstroms' home a time or two. Millie used to sing in the choir, and she'd hosted the salad course of a progressive dinner for the singers. That was before Brian was born. Or maybe he'd just arrived. Twenty-five years in a town of ten thousand blurred events.

She parked in the Bergstrom driveway and followed Brian up the sidewalk and through the front door.

"Grandma?" he called.

"In the kitchen," came the reply.

Allen sat in a blue vinyl kitchen chair with one hand bracing his lower back. Millie hovered with an ice pack, unsure where to apply it. Angela had little experience with these things. This was a two-story home. How in the world had Millie, with her slight build, gotten her husband off the attic landing, down the main stairs, and into the kitchen when clearly the best he could offer was a painful shuffle?

Allen braced himself and leaned forward, wincing.

"I'm happy to help," Angela said, "but I wonder if we shouldn't call an ambulance, after all. A back injury can be serious."

"I've already done the hardest part," Millie said. "I got him down here, didn't I? And Brian got you. No telling how long we'd be waiting for them to come all the way from the hospital."

Allen exhaled heavily before groaning. "Do I get a vote?"

"Of course." Angela forced herself to look at him.

"We're only ten feet from the back door," Allen said. "There are no steps down to the driveway."

"Our car is in the garage," Millie said. "You can come right up to the door with yours."

"Okay, okay," Angela said. "I will go out and pull up as close as I can get, if you're sure an ambulance wouldn't be a better way to travel."

"We've already been to that rodeo," Allen said. "They charge an arm and a leg. I'm not dying. It's just my back."

Visions of paralysis floated through Angela's mind.

"He knows he has disc issues," Millie said. "He tries to do too much."

"He's had this before?" Angela said.

"Yes. He needs the hospital to get the pain under control—and to make sure it's not a different disc. Or that nothing's broken."

"Nothing's broken." Allen exhaled through gritted teeth.

"If you're sure," Angela said.

"Brian," Millie said, "get your grandpa's jacket off the hook."

"Don't fuss," Allen said. "I can't put a jacket on right now."

"A quilt, then. Quickly, Brian."

Angela hustled out the back door and down the driveway to where she'd left her car. She popped the trunk, scooped her clutter out of the backseat, and dumped it into the trunk. No matter how many times she resolved to stop treating her vehicle like a high school locker, she never shook the habit of leaving things in the car.

By the time Angela got her car pulled up to the kitchen door, Allen had his long arms slung over the shoulders of his wife and grandson. Angela jumped out to open the rear doors. Allen leaned against the car, waved off further assistance, and lowered himself in. Millie and Brian ran around to the other side.

Angela backed out of the driveway.

"Watch the bump at the end of the block," Allen muttered.

Angela was glad for the warning.

The hospital was eight-and-a-half tedious miles away. Spruce Valley had a few doctors, but it couldn't support even an urgent care center that was open on the weekends. No one spoke. Allen groaned intermittently. Angela could not interpret whether that meant he wished she'd drive faster or slow down for the potholes.

Finally, she pulled up under the overhang at the emergency department entrance.

"I'll get help." The automatic doors opened, and Millie darted into the building. She was back with a wheelchair and an orderly who looked like he knew how to handle a man of Allen's stature.

"I'll park and meet you inside," Angela said once Allen was in the chair.

The doors whooshed open again and swallowed the patient and his entourage. Angela breathed in and out three times with deliberation before putting the car in gear and navigating into the parking lot.

An MRI to confirm the suspect disc.

Hopefully some painkillers—and hopefully Allen would agree to take them.

Follow-up with an orthopedist and perhaps a neurologist because of trapped nerves. Since this was a reoccurrence of a known problem, it might be time to discuss surgery.

Then they'd have to get him home. Angela hadn't seen much of the house and couldn't remember if there was a place Allen might sleep on the main floor.

There was a lot to figure out.

But clearly Allen would not be climbing any ladders to hang lights up and down Main Street.

CHAPTER 9

Candles. And paper lanterns. These were the subjects on Angela's mind when she woke on Monday morning because they were two items she was sure would not have been among the ruined boxes in the church basement.

The evening had been long. Every step at the hospital involved a separate wait, and once they were back at the Bergstroms', she couldn't just drop them off. Allen was medicated, which was in his best interest for the next few days. He'd have to see an orthopedist about the surgery question. In any event, he was in no condition to climb stairs, so sleeping arrangements had to be sorted out. At least there was a main-floor bathroom. Obviously Allen couldn't be left on his own. Angela and Brian took sheets and blankets from an upstairs closet and made up two deep leather couches in the main-floor family room for his grandparents to sleep on.

By the time Angela got home, Blitzen was desperate to go outside. It was silly not to have a doggy door. As soon as this Christmas business was over, she'd find somebody who could make her existence more dog-friendly. For now, she stood outside watching Blitzen for a few minutes so she could let him back in.

In the meantime, she had six days.

Six days.

It didn't seem reasonable to ask Millie about the lights that were probably still strewn on the attic stairs, although Brian might yet round them up. All she was certain she had to work with were Simon's two horses. This was not exactly forward progress.

For years she and Carole had debated the advisability of

distributing candles during A Christmas to Remember. The number of things that could catch fire, and the concentration of people, argued against it. Yet people had come to expect them. Some would only light them while the sleigh took its route. Others carried them home to incorporate into their family's traditions. Angela had thought candles would be one detail she'd conveniently overlook, but she had to produce something more than horses. Besides, she was fairly certain that the annual order was automatic and that if she went into the candle shop on Main Street and inquired, she would discover seven hundred and fifty white Christmas candles awaiting her. They would be Elinor's annual contribution to A Christmas to Remember.

So she ate a quick breakfast, gulped the coffee that she had nearly let get too cool, walked Blitzen, and headed to Main Street.

The mixed fragrances of the candle shop always confused her senses. What was she supposed to be smelling? Clove? Evergreen? Cinnamon? She moved through the shop toward the counter, reading signs to help her distinguish fragrances. Balsam and fir. Chestnut. Juniper. Mistletoe.

Behind her the shop's bell jangled. She didn't remember it ringing when she came in, though of course it had been there for as long as Elinor had been running the shop, which was at least fifteen years. Angela glanced back over her shoulder. No one had followed her in. Someone must have just left. She angled toward the counter once again.

"Did you see him?" Elinor said.

"Who?"

"That young man? He walked right past you."

"I guess I didn't notice." Angela had been too busy mentally sorting fragrances. They still jumbled together.

"You had to have seen him." Kim, an alto in the church choir raised an insistent tone.

Angela shrugged. "I wasn't paying attention. I have candles on the brain this morning."

"I suppose he might have slipped down the other aisle." Kim twisted her lips to one side. "I've never seen him before, and I thought I knew everyone in this town."

"We get a lot of visitors at this time of year," Angela offered.

"That's right," Elinor said. "And it's good for business. That man spent seventy dollars in here."

"I bet if I wander down the street I'll see him again," Kim said.

"Maybe." Elinor straightened a stack of discount flyers on the counter.

Kim wandered away.

"Are you sure you didn't see him?" Elinor whispered.

"No," Angela whispered back. "Why is he so important?"

"There's something about him. I can't quite put my finger on it."

"Kim seems to feel the same way."

"Mmm."

"I came for candles," Angela said.

Elinor raised her eyebrows. "It's a candle shop."

"For A Christmas to Remember," Angela said. "I've been asked to organize things. I know you usually had some for Carole."

"Of course. I've had them for weeks, actually. I kept getting a different answer about what to do with them, so I set them aside."

"I'll be happy to take them off your hands, then."

Elinor surveyed the shop, which was now empty except for the two of them.

"Come on back in the office and we'll get them."

Elinor's office looked about as organized as Angela's trunk, but she seemed to zero in on one particular corner of the desk and lifted folders and catalogs.

"They were right here a few days ago," Elinor said. "Three boxes of two hundred and fifty each. One of the girls must have moved them."

"Can I help you look?"

"Just give me a moment." Elinor's eyes darted from the top of the filing cabinet to an overloaded bookcase to a side chair. She moved a few more things, revealing only more clutter. "Oh, no."

"Oh, no what?" Angela stepped closer to Elinor as she turned to the area behind her desk.

"The radiator." Elinor moved a stack of magazines from the metal covering fitted over the radiator.

Three boxes were laid side by side.

Elinor slapped her forehead. "The girls come in here on their breaks. I am forever telling them not to touch anything."

Angela's stomach hardened. Seven hundred and fifty candles on top of an ancient radiator.

Elinor picked up one box and moaned. "I can tell already."

"Tell what?" Angela wanted to hear the words. She was not in the mood for assumptions and ambiguity.

"I'm afraid they're ruined. Melted together into three great globs." Elinor dropped a box into the metal trash can. It thudded with a heaviness of confirmation.

Six days, and now no candles.

"I feel awful," Elinor said. "I should have insisted someone tell me what to do with them before now."

Or you might have put them someplace safe in the meantime. Angela swallowed the words that came so close to passing her lips. Who would keep candles on a working radiator in the middle of winter?

"Give me a moment." Elinor reached for the phone on her

desk. "I can make a call. It's my mistake, so I'll make it right. If I expedite the shipping, we can still have candles on time."

Angela eased out breath while listening to one side of the phone conversation.

"Barbara, Elinor here. I need a favor. . .seven hundred and fifty of the traditional white, as fast as you can get them to us. . . Of course it's a popular item. . .mmm. . . I see. . . Just a minute."

Elinor raised her eyes at Angela. "They're sold out of the white. I should have expected that. But we can get a nice variety of shades of blue if we don't mind a bit of irregularity in the wicks."

"Blue?" Angela rubbed her forehead. "I don't know."

"Could be fun," Elinor said. "Shake things up a bit."

"No red? Or even green?"

" 'Fraid not. We could mix in a little purple."

"No," Angela said quickly. Purple mixed with blue? It would look like a confused Advent. "Just the blue."

"Barb? We'll take the blue. . .day after tomorrow, then." Elinor hung up the phone. "You'd have a hard time finding a better option."

Angela didn't doubt it. "Thanks for your help. I'll stop in again day after tomorrow."

She kept herself from racing out of the shop, but she took a direct path out to the sidewalk. The paper goods store was two blocks down, which gave her some time to regain her composure. Carole always spoke of the paper lanterns as a standing contribution as well, but what if someone had assumed that her passing meant an end to the contribution to the community event?

Inside the paper goods store, which was more cramped than the candle shop, Angela's eyes sought the owner's gaze but instead were met with the inquiring expression of Kim once again.

"Did you see him?" Kim asked.

"Sorry, no."

"He was just here," Kim said. "He seems to be visiting all the shops."

"Christmas shopping," Angela said.

"You've probably seen him and didn't realize it."

"Possibly." What difference did it make if she'd seen a strange man visiting town for the holidays?

"He's mid-twenties, sandy-haired, a bit scruffy looking."

Angela shrugged.

"He's staying at the B&B. I've heard that from three different people."

"Makes sense, doesn't it?"

"Alone? At Christmas?"

"He could be visiting relatives but not staying with them."

"I doubt it. Someone would know."

"Well," Angela said, "I hope you solve your mystery."

The young man behind the counter, Travis, had once been one of Angela's first students. He always looked slightly sheepish when he saw her, as if she had caught him not practicing all these years later, though he must be pushing forty and had taken over the shop from his parents.

"Rowena told me you might be by," he said. "I tried to give her the lanterns a couple of weeks ago, but she said you were in charge this year."

Why did every other conversation seem to confirm that she'd been the last person in town to find out she was in charge of A Christmas to Remember?

Travis was more organized than Elinor had been. He reached beneath the cash register and pulled out two large bags to hand to Angela.

"You remember how to open them?" he said.

"I'm sure I will." Over the years, she'd opened hundreds of

these with Carole, though at the moment she couldn't recall how long the task took. They always did it together, and time never seemed to matter. A lot of years, others helped as well. Angela could make a few calls and rustle up a few volunteers. Opening the lanterns would be the easy part. Hanging them above the shop doors would be more time consuming.

At her car, Angela peeked into one bag to make sure she was transporting the right items home. A snowy white color reassured her.

As soon as she turned her key in the back door she heard Blitzen's movement. He skittered across the floor to greet her with his usual enthusiasm, and she felt heartened enough to make a turkey sandwich and chomp into it with some enthusiasm of her own. She took the half-eaten sandwich into the living room, where she spilled the contents of one bag from the paper goods store onto the sofa. Chewing an ambitious mouthful, she slit open the packaging around a dozen paper lanterns hoping to pop one open into shape. Instead it leaned to one side and sagged. Blitzen approached to inspect, and Angela gently pushed his head away before picking up the lantern with both hands and turning it in multiple directions. It was sliced clean through in at least two directions where there ought not to have been any scores, much less cuts.

This was not the sort of thing that could happen to only one item on a manufacturing line.

She took the next one out of the package.

And the next.

And the next.

She opened the next dozen.

And the next.

And the next.

By this time she could tell just by looking if the cuts were wrong.

And they all were. Every package in that bag was wrong.

She opened the other bag from the shop and dumped out the dozens of lanterns. Wrong. All wrong.

She tossed an unopened dozen across the room. Blitzen cheerfully fetched it and brought it back to her, dripping with drool.

The lanterns had been sitting in those bags under the cash register for weeks, and no one had inspected them when there was still time to replace them. Now she had nothing.

No sleigh. None of Carole's decorations. No Nativity scene. No carolers for the corners. No lanterns. No candles—well, blue ones. Who knew what those would be like? Maybe there were lights, and maybe there weren't. Who knew how many? And who would put them up?

She hadn't wanted to do this at all. Now she couldn't even do it the simple way. And she had six days.

Kenneling Blitzen wasn't her favorite idea, but she was tempted, if it would mean she could throw in the towel, drive to the nearest airport, and buy a ticket to whatever flight would get to a beach where she could wait out Christmas in peace.

CHAPTER 10

"B litzen, I need a phone." Angela abandoned her sandwich and headed for the kitchen. "And phone numbers."

Her call list for the afternoon instantly changed from soliciting hands-on help for lights and garlands and lanterns to the four members of the event committee who had shackled her to serial frustrations. It took some digging, but she finally found an old e-mail from Rowena Pickwell that contained contact information for Ellen, Nan, and Jasmine as well.

She used her pleasant inside voice but persisted until she had spoken to all four women and obtained their promises to meet her at three thirty at Main Street Church, in the same room where three days earlier they had stunned her with their expectation.

"Let's get ready, Blitzen," she said, scratching under his jowls. "That's right. You're coming."

Angela got to the church early and unlocked the side door the others would likely use to come in from the parking lot. With Blitzen on a short leash, she stuck her head in the church office to let the secretary know the group would be in the building for a few minutes and then slipped down the hall to the old library and flipped on the lights. Bringing Blitzen was the right decision. Gripping the leash gave her something to do with one or both hands, and she could be sure someone in the room was on her side. Angela chose to sit at the head of the table. This time the meeting was hers to run, with the evidence recorded on her yellow legal pad in front of her.

Rowena's clipped steps were the first to come down the tile

in the hallway. Angela sat up straight in her rolling black vinyl chair.

"Thank you for coming on such short notice," Angela said.

Rowena let her navy wool coat drop from her form and laid it in a chair against the wall. "You insisted it was urgent."

"It is."

Rowena chose a seat at the far end of the table. "Ellen is in the lobby. I asked her to make a couple of phone calls while we were waiting."

Angela nodded. "We'll wait for everyone to arrive."

Jasmine blew in and sat on the edge of a chair without removing her down jacket or letting her purse strap slide off her shoulder. "I don't have a lot of time. My son has a skating party in an hour."

"I hope this won't take long," Angela said.

"Let's get down to it, then."

"Nan should be here soon. And Ellen's just in the hall."

Jasmine pushed up her jacket sleeve and looked at an expensive watch. Angela shifted in her chair. Blitzen tugged against the leash and poked his head out from under the table.

Ellen came in and opened a folder. "Will you want the minutes?"

"Thank you for always being prepared," Angela said, "but I don't think that's necessary."

"Perhaps unofficial notes," Rowena said.

Rowena perched her glasses on the end of her nose and scrolled through several screens on her cell phone. Angela reached down to bury a hand in Blitzen's coat.

"I don't think I can stay much longer," Jasmine said.

"Nan promised she was coming." Angela picked up her blue pen and authoritatively underscored a line on the yellow pad, unsure how much longer she could stall but certain she wanted everyone to hear the realities.

"Sorry, sorry, sorry." Nan was finally there. "I couldn't extricate myself from a conversation with Kim about that stranger around town."

Angela flipped her eyes up and resisted the temptation to be distracted.

"I wanted to give you all an update. We have some decisions to make."

Jasmine's eyes darted around the room. "I was under the impression we had given Angela all the authority she needed to carry out the responsibilities."

"I appreciate your trust in me," Angela said, "but I've run into extenuating circumstances."

Rowena looked up from her phone. Ellen's pen was poised over her notepad.

"First of all, we will not have the traditional sleigh," Angela said, "although Simon Masters generously will make his horses available."

"To pull what?" Nan asked.

"Nothing. The sleigh is in need of replacement. If we want to continue that tradition, I recommend the committee allocate funds for this purpose before next year."

"What about this year?" Jasmine said. "My children love the sleigh."

"No sleigh. It's broken and beyond repair, but I'm sure your children will enjoy the horses." Angela checked off the first item on her list. "Second, yesterday, Allen Bergstrom and I discovered a water leak in the room downstairs where most of the decorations used from year to year were stored. They are ruined. None of them are salvageable."

"What do you mean?" Rowena's cool voice sharpened.

"Everything is waterlogged and mildewed."

"Surely if you went through things more carefully. . ."

"I'm afraid not. That leaves us with no lights, no garland, no Nativity, no wreaths, no carved carolers, none of the large boxes for wrapping to decorate, no—"

"I believe we take your point," Rowena said.

Ellen scribbled notes. Angela checked off her second point.

"Third, Mr. Bergstrom, who usually oversees hanging the lights, has injured his back and will be unavailable to assist with the task. This of course includes any lights normally used on the tree at the end of Main Street." She checked off another item. "Fourth, the traditional white candles have been melted. It's likely we will receive blue ones in time, but I wanted to inform you of the change. Fifth, there will be no paper lanterns this year."

"We always have paper lanterns," Nan said. "It surprises visitors. It's part of the charm."

"Not this year. I picked them up today and discovered that every single one is faulty, and I am confident that we won't be able to replace them. They are a special-order item, and we'd have to have them by day after tomorrow to have any hope of hanging them."

Angela checked off her final items and laid down her pen.

Ellen raised a hand. "So we have the horses and the blue candles. Is that correct?"

"That's correct," Angela said.

"You can't be serious," Jasmine said.

"Facts are facts," Angela said.

"But you can't expect the town to just skip Christmas. Families depend on it. Their visiting relatives expect it. A Christmas to Remember is one of the biggest commercial draws of the year."

"I'm telling you where things stand," Angela said. "We will not be able to do everything we're used to doing. We only have six days. I'm afraid we face the decision of calling off the event or scaling it back considerably—and we'd still all have to pitch in. I'm sure I could still arrange some children who would enjoy singing carols. They would just have to walk down Main Street instead of being in the sleigh."

"You know," Nan said, "Kim just wouldn't let go talking about that strange young man, and now I wonder if she doesn't have a point."

Angela scrunched her eyebrows toward each other. "I'm sorry?"

"We've been putting on A Christmas to Remember, in some form or another, nearly as long as any of us can recall. Why should it all fall apart this year?"

Because of a broken axle. Because of an unseen water leak. Because of candles buried under magazines on a radiator. Because of paper goods somehow slashed before they ever left the factory. Hadn't Angela just explained all this?

"There could be a connection," Nan said. "A stranger comes to town, and all of these maladies?"

"We have many strangers in town at this time of year," Angela said.

"But no one knows him."

That's why he's a stranger.

"I heard about him," Jasmine said. "He checked into the B&B a few days ago, but he hardly spends any time there. And he's not visiting anyone."

"Why is he staying so long?" Nan asked. "His registration is open-ended. Whoever heard of such a thing in Spruce Valley? We're a lovely town, but it only takes an afternoon to see the shops and another to walk the countryside."

"Precisely," Jasmine said.

"I heard he was from New Zealand," Ellen said.

"Australia," Jasmine contributed.

"No, no, I'm sure it's New Zealand." Nan was twiddling a pen, just as she did in every meeting she attended. "Greg. Gabe. Gary. I can't remember the name I heard, but it was something like that. If I know Kim, she'll have sniffed it out by now."

"Do I need to put all this in the minutes?" Ellen asked.

"It's not necessary," Rowena said. "Do we know anything else about this man?"

"I haven't seen him myself," Nan said.

"The event," Angela said. "We need to make completely new plans."

"Someone will have to watch him to be sure he doesn't do it again," Jasmine said.

"Do what again?" Angela asked.

"Why, foil our plans at every turn."

"I don't think he could have caused a water leak in a locked closet," Angela said. Blitzen stood on all four legs and put his head in her lap. "Or sabotaged a paper factory three states away."

"You never know," Nan said. "Stranger things have happened. He knows too much about Spruce Valley for someone who has no connections to the town."

"Then why would he want to hurt the town?" Angela asked.

"That's exactly what we should be thinking about," Nan said. "His interest goes below the surface of the visitors we get, and that makes it suspect."

This was not going as Angela had planned, and she was sorry she'd let herself get sucked into the speculation. "Maybe we can make some concrete plans, just far simpler. It can still be a nice event full of homespun charm."

"Ellen, do you have that list?" Rowena asked.

Ellen passed a sheet of paper to Rowena, who in turn slid it down the table toward Angela.

"I took the liberty of asking Ellen to assemble some names,"

Rowena said, "and make a few preliminary phone calls. Just in case you found yourself in need of assistance."

Angela scanned the list. Most of them were men, presumably to help with the ladder work up and down Main Street. She could scratch out Allen Bergstrom's name. A list of volunteers, however, did nothing to solve the lack of decorative supplies.

"You could drive over to Marksbury," Nan said. "They have a couple of big box stores that are probably marking down Christmas decorations left and right."

Possibly. Angela had thought of this. But there was no telling what she'd find, or in what quantities.

"I assume there would be a budget," she said.

Jasmine tugged the zipper up on her jacket, an announcement of her impending departure. "I'll ask Jake. My guess is he'd be willing to cover another three hundred dollars as long as he gets a receipt that he can write off."

Three hundred? That hardly seemed sufficient to decorate a town for Christmas with all the charm and taste that its occupants would be expecting.

"There's always Buford," Ellen said.

"If one becomes desperate, I suppose so," Rowena said.

"He only has space for one rack by the cash register, but his sign says he has much more in the back room. Just ask. That's what it says."

Angela had not even flipped through any of the items Buford was selling out of his diner. Nothing he sold was nearly as nice as what Carole would have stocked in her Yule-Tidings Shoppe, but even seeing the way he'd moved in to corner the market made her wince. He hadn't known Carole the way she had. He saw only the opportunity her absence left. Angela might have to swallow her feelings and at least ask to see Buford's Christmas stock.

"I'll have to scoot," Jasmine said. "My son gets anxious if he's late to a party."

"I'll walk out with you," Nan said. "Angela, I'll see you for choir practice on Wednesday."

Angela nodded.

Rowena stood and picked up her coat, so Ellen did the same. Blitzen pulled briefly against his leash, curious about the activity in the room, but Angela held him firmly for a couple of minutes until they were once again alone.

"Gabe," she said softly. "Gabriel. And New Zealand."

Her determination to leave this meeting with a stronger fix on replacement ideas and help had fallen to the side at the first mention of the man's name.

Little Gabe. Would she even have recognized him if she'd passed him on the street? There was no reason he would know her by sight. If it was even him. And if it was, Nan and Jasmine asked good questions. Why had he come?

Angela placed Ellen's list between the top two pages of her yellow legal pad and decided to drive past the B&B on her way home. It couldn't hurt to see if she might spot him.

CHAPTER 11

B litzen had been out once that morning already, but he was scratching at the back door, so Angela opened it and granted his release. December was not a time when bunnies would agitate the neighborhood pets with their darting presence, but he might have spotted a squirrel to chase. Angela didn't see one, but Blitzen might as well enjoy the yard, because he was likely to be inside the house for most of the day again.

Angela had no better plan than she'd had after yesterday's meeting or after she once again started with a fresh sheet on her legal pad, though she had jotted down the names of several large stores in Marksbury. She might start the day with some phone calls to determine if driving over there and schlepping through the crowds five days before Christmas would be worthwhile. Losing half the day and perhaps coming home with little to show for the effort would not advance the cause of A Christmas to Remember.

Her oatmeal was ready. Angela took it off the stove and carried it to the table. Her iPad was within reach, so she began looking up phone numbers. The more she thought about it, the more she was inclined to think that Christmas decorations would be picked over by this date, but at least she'd be able to say she'd inquired if anyone questioned her judgment. Two mouthfuls of warm oatmeal slid down her throat, and her forefinger was ready to start punching numbers in the phone when the commotion at the front door began.

Nora was the only person who knocked in that manner, and Blitzen's muffled bark verified Angela's suspicion. Abandoning the phone on the table, she paced to the front door and yanked it open.

"I've saved your dog," Nora said. "Again."

"Saved him from what?" Angela said.

"He was loose and in the company of a stranger. You really must have someone look at your fence. The gate was wide open this time."

Angela leaned forward and took hold of Blitzen's collar. "Thank you—again—for bringing him back."

"The stranger is still there." Nora nodded her head over her shoulder. "You could lose your dog, you know."

Angela looked across the street and down a few yards. A young man stood with his hands in his jacket pockets, his shoulders hunched slightly against the morning cold.

Nora wore no jacket.

"You must be freezing," Angela said. "Don't worry. I've got Blitzen."

"One more thing," Nora said. "I understand you may be in need of some lights."

Angela's interest perked up. "Yes?"

"We had to break up my father's house a few months ago and move him. He always had to have more lights than anyone else in the neighborhood. They're taking up space in my basement. You're welcome to them."

"Nora! Yes!"

"There are thousands. I don't even know how many."

"We need them! Yes, please."

"All right. I'll get them out and bring them over." Rearranging her cardigan, Nora descended the porch steps and crossed the yards.

Angela had never seen so much of her neighbor as she had since she took in Blitzen. The dog did seem to get out a lot, so she ought to be thankful for a vigilant neighbor—especially one willing to confront a stranger for the sake of the dog.

Of course, Nora would not know that this was not really a stranger.

Angela let the dog in the house but remained outside when she closed the door. Tightening her own sweater around her midsection, she looked at the young man. Mid-twenties. Sandy-haired. This must be the man Kim had tracked around town for the sake of her own curiosity. Still on the other side of the street, he moved so that he was directly across from Angela's front door. Watching the house. Watching her.

"It's cold out here," she called out. "Would you like some hot cocoa?" She wanted to call him by name. What if she was wrong?

He nodded and came up the walkway.

Never in her lifetime had she imagined this would be the way. Inside, she took his jacket and hung it from the antique brass coatrack just inside the piano room and tried not to stare. His face was familiar, his features echoing two generations removed. The boyishness she had known was still there. A thousand questions swirled, but she didn't give them words, lest what she saw in his face was only what she wished was there.

"I'll make some cocoa on the stove," she said, gesturing that he should follow her into the kitchen. Blitzen circled him three times before they got there but offered no objection to Gabe's presence in the house.

"I wanted to come sooner," he said. "I wasn't sure how."

So it was him. Angela's hands trembled as she took milk from the refrigerator and poured it into a pan to warm. The tins of cocoa and sugar were on the shelf above the stove.

"Have you found things as you expected?" Angela stirred, allowing herself only a glance at the young man sitting at her kitchen table when she would have liked to study his features further. Would he be uncomfortable if she looked him in the eyes and tried not to blink?

"I wasn't sure what to expect." With two fingers he stroked the bowl of oatmeal she'd abandoned when Nora turned up at the door. "I suspect I've cost you your breakfast."

"The cocoa will make up for it." Angela reached for two large mugs, sure that she'd made plenty to fill them both. She stirred awhile longer, making certain her morning offering would be hot without letting it boil.

"It's good to meet Blitzen," he said. "I hadn't imagined that I would."

"You mean when you turned up on my street?"

He shrugged. "Or ever."

His accent was charming. Anytime she saw a film with actors from New Zealand, she'd wondered if he would sound the way they did.

"I'm hoping for snow," he said. "Keen for a white Christmas and all that."

"It might happen." Angela poured the cocoa into the mugs. "Even without snow, it must be quite different than Christmas in the middle of summer."

"Yes, quite." He took the snowy white mug she offered. "I hope I'm not keeping you from anything."

"To be honest I'm not sure what my day holds." Angela pulled out a chair and sat opposite him. He was really here. Carole's absence stabbed her afresh. "How did you get out here this morning? I didn't see a car on the street that I didn't recognize."

"I walked. I wanted to have a look, and maybe just that. I didn't know Blitzen would come running out."

"If you saw how he got out, you'd be doing me a great favor to tell me."

"Sorry. He was just suddenly there. And then your neighbor."

"It's quite a ways to walk from the B&B." Angela took a long sip and looked at him over the edge of her mug.

He chuckled. "So you've heard."

"Everyone has."

"Kim. Isn't that her name?"

Angela nodded.

"It's not so far to walk," Gabe said.

"Three miles."

He shrugged.

"I'm going into town," Angela said. "You can ride back with me, if you like."

"Are you sure?" He tapped the legal pad on the table. "Looks like you have things on your mind."

"I have five days to pull a rabbit out of a hat," she said. "That's counting the day of the event. And I have neither a rabbit nor a hat—nor that fancy wand magicians use."

"I'd like to help," he said, "if you'll let me."

Now she did look at his golden eyes and kept herself from blinking. "I'd be happy to have help."

"What's first?"

Angela glanced at her list of phone numbers and discarded the idea of using them.

"Let's start by going down to the church," she said. "At least some things are within my control there."

In a car, the three miles into town weren't a long distance, but Angela gave Gabe the overview of A Christmas to Remember— at least this year's version. When she parked and they walked together toward the church, a few heads on Main Street turned. Angela waved as she would have on any other day and turned her key in the lock.

"I have to organize the choir folders," she said, leading the way to the rehearsal room. "Experience tells me that come

Christmas Eve, people tend to still have music from the fall in their folders. It makes for a lot of noisy paper shuffling during a candlelight service."

Angela pulled the stack of black folders from the rack, knowing that a few were missing. Lea Sabatelli, for instance, liked to take her music home and pick out the soprano line on her piano. Angela was glad she did. Lea was the strongest soprano in the choir, and when she was confident the whole section benefited. For years Lea had been leading a stunning descant line when the congregation sang "O Come, All Ye Faithful."

Gabe followed Angela's lead, pulling out music that was not Christmas-themed and rearranging what was left, Sunday morning's anthem on the left and Christmas Eve music on the right.

"Ah, an empty sheet of paper," Gabe said.

"Lois," Angela said. "She always means to write things down."

"I should leave it, then."

"She gets a new sheet every week anyway."

Gabe removed the paper and closed the folder. "Could you use another tenor?"

"Always! Have you ever heard of a church choir that doesn't need more tenors?"

He laughed softly. "You haven't even heard me sing."

"Come to rehearsal tomorrow night, and we'll work that out."

Angela opened another bulging folder that still held music from last Easter.

Gabe fiddled with the blank sheet of paper he'd found and began humming "Lo, How a Rose E'er Blooming" at the unhurried tempo Angela loved best. She paused, closed her eyes, and listened. She hadn't paid much attention to Christmas music outside of choir rehearsals this year, but with Gabe beside her now humming melody and her mind supplying harmony, she was grateful for the unexpected moment. By the last line of the tune, the notes in her mind took form in her throat, and they finished humming the carol in tandem.

Angela opened her eyes. Gabe handed her the paper—folded perfectly into an origami lantern. She gasped.

"Where did you learn to do that?"

"I don't remember. I've been doing it all my life. It's very easy."

"I could use about six dozen by Friday morning."

"No problem. We just need some decent paper."

"Travis at the paper goods store will have something, surely."

"I know the shop you mean," Gabe said. "I'll go this afternoon and see what he has."

Angela nodded. Finally someone offered to help. "I'll make some calls to ask some children to sing carols. I'm sure I can find enough older kids who know the words, and the younger ones can come along for the fun. And I'll see about the lights. I might have some, though I still have to arrange help to string them."

She'd been meaning to call the Bergstroms anyway, to see how Allen was doing and whether he'd need surgery. Their Christmas certainly was going awry. But Millie would still be glad to have the lights out of the house, and Angela could also use the ones she hadn't bothered putting up around her own home this year. A few phone calls might yield more. She'd never find enough to do something grand with the tall spruce at the end of Main Street—or anything at all. That reality remained unchanged.

"A Christmas tree lot might have some greenery they've trimmed away," Gabe said. "I'll check. And I'll help hang whatever needs hanging."

"Would you?"

"Of course."

"I know where we can get ladders."

"Why don't we meet tomorrow morning at Buford's for

breakfast?" Gabe said. "We can see where we are. I'll bring the paper for the lanterns. If you don't like it, we can return it."

Angela nodded. She was going to have to buckle down and ask Buford what he had in his back room anyway—but not until she knew what she and Gabe could come up with today.

Help was a wonderful thing.

Chapter 12

A ngela arrived early for breakfast at Buford's, already buzzing from two cups of coffee at home. She didn't know if Gabe was the sort to be early or late, but she was already squirrelly at home even after expending excess energy by letting Blitzen tug her around the neighborhood for an extra twenty minutes. It couldn't hurt to grab a table and wait for Gabe at the restaurant.

Christmas on a beach still held some appeal. She'd have to ask Gabe what that was like, and if he'd ever taken a solo vacation at Christmastime before. He was here alone now. Didn't his parents like to have him home? Maybe he'd traveled internationally other years, or maybe a beach in New Zealand was his usual tradition. If he hadn't shown up on her street twenty-four hours earlier, she couldn't be sure she wouldn't have flown the coop. If one more thing had gone wrong—it still might, but at least she had someone to talk to who was more interested than the official committee.

She'd talked herself hoarse the previous afternoon on the phone. She had forty piano students, representing twenty-seven families. In addition, another twenty or so families at Main Street Church had children who could sing on the street. Expanding the age range at least through middle school would give her some strong singers as well as kids who could be trusted to herd the younger ones and keep an eye out for candles getting too close to hair or hats. Without the limitation of the wagon's size behind the horses, anyone could follow behind. Some families already were out of town. Angela caught parents on their cell phones across the state or across the country. Others were getting ready to leave to join family gatherings elsewhere. But most were staying right there in Spruce Valley and wouldn't think of missing A Christmas to Remember.

Liz Bergstrom had assured her that despite his grandfather's injury, Brian had collected the lights from the elder Bergstroms' home; screwed in every bulb; plugged in the strings; counted three thousand, four hundred and sixty-seven working lights; and brought them all home. If Angela wasn't going to hang them somewhere, Brian was. In her own basement, Angela found assorted strings, evidence that in past years Carole's enthusiasm for Christmas had been catching. She didn't count them. Perhaps between the two collections there were five thousand, which sounded like a large number but would be hardly enough to catch anyone's eye if stretched out down all of Main Street. But it was something, and she'd figure out a plan. They might have to call this year The Christmas Everything Changed.

Her cell phone rang just as she found an empty booth.

"This is Brian."

"Hello, Brian."

"My mom said I should call you."

"I heard about the lights." Angela shirked out of her jacket. "Thank you."

"She forgot to tell you about the ladders. My dad promised he would make sure you have the ladders."

"Thank you, Brian." Angela had an urge to learn to play the saxophone just so she could teach this boy herself.

"And I'm going to help. I'm not afraid of heights."

"I'm glad to know that, because ladders make me feel wobbly."

"Don't forget to call me." His plea was plaintive, the tremors of a child left behind by adults in the past.

"I won't," Angela said.

"I really want to help."

"I know."

Buford approached with a pot of coffee as she tucked her phone away. Angela's previous consideration of switching to decaf faded against his determination to fill her cup.

"Thought maybe things would be looking a little more like Christmas," he said.

Angela puffed out her cheeks and shrugged. "A few things have gone wrong."

"I've heard. Candles. Paper. Lights. Sleigh." He paused to chuckle, which irritated Angela. "Pretty much everything, from what I've heard."

Angela didn't answer. Neither did she drink his coffee.

"I also heard you've been hanging out with the stranger who is trying to ruin our Christmas," Buford said. "He's wrecking everything he can get his hands on."

Angela tilted her head. "Why would a stranger come to town and try to ruin our Christmas?"

"A grudge," Buford said. "Or he's just mean. He was in the candle shop right before Elinor found those candles on the radiator."

"I think the candles had been there quite a while," Angela said. They wouldn't have melted in just a few minutes.

"Somebody slashed all the paper lanterns." Buford set the coffeepot on the table and leaned against the booth bench opposite Angela. "Seems like something he would do."

Angela couldn't stop the scoffing sound that escaped her mouth. "If he's a stranger, how do you know what he'd do?"

"I guess he's not a stranger to you, now is he?"

Four days ago, on a biting morning, Buford offered her the kindness of some hot chocolate. Now he was snapping about someone he didn't know.

Well, she knew Gabe.

Angela looked past Buford to the area near the cash register. Without Carole in town to corner the Christmas decoration market, Buford had jumped at the opportunity for extra seasonal profit. His strategy seemed to have worked. The racks were picked over.

"The committee suggested I check with you about decorations," Angela said. "But it looks like you've done a nice business for yourself."

"There's more in the back. I got another shipment yesterday, as a matter of fact. Can't decide if I should just save it for next year. Folks might be done buying for now."

A whole shipment? Angela perked up.

"As you know, I may be in need of some items," she said. "Might you have any long garlands?"

"I believe so."

"Wreaths?"

He nodded.

"Could I have a look after I eat?"

"We could arrange that."

"Thank you, Buford." Angela picked up her coffee. "Oh, here's my breakfast date now."

Gabe hustled through the front door. Angela waved, and he headed her direction.

Buford picked up his coffeepot and eyed Gabe. "Figured you'd be eating at the B&B. After all, one of those *B*s stands for *breakfast*."

Gabe grinned. "Maybe I'm secretly writing restaurant reviews."

Buford glared. "Coffee?"

"Sweet as, mate?"

The unfamiliar expression threw Buford off balance.

"He means yes," Angela said.

Buford poured.

Angela arranged her silverware. "How about two orders of your cream cheese French toast with bacon on the side?"

Gabe nodded. "That sounds delicious."

Buford withdrew.

"Thank you for coming," Angela said.

"The Christmas tree lot didn't have as many scraps as I'd hoped, but I did find some paper." He slid a few pieces out of a bag. "What do you think?"

"Mmm. Blue?"

"A very tasteful pale blue," Gabe said, "suggestive of evening. It's got a nice texture, and it's sturdy. Also, the tree lot did have cans of spray-on flocking, so we can give it a snowy look."

Angela nodded. "Your inner artist is showing."

"I hope so."

While they waited for breakfast, he showed her how to fold a sheet of paper into a lantern and where they could punch holes to string them up.

A vision formed in Angela's mind, and it did not involve a beach.

CHAPTER 13

A ngela pushed away her plate, leaving only a few bites of French toast crust. "Thanks for breakfast. I'd better see what Buford has in the back room."

"I'll go with you," Gabe said, "if you don't mind."

"Mind? I'd welcome it."

Gabe had the ticket for their meal tucked under his own plate a few minutes ago, though Angela had not intended to argue with him about it. They gathered their things and walked to the front of the diner, where Gabe paid for breakfast and Angela waved down Buford.

Buford pointed his chin at Gabe. "Is he coming with you?"

"Yes, as a matter of fact."

"Why?"

"Because I'd like him to." She met Buford's eyes.

Angela had lived in this town longer than she'd lived any other single place in her life. It was a friendly place. Small towns had a reputation for rumors and everybody knowing everybody else's business, but Angela gave people the benefit of the doubt. Not everyone was like that. Not even most people were like that in Spruce Valley. Half the businesses up and down Main Street depended on day or seasonal tourism in some way. The town was small, but it wasn't a self-sustaining economic bubble. So why had a cluster of people decided to blame events on a young man from New Zealand patronizing their businesses? Answering that question was not on her to-do list for the days between now and Christmas Eve—four days—and she would spend as much time with Gabriel as she wanted to.

Gabriel.

The name she had first known him by. Then it was Gabie in the toddler years. Did anyone still call him that?

She turned to Gabe. "Ready?"

He nodded and fell in step behind her as Buford led the way through the kitchen. Angela had been in the diner's back room a few times over the years. Once, in a spring when she had a burst of energy, she organized a private post-recital party for all her students and their families at the diner. Part of negotiating the cost down had been agreeing to arrange a few volunteers to help with setup and cleanup. The reasons for the other visits escaped her memory now, but one of them had involved Carole. As soon as Buford pushed open the metal door and the smell of cardboard and plastic infused her nostrils, Carole's favorite fragrance met it there.

The room, which wasn't large, was unadorned cement from floor to ceiling, with cinderblock-and-board shelving to maximize the storage of restaurant supplies along three walls and refrigerators and freezers along the fourth. In the middle of the space were eight large boxes stacked in four sets of two rising as high as Angela's chin with barely enough room to maneuver around them. All of it was stamped CHRISTMAS in large letters.

"Buford!" she said. "This is great! I had no idea you would have so much. I should have asked sooner."

"I told you, I just got it yesterday. There wouldn't have been anything for you to look at." He reached into the corner of a shelf for a box cutter and handed it to Angela. "Feel free to open anything. Just try not to make a mess."

"We'll be careful," Gabe said, already pulling down one of the upper boxes into the cramped space.

"I'll be back," Buford said. "We can talk about a deal."

"Many of the businesses are making donations," Angela said.

Buford shook his head and stretched his mouth in a grimace. "Not sure I can go that far. But I'll make it worth your while."

The metal door swung closed behind Buford's return to the kitchen just as Gabriel sliced through the strapping on the first box. Angela stepped closer to help hold the flaps back while they inspected the unexpected treasure.

She blinked, lifted a flap, and looked at the labeling on the side of the box more closely.

"It says 'Blue'."

"And it's telling the truth."

"Blue Christmas decorations."

"It takes all types."

"It's a box of blue Christmas garland."

"That it is."

"I can't use that."

"Can't you?"

"Can I?" Angela made herself put one hand inside the box and lift a length of garland wrapped around stiff cardboard. It felt the same as any other artificial garland—better than many that she'd examined in hobby and craft stores.

But it was still blue.

"Gabe, it's blue," she said.

"Sweet as, mate."

Angela stared at him.

"Yes," he said. "Yes, it's blue."

She dropped the garland. "Maybe in New Zealand, beach tones suit expectations at Christmas, but this is Spruce Valley. People expect evergreens, and you'd better have a good explanation if you show up with fir or pine rather than spruce."

Gabe shrugged. "I'd say you have a good explanation, wouldn't you?"

"For myself, perhaps."

"You did tell me the candles were blue."

She twisted her lips. "Not because I want them to be."

"Blue candles. Blue paper. Blue garland. I see a theme."

"Not an attractive one."

"It's Christmas! It'll be stunning."

She couldn't imagine it. A blue Christmas? Not a silvery, sparkly blue in someone's living room, to suit personal taste, but for the entire town? Sliding to one side, she read the sides of several more boxes before shuffling farther to read the rest.

"They all say blue. Garland, wreaths, and bows. They all say blue."

"Yes, I noticed." Gabe tapped another box.

"Did Buford really think he was going to sell this much blue Christmas decor?"

"Maybe he didn't know it was blue," Gabe said. "He's a man who's keen on a good deal, wouldn't you say?"

"I would, as a matter of fact."

"He was offered a good price and believed he could turn a profit."

"Even in blue." Angela sighed.

Gabe rubbed his hands together. "I love a creative challenge."

"I might, too, with a bit more notice." And with a bit more notice, she could have been creative within the traditional bounds of Christmas observation in Spruce Valley.

"This is Wednesday morning, and we've only got until Friday evening."

It was impossible. The whole mess was impossible. What was she thinking when she allowed herself to be optimistic? They could fold and flock a few paper lanterns, but it would take hours to string them up and down Main Street, not to mention the lights. Brian was sweet, but he was an eleven-year-old. Did he understand enough about electricity to be careful? Where did all the lights even get plugged in? How was it she'd never paid attention to that detail? She couldn't be certain how many children would turn up to sing carols in the street, and for all she knew one of the horses could go lame.

"Can we open the rest?" Angela asked. "Just to make sure they're not mislabeled?"

"Never hurts to be sure." Gabe picked up the box cutter and began slicing.

Blue.

Blue.

Blue.

Blue.

Blue.

Blue.

Blue.

Eight boxes of blue Christmas decorations.

"This is not the tasteful pale snowy blue of your paper," Angela said. It was the penetrating blue of a sports logo, as if a manufacturing plant had leftover paint and spilled it into the machinery churning out what should have been green—or at least silver or gold—Christmas items.

She could ask Gabe to look after Blitzen and she could still catch a flight to a beach. She could cancel the choir anthems for Christmas Eve and offer a tantalizing amount of money for one of her more than competent teenage piano students to play carols for the church services.

"It'll be all right," Gabe said softly. "I won't leave you in the lurch."

She blew out her breath. He was a guest in Spruce Valley. It wouldn't be right to leave him in the lurch, either.

"I'm just having a hard time these days," she said.

"I know."

And he did. She knew that.

"At least it would give us quite a bit to work with," she said.

"Now you're talking."

"I still have nothing for the old spruce at the end of Main Street. Even if I did, it would be more than a three-day project."

"One thing at a time."

Buford came whistling through the door. "Solves your problem, right?"

Angela caught Gabe's eye. "We're considering the options."

"We both know you don't have any others, don't we?"

She sucked in her lips for a few seconds and said, "There is the small matter of the color."

"Blue," Buford said. "Original, I'd say."

"Your diner is done in yellow and purple," Angela said. "I've never noticed you to be partial to blue."

Buford laughed. "I'm not partial to yellow or purple, either. Economics."

"As I mentioned, many businesses make donations. We don't operate with much of a cash budget."

"You don't expect me to take a loss, do you?" Buford put his hands in his pockets.

"Your accountant would say it would be a nice tax write-off," Angela said. "End-of-year giving."

"I give to the Methodist Church causes all through the year," Buford said. "And the Boy Scouts and the Girl Scouts and the YMCA and refugees coming from war-torn parts of the world. I'm not heartless, but I try to be a good steward just as the Lord impresses upon all of us."

"What did you have in mind, Buford?" She suspected his donations to Scouting were in exchange for popcorn and cookies.

"I got a very good price," he said. "The supplier was eager not to have to store them and have them in inventory when their tax liability is assessed."

"Mmm." Angela was listening. "Surely you can still take a small percentage off."

Buford shook his head. "No, but I'll add on only the smallest percentage necessary to cover my own costs for transportation and storage."

Angela looked around the back room wondering what storage expense he could have incurred since yesterday afternoon.

"Seems to me I'd be doing you a favor if I got these boxes out of your way," she said. "I'll get the dolly from the church and get them out of here before your lunch rush starts. You won't have any more storage expense or inconvenience, and it would be more than fair for the committee to pay what you paid."

Gabe folded in the flaps of the garland box. "She strikes a hard bargain, wouldn't you say?"

Buford grunted. "I'll go in the office and get the paperwork so you can see for yourself that I'm agreeing to your terms. But I'll need the committee's check before the week is out."

CHAPTER 14

G abe's rental car was too small to be much help with the size of the boxes in Buford's storage room, so it took three trips with Angela's car for the two of them to transport the cartons to the church, where they lined them up against one wall in the hallway outside the sanctuary. Angela rummaged through a closet and found tablecloths she was certain no one would be looking for and draped them over the boxes. Eventually people would find out that everything was blue this year instead of evergreen with red velvet ribbons, but they didn't have to know today, so she lettered several PLEASE DO NOT TOUCH signs and taped them in plain sight.

The racket from downstairs provided an incessant reminder of why Angela had agreed to eight cartons of blue Christmas decorations. Allen Bergstrom was following his doctor's instructions to take it easy, but the rest of the property committee was hard at work. A construction disposal bin was positioned outside the downstairs wide double doors, and the committee, along with a couple of hired younger men, were hauling out load after load. From what Angela could see and overhear when she ventured halfway down the stairs, the unanimous decision seemed to be to discard everything in the storage room except a couple of ladders and a metal file cabinet. Whatever wasn't ruined by the dampness was so long forgotten that there wasn't any point in keeping it. They'd clear the room, fix the broken pipe, put fresh paint on the walls, and have the whole business put back together by New Year's.

Angela watched as the carved carolers were dragged out and

thudded into the bin.

One of the hired disposal workers cracked a joke about the thousands and thousands of lights. Twenty-five thousand. Angela remembered now that Carole had given that estimate once.

She couldn't watch anymore and turned to go back up the stairs.

Gabe was in the foyer with his stack of sturdy blue paper.

"I could fold the lanterns, if you point me to a space," he said. "No point in going back to the B&B to do it when we'll want them here, right?"

Angela nodded. "This does seem to be turning into command central."

The meeting room made the most sense, and she led the way. The lighting was good, and the table's polished surface would be safe for a delicate project.

"Want to try again?" Gabe said, spreading paper on the table like a deck of cards.

It was tempting.

"I'd better make some calls," Angela said. In her coat pocket, she still had the folded sheet of paper Rowena had slid across this same table two days earlier with the names and numbers of men who had given at least preliminary consent to help set up A Christmas to Remember. It would all have to be done tomorrow and Friday, but at least it wouldn't come down to Gabe, Brian, and her. At least some of these men had helped in the past. The tasks would be different this year, but they knew the general idea and between them they should be able to round up vehicles and equipment. Angela paced the hall as she worked her way down the list and wrangled more firm consent to help.

But not from everyone.

She tried not to begrudge people their reasons for bowing out. Neither did she get the block of hours she was hoping for, but the voices of experience assured her that if they had the right ladders and enough of them—she made a note to call Ned Bergstrom—the crew would know what to do. Most of the nails and hooks they used stayed up year-round, a detail she'd never noticed but that would be easy enough to confirm.

Angela strode back to the meeting room and paused in the doorway, stunned at the progress Gabe had made with the lanterns. Several dozen already stood sentry on the table, lined up in precise rows showcasing their exact folds and tucks.

"Impressive," she said. "Was I really gone so long?"

"Sit," Gabe said. "I'll show you again."

"I don't know. I won't be good at it."

"You might be."

"I should run home and let Blitzen out. And feed him."

"Just one." Gabe slid a sheet of blue paper toward her.

Tentatively, she lifted it with two fingers.

"Here's your first fold," he said, showing her.

His technique was swift and certain. Hers was slow and clumsy. But he waited for her at each step, encouraging her to crease her folds and press the corners, and more quickly than she might have imagined she'd folded her first lantern.

"One more?" he said, his eyes twinkling.

She glanced at the wall clock. "One more."

Angela still had to watch Gabe's movements closely, but they produced another pair, and he added them to the lanterns marching across the table.

"See?" he said. "Don't you feel better?"

She sucked in a breath and gave a laugh. "You know what? I do." Her pulse had slowed, and her shoulders had lowered.

"Art does that to people," Gabe said.

"Are you an artist—in your real life?"

"Art is something that happens in your soul." He tipped his

head at her. "You know that because of your music."

"I teach piano lessons and direct a church choir."

"Are you telling me you never let loose with Bach's Toccata and Fugue in D minor when no one is listening? With all the stops out?"

She laughed again. "Sometimes. When I've finished practicing the service music for the week."

"This is what I'm talking about."

She stood up. "I still have to go let Blitzen out and feed him."

"I'll be here when you get back."

"Will you?"

"Of course. It's choir practice night, isn't it?"

"Yes. Yes, it is. You can make it?"

"If I'm going to sing on Sunday, I certainly ought to practice once."

"Gabe, I can't begin to express my thanks. You've been so much help. And not just everything you're doing. Just having *you* here. It means everything."

"You knew who I was right from the start, didn't you?"

"I like to think I would have recognized you if I'd met you on the street," Angela said. "Carole always kept photos on display, but it's hard to be sure. When I heard there was a man named Gabe from New Zealand. . ."

She didn't care if Gabe saw the tears in her eyes or heard the waver in her voice.

He reached for a box of tissues and handed it to her.

She blew into one. "Your great-aunt Carole would surely love to know that you came, that you somehow knew someone on the other side of the world needed you because she couldn't be here, and you came."

"Careful, or you might have to pass that box back to me," Gabe said.

"What a pair we are."

"We both loved her, and she loved the both of us," Gabe said. "In my whole life, I've never had a Christmas morning without a phone call—or a Skype call these last few years—from Great-Aunt Carole. Being with you is the right thing."

"Your whole life is almost as long as I knew her."

"Then we shall carry on the tradition of knowing each other, and she'd be pleased as punch."

Angela smiled through tears. "She would."

Gabe waved her off. "Go feed the pooch. I imagine I'll have these finished when you get back, and we'll have time to grab something to eat."

"Not at Buford's."

He grinned. "Somewhere with good meatballs."

She spotted the blue tubs on her porch half a block away. Nora's lights. Untangling them might take half the night, but she'd take all the lights she could get. From now on, she would be grateful for her neighbors.

Two and a half hours later, Angela once again unlocked the church building and flipped on lights, this time down the hall leading to the choir rehearsal room. Once they'd run through parts and sung through all the anthems both for Sunday morning and the candlelight Christmas Eve service in the evening, they would move to the sanctuary and practice everything one final time with the organ. This was the system she'd been using for years.

"Where shall I sit?" Gabe asked.

Angela pointed. "The tenors are there. You might want to sit on the end and leave plenty of space."

"Ah, yes. People have their usual spots."

"They get used to hearing each other a certain way. I find the harmonies work best if I don't scramble it up too much."

Angela handed Gabe a music folder and made a mental note that before Sunday she'd have to find a robe for him to wear. She had a hunch he was a more-than-competent sight reader, and most of the music was traditional enough to be familiar. As she spread her own music on the piano, other singers drifted in.

"Goodness, we have a visitor."

Angela looked up.

"Hello, Kim. I think you've met Gabe around town the last few days."

Gabe gave his best boyish grin. Angela stifled her smile as she watched Kim fumble to respond.

"Gabe is going to be in town through Christmas," Angela said. "Isn't that nice? He asked if he might sing with us. How could I turn down someone who wants to sing at Christmas?"

"Hmm." Kim took her music folder from its slot and found her seat in the alto section.

The rows filled in. Nan found her seat in the soprano section yet angled her eyes at Gabe. Travis, from the paper goods store, gave Gabe a fist-bump greeting before sprawling in position to anchor the basses. Most weeks someone was missing. As starting time approached, Angela grew slightly anxious that Lea Sabatelli hadn't appeared, but she reminded herself Lea had phoned her just the other day with questions about the music. She might be a few minutes late, but she was as mindful as ever about learning her part well.

Absently, Angela started picking out with one finger the tune to "Once in Royal David's City," trying to fill her mind with the full and beautiful sound of her favorite recording of the great processional hymn. Someday she hoped to have a choir robust enough to sing it the way it was meant to be sung, including a soaring descant. *Once in royal David's city stood a lowly cattle shed*, she heard in her mind.

She hadn't expected anyone to sing it tonight.

It was Gabe. "Where a mother laid her baby in a manger for his bed."

Angela's fingers found the four-part harmony under his voice.

"Mary was that mother mild, Jesus Christ, her little child."

My, what a voice he has. He had stilled the room.

The door flung open again, and Lea rushed in.

"I'm so sorry! I never meant to be late."

"It's no problem," Angela said, relieved. "We're just getting started."

"I was in the middle of making supper when I got the call."

Several of the women gasped.

"The baby?" one of them said.

Lea nodded rapidly. "A month early! Who would have thought? Of course, babies do come early. You just never think it's going to be your own grandchild who comes early."

"She's all right?" Kim asked.

"Perfect!" Lea said. "Mommy is, too. We're all very excited. I've been on the phone and was able to change our flights. You'd think it would be impossible this close to Christmas, but we managed. Of course, we had to pay a premium, but it will be worth it to be there. Mick and I are both flying out first thing in the morning. I just wanted to let you all know the good news and drop off my music in case someone else needs it."

"Congratulations, and safe travels." Angela forced the syllables out. She could hardly begrudge Lea a grandmother's joy. Yet there wasn't another soprano like Lea in Spruce Valley. No one could carry the Christmas Eve music the way she could.

Lea hustled out as quickly as she had come in.

"We'd better get started," Angela said. The morning anthem would be a piece they were also singing during the candlelight service. They might as well get to work.

Angela went through the motions of rehearsing the individual parts, asking if there were particular measures people wanted to hear again, and then putting it all together. Altogether there were four anthems. With each one the soprano section grew more timid, one by one their voices dropping out before the highest notes—except for the one singer who was least able to hit the high notes but also least able to admit this reality. The descant that should have been the most dramatic stanza of the service was headed for disaster. Without Lea, the confidence of seven other sopranos whooshed out of the room.

The choir was the one part of Christmas Angela thought she had under control.

Things couldn't get much worse.

CHAPTER 15

T here's his truck now. Looks like you can relax."

Angela didn't appreciate the tone behind Pete Nicholson's half smile. Condescension wouldn't solve practical issues, and the clock was ticking for the event only two days away. But she swallowed the urge to set Pete straight. She needed his help. Only four men had agreed to string lights, and only three of them had promised to stay on task past lunchtime. Pete lounged against a light post. The others had ducked inside Buford's for some coffee. Angela had expected they'd get it to go and come back outside. How they planned to juggle hot coffee with climbing ladders and hanging lights, she didn't know. But they hadn't come back. The only explanation was that they'd sat down inside and were probably on their second refills.

Ned Bergstrom pulled his pickup to the curb beside Angela and Pete, outside Main Street Church, and hustled out of the driver's side.

"Sorry." Ned let down the gate at the back of the truck's bed. "Had to stop by my parents'."

"How is your dad?" Angela asked.

"Not well. In a lot of pain, and Mom's not managing well. I've got to get decent beds downstairs for both of them—today. The doctor is talking about surgery. At this rate, he won't be able to get upstairs for weeks, and she can't be running up and down to see what he needs at night."

"That will exhaust her."

"Wish I could help with the lights," Ned said, "but I can't stay. You understand."

"I do understand," Angela said. "And Brian was right when he said Allen had all the right ladders."

"My mother may never let Dad go up on a ladder again." Ned pulled one ladder out of the truck, and Pete took another.

Angela gasped. "Brian."

"What about him?"

"He wanted to help with the lights. He made sure I knew he wasn't afraid of heights."

Ned slapped his forehead. "He told me, too. My mother called so early, I left the house before he was even up."

"He'll be very disappointed if we do this without him."

"I can't stay to help, though," Ned said.

Angela spun toward Pete.

"What?" Pete said, leaning a ladder against the light pole. "You want me to babysit?"

"It's not babysitting," Angela said. "He's a good kid, and he wants to help."

"You know my boy," Ned said. "He tags along with my dad every chance he gets. If you don't want him up on the ladders, he can at least hand you tools."

Pete rolled his eyes. "Sure. Why not? But I'm gonna tell him the rules, and if he gets out of line, you can expect your cell phone to ring."

"And I'll answer it," Ned said. "I'll go get him right now."

"No," Angela said. "Go take care of your dad. I'll call Brian and run out to pick him up."

"Thank you," Ned said. "And thanks for remembering him. I would never have heard the end of that."

Ned pulled away, leaving Pete with the pile of ladders.

"So where are these lights?" Pete said.

"Right inside the front doors of the church," Angela said. "Start with the six blue tubs. The doors are unlocked."

She looked down the street toward Buford's.

"They're coming," Pete said. "I already sent them a text message. Get the boy, and then you can skedaddle."

"Skedaddle?"

"We don't need supervising."

"You'll call me if you have questions?"

"We won't have questions. We do this every year. Just get the boy."

When Angela returned twenty minutes later, with an ebullient Brian, Pete remained in charge of the crew. They were still drinking coffee, which made her nervous considering the limited time they had committed to the task.

But also on the sidewalk was Gabe, holding two large steaming coffees. He handed one to her as the other men, with Brian in tow, carried tubs and ladders down the street.

"I hope they know what they're doing," she said.

"I might just happen along Main Street a little later this morning," Gabe said. "Shopping. Enjoying the season."

"I would be incredibly appreciative if you would!"

"I have another idea as well," Gabe said.

"Yes?"

"I'll sing gentle falsetto with the sopranos on a couple of pieces. You don't have many tenors, but they seem to know what they're doing. Most of the time, they just have to find G and stay right around it, and they do just fine."

Angela laughed. "Tenor parts are like that sometimes. But singing with the sopranos?"

"Just a little support, especially on the descant. They're used to having someone to reassure them they're on the right track."

Angela sipped coffee. "It might work."

"It's settled. Now one more thing."

"What's that?"

"I have my rental car right over here. I'd like you to take a short drive with me."

"A drive? I don't have much time."

"It's not far. It's important."

She met his eyes. He'd asked nothing of her in the last few days, and he'd done so much for her. She nodded. The time had come.

They didn't speak as he drove. Down Main Street. Right on a side street. Over a few blocks. Cutting over on an angling street across the back of town that Angela didn't allow herself to traverse anymore. The edge of the oldest homes in Spruce Valley.

Angela's throat thickened.

He parked in front of Carole's house.

Angela had only been past it a few times since helping to clear it out months ago. She'd forced herself to create new mental ruts to follow as she navigated to all her usual locations around town, routes that didn't take her past the home of her deceased friend. Other people lived there now.

They sat in silence. Angela finally heaved a heavy breath.

"She saved my life, you know."

"I didn't know," Gabe said. "When my grandmother moved away, I don't think she ever knew she'd spend the rest of her life living in New Zealand. But even when I was a pip-squeak, she brightened at Great-Aunt Carole's letters and the news about her friend Angela."

"It was a highlight of Carole's life when your parents brought you to meet her. I'd just moved here with my husband. Carole had us over to meet you. I think you were four, maybe five."

"I barely remember," Gabe said. "Sometimes I think it's my parents' stories I remember more than actually being here."

"I hadn't been married long when I moved to Spruce Valley," Angela said. "Carole took me under her wing. Not long after your visit, my husband died. It was Carole who sat with me and never once suggested it was time to move on. Even without saying so, she managed to make me believe I could still go on to have a happy life."

"And you have, haven't you?"

Angela nodded. "I have. I really have."

Most of Spruce Valley had long forgotten Carole had a sister who moved to New Zealand and never returned. But Angela still had the photo albums of Carole's only nephew and his only son—Gabe. She hadn't known what to do with them when they cleared out the house.

"I loved your great-aunt very much," she said. "Losing her. . . well, it's stirred up every other loss I've ever had. My father who abandoned us. My mother who died when I was thirteen. My husband. The children we never got to have. She loved Christmas, and she made sure I did, too. But not this year. It's been too dismal—until you came along."

Angela was still nursing the large coffee he'd handed her on Main Street, though now she was twisting the cup around in her hands more than she was drinking the liquid.

"I've always wanted to come back to the States," he said, as if reading her mind. "I'm her only heir. Her will seemed to give me a good excuse. I wanted to see the house before selling it, see if I truly remember that visit when I was little or anything else about Spruce Valley. The bank accounts and life insurance aren't complex, but they still have to be dealt with."

"But have you even been inside?" Angela asked. "There are renters."

"Not yet. The lawyer will arrange a time after Christmas. I don't want to upset anyone's holiday."

"Will you give the renters a chance to buy the house?"

"I'm not sure. Maybe I'll live in it."

Angela turned her head to look at him. "Live in it?"

"I have to live somewhere."

"You're thinking of staying?"

"I hear the choir director could use another tenor in the long term."

Angela laughed and wiped tears from her eyes.

"We have a busy day ahead of us," Gabe said, "but I want to take you somewhere tonight."

"There's so much to do."

"And I'm going to help you with all of it. I am at your disposal. I'll flock the lanterns. I'll make sure the lights are being hung properly, and I'll introduce myself to Mr. Masters to see if he needs help with the horses. I'll check with Elinor to make sure the candles have arrived."

"Blue candles."

"Blue candles. Tomorrow I'll deal with the blue garland. That's all for the town. Tonight is for you. For your spirit. This is the longest night of the year in your neck of the woods—though not in mine—and I've discovered a lovely tradition called Blue Christmas."

"You're joking."

"I'm not! It's a church service. There's one in Marksbury. Come with me."

CHAPTER 16

The church in Marksbury was unpretentious. Tending toward a boxy shape, it was nothing like Main Street Church in Spruce Valley that had occupied its corner for more than a hundred years. Angela had never even noticed this building before.

"How did you find out about this?" Angela asked.

"I'm a soft touch for the local 'Things to Do' flyers." Gabe put the car in gear and removed the key from the ignition.

Angela knew the flyer he was talking about. All the shops on Main Street had them on their counters. She hadn't perused one in years, but the stacks seemed to disappear every month before the new issue came out. Obviously people did pick them up.

They got out of the car, and Angela tucked her hands into the pockets of the long woolen coat she'd chosen that night, an extravagant gift from Carole several years ago. Darkness had come hours ago and would hover long after everyone in Spruce Valley and surrounding towns was up and moving tomorrow. At this time of year, some people rarely saw daylight on workdays.

It was indeed the longest night of the year.

Inside, in a foyer lit only by several arrangements of candles, someone handed them each a bulletin and a blue votive candle. Electric lights in the sanctuary were turned on but dimmed to a level to accommodate reading the bulletin while inviting a pensive mood. Angela chose a pew two-thirds of the way back before Gabe could get ideas about sitting down front in a strange church. She was there. That was hard enough. The sanctuary did not fill up, but she hadn't expected it would. Three days before Christmas Eve, most people were still in the malls, or home wrapping packages, or driving around the neighborhoods with their children to *ooh* and *aah* at the lights on this longest night of the year. In Spruce Valley, perhaps they were arranging logs and kindling in their fireplaces and talking about where they would stroll during A Christmas to Remember. Those who gathered in church on this night were those whose hearts clenched at the thought of Christmas, just as Angela's did.

Not even a week had passed since the committee had been unceremonious about laying the success of the event in Angela's lap. Only Gabe's presence, and Carole's memory, kept her moving with her tasks. She would just have to steel herself for all the questions that would come about why everything was so different this year.

A blue Christmas. It wasn't what she wanted for the town, and her gut told her this service, with its blue title and blue candles and blue bulletin, would rub salt into the wound. Sitting back in the pew, she took several deep breaths and let them out slowly.

The leaders who stepped forward from the first pew were soft spoken with a genuineness in their voices that surprised Angela. There was no cheery "Merry Christmas" greeting, no grand music of the season, no processional with its pomp. She heard only warmth and acknowledgment of pain. The leaders stood side by side in front of a table draped in a blue cloth that puddled on the floor.

"We all need comfort at points in our lives, for seasons or for long stretches," one leader said. "You have done the brave work of coming tonight in search of comfort and hope. God's people yearned for the consolation of the long-awaited Messiah, and the writings of Isaiah to disconsolate hearts gave hope-filled images of God's redeeming presence. Christmas can be a time when many are in need of that reassurance and comfort, and that is why we have gathered tonight."

He gestured for his coleader to continue the welcome.

"Tonight is the longest night of the year," she said. "Outside these walls, the world awaits Christmas only four days away. Voices ring with excitement and plans and the passing of favorite recipes from one generation to the next. Music plays from the stereos. Tables are set for festive meals. Yet inside these walls are the truths of depression and sadness, mourning and struggling. Like the long-ago people of Israel, we yearn to know hope once again. Some have come in reluctance and anxiety. Some have come because they have been here before and yet still find grief in these days. Some have come because they have tried everything else and are on the brink of believing hope no longer exists."

The two leaders stepped apart and took up new positions on the sides of the tables.

"My name is Rich," the first leader said, "and this is Lucy. Our service will be brief. After it concludes, we invite you to remain in the sanctuary until you are ready to depart. We are not on a schedule. Lucy and I will be here to speak with you if that's what you'd like."

"If you feel blue tonight," Lucy said, "make no apology. We do not ask you to put a smile on your face if there is no smile in your spirit. We do not ask you to sing with your voice if there is no song in your heart. We see no shame in tears. Tonight we gather from our individual isolation to be companions in the seasons of life that have brought us here."

The lump in Angela's throat thickened even as her spine curved in growing surrender. It was as if these two strangers, leading a type of service she had never heard of before, were looking right into her. What surprised her most was that she didn't want them to look away.

Rich turned to the table and lit a large white pillar candle.

"Beginning tomorrow, we will see daylight more and more each day. It will be measured in moments at first. Gradually we will realize that the moments have gathered into an hour, then two, then three. Hope begins anew in that flicker of a moment. We turn toward God now, no matter how tiny the flicker in our hearts, to ask God to burn the flame of hope when we cannot do it on our own. Pray with me."

Angela's breath caught as she closed her eyes and listened to the words of the prayer, which didn't shy away from pain or solitude or discouragement. Neither did they shy away from promise or redemption or restoration.

"The fortieth chapter of Isaiah tells us, 'Comfort, comfort my people,'" Lucy said. " 'Speak tenderly to Jerusalem, and proclaim to her that her hard service has been completed, that her sin has been paid for, that she has received from the Lord's hand double for all her sins. A voice of one calling.'"

Rich's voice continued the passage. " 'In the wilderness prepare the way for the Lord; make straight in the desert a highway for our God. Every valley shall be raised up, every mountain and hill made low; the rough ground shall become level, the rugged places a plain.'"

" 'And the glory of the Lord will be revealed,'" Lucy read, " 'and all people will see it together. For the mouth of the Lord has spoken.'"

Prayers.

Readings.

Carols of love and light.

Four blue pillar candles lit to remember those loved and lost, the pain of loss, those gathered in loss, the gift of hope even in loss.

The invitation to carry votive candles forward and light them to remember particular individuals. Angela gripped her candle and stepped out of the pew. Gabe rose and walked behind her up the main aisle toward the table at the front. They set their votives down together, took small white taper candles, dipped them into the strong flame of one of the blue pillars, and lit the votives. Standing side by side, they waited until their flames burned certain. The line continued moving forward as they receded. Soon the table shown with the brilliance of grief and gratitude magnified.

And the final words of the evening, once again from Isaiah: "The people walking in darkness have seen a great light; on those living in the land of deep darkness a light has dawned."

Angela sat quietly while others trickled out of the sanctuary, as reluctant as she was to leave this place of solace.

She knew the words of scripture well.

When she left this place, would she also know the dawn of new light?

CHAPTER 17

The movement felt good. Peace from the evening before still hovered in Angela's spirit, and now she let Blitzen lead and set the pace. A gray sky might yield snow. More likely it would just be a drab day, and an extra layer beneath her jacket had proven to be wise. Mingling with peace from the blue Christmas service was the exhausting emotional release of staring at her emotions and not bolting. She missed her best friend and grieved her passing. She was allowed this, even at Christmas, even while organizing A Christmas to Remember. In a room full of strangers, each one with a private reason for being there, she'd felt less alone.

On this final day before A Christmas to Remember, details still awaited. Touch base with Simon about the horses and where to bring them. She hadn't been too worried about food vendors, because there were several small businesses along Main Street that served food and other groups were regulars at the event to raise funds for their causes, but it wouldn't hurt to double-check so she would know the answers when people asked the questions. Buford would offer a never-ending supply of cocoa and steaming coffee on various street corners. The women's ministry at Main Street Church baked Christmas cookies and packaged them attractively for their primary fund-raiser for the coming new year. The bakery would sell an array of other baked goods but honor a tacit agreement with the women's ministry not to compete for cookie sales. The candy shop would stay open late primarily for its fudge case.

Angela also needed to verify she had enough people to pass

out the blue candles at various stations, and they would need signs cautioning people to handle the flames responsibly. They should only be lit during the parade and only outdoors. The fire department would have a visible presence to enforce safety rules. And she hadn't talked to Simon Masters about his horses. For her sake, she wanted confirmation he would come to the street corner where she would be awaiting. She'd spent more time on the phone in the last five days than she had in the last five years.

She was nearly home after a particularly vigorous walk when she caught sight of her neighbor Nora watching out the front window and waved. Rather than simply wave back, Nora barreled out her front door in a loose coat she might have selected for its proximity. When Angela saw her coming, she stopped. She was the one who'd waved. She couldn't now act as if she hadn't seen Nora. Blitzen resisted the tightening hold of the leash, but Angela gathered enough of the leash to keep him under control.

"Thank you again for the lights," Angela said. "So many! They will definitely be put to use."

"I'm glad to hear it," Nora said. "Please feel free to keep them."

"It will be a good start for rebuilding our supplies."

"When I heard you were in charge of A Christmas to Remember," Nora said, "I assumed the big spruce was beyond your plans. The event is tomorrow, after all."

"You assumed correctly," Angela said. "I imagine a lot of people also heard about the water damage at Main Street Church. A number of things will look different this year."

"But the scaffolding," Nora said. "If you aren't planning to light the tree, why is there scaffolding?"

"Scaffolding? I didn't arrange any scaffolding."

"Someone did."

"That can't be right."

"Saw it with my own two eyes when I took my husband to

the train station early this morning."

"Thank you, Nora. I'd better make some calls."

Angela tugged at Blitzen's rope, but he seemed more interested in following Nora up the walkway to her home than following Angela. He weighed seventy pounds, too heavy and strong for her to just pick up and carry to the next house over. She pulled on the leash, and he kept his resistance taut as he turned around to face the other direction.

"Come on, Blitzen," Angela said. "It appears that the best part of the day is now over."

He looked at her with his best sad puppy look.

Angela removed one glove to rummage in her jacket pocket and came up with several dog treats from a previous outing. It wasn't much, but it might be enough to buy his compliance.

The plan worked. Angela left him in the kitchen as she always did before jumping in her car for the three-mile drive into town.

Sure enough, scaffolding surrounded the tree. A system of ladders and platforms gave access to all sides. No one was using the scaffolding, and she saw no signs of supplies nearby. Whoever had put it up would have to take it down immediately. It would be disappointing enough to the crowd the next evening not to see the tree decorated without drawing attention to the fact by parking scaffolding there.

Angela scrolled through the contacts list on her phone looking for any likely suspects. She settled on Pete Nicholson.

"He's sleeping right now," Pete's wife said. "He was up most of the night with some last-minute work."

Angela winced. If the hours Pete had given her yesterday morning meant he had to work during the night, her debt of gratitude just tripled in size.

"If you think of it," Angela said, "please ask him to call me when he wakes up."

Next she popped into a couple of businesses close to the big spruce. Both the thrift store and a small frame shop were at the end of Main Street directly across from the big spruce. Surely someone working inside would have glanced up at some point and noticed the arrival of the scaffolding. It would have involved a sizable truck.

Inside the thrift store, she flipped through a rack of red sweaters. Ginny was minding the shop.

"It's not too late for a Christmas sweater," Ginny said. "They're half off."

"I just stopped in for a look-see," Angela said, glancing out the front window.

"What time will the crew start?" Ginny said.

"Crew?"

"For the tree."

"I'm still sorting that out," Angela said. "Did you happen to notice when the scaffolding went up?"

"Last night. I stayed late to catch up on bookkeeping and noticed the trucks. Everything went up so fast. Obviously these guys knew what they were doing."

"Did you recognize who they were?"

Ginny shrugged. Nobody in Spruce Valley has scaffolding like that. I'm pretty sure it's rented from a place in Marksbury every year."

"Was there a company name on the trucks? Or a logo?"

"Probably, but I couldn't see it. It was dark."

"Yes." Angela removed her hand from the only sweater that vaguely tempted her. "I'd better see what's happening."

Next door in the frame shop, she learned only that the young woman behind the counter had not been working yesterday. She arrived at work in the morning, saw the scaffolding, and assumed it was for A Christmas to Remember.

This was all a horrible mistake. The scaffolding had to come down, or at least be moved out of the way, even if she couldn't track down who had put it up. She needed help. And the expense—who would have approved this?

She pulled out her phone, found Gabe's number, and hit the CALL button.

"I've just picked up Brian," Gabe said. "We're going to hang the garlands and wreaths."

"That's great," Angela said. "Thanks for taking him under your wing."

"I also wrangled some more flocking."

"Even better," Angela said. "I'm afraid I need your help with something else."

"Whatever you need."

"I don't know who is responsible, but there's scaffolding around the big spruce. We have nothing to put on the tree. I can't have all those ladders there tomorrow night."

"You can leave that to me," Gabe said.

"I don't think it's a one-person job."

"I'll take care of it," he said. "I promise it won't be there tomorrow night. See you later."

Gabe's voice held too much cheer for the circumstances, but he ended the call, so Angela couldn't further reiterate the importance of removing the scaffolding.

Angela walked down the street to a coffee shop where she could have the second cup she'd intended to have at home before the large metal snafu hijacked her morning. She could sit, sip coffee, and make her calls to the various vendors. An hour later she had reassurance that everything was in order.

Today, and then tomorrow, and whether the event was a triumph or a catastrophe, at least it would be over.

When she went outside again, Brian grinned at her from

inside Gabe's rental car. The window came down, and Gabe leaned over Brian to speak to her.

"Got time to help us a bit? We'd love to have you. We need someone to let us into the church."

"It's a tempting offer." Angela's eyes lifted to the scaffolding two blocks away.

"I'll take care of the problem you mentioned," Gabe said. "You can trust me on that."

During the last few days, it had been hard to trust anyone for anything. But Gabe hadn't let her down. It was unfair to presume he would just because others had.

Angela got in the car, and Gabe accelerated.

"I thought we'd start at the church and work in the other direction first and then come back this way."

"And work right up to the tree," Brian said.

The tree.

They went to the church for a ladder and a supply of wreaths and garlands. Gabe opened the trunk of his car and pulled out a dolly that unfolded to a small flatbed that would easily hold a box of wreaths and a box of garlands and a supply of flocking. When the boxes were empty, they could roll it back to the church and reload.

They made steady progress. Gabe carried the ladder and Brian pushed the cart. Angela was in charge of a box of small nails and a spool of fish line. During one break, Angela paced down the street to Buford's for three sandwiches, three bags of chips, and three bottles of water. Then they worked in the other direction. Gabe patiently let Brian do as much of the work on the ladder as he wanted to, and Brian had the perfect touch with the spray-on flocking.

Angela looked up and down the street as they were near the end of the task. It didn't look terrible. In fact, it was inviting.

Tomorrow the lanterns would go up, and when the lights lit the streets, it would look even better.

For the sake of Carole's memory, Angela hoped the event would not be a disaster, after all.

They were down to the last three wreaths when Gabe said, "Angela, would you mind very much running back to the church for the wire cutters? I had them earlier, but I must have left them at lunchtime."

"We've done very well without them," Angela said. The wire on the garland was easy enough to twist and snap, and they were nearly finished.

"Still, I'd like to have them for some touch-up work."

"It'll be dark by the time I get back."

"True. Maybe you know where to grab a flashlight at the church?"

He was persistent.

"I left my car not far from here this morning," Angela said. "Maybe it would be faster to drive."

"If you think so," Gabe said.

Angela looked at Brian. "Would you like to come along?"

"I need Brian here," Gabe said.

In fact, Angela didn't know where to find a flashlight at the church. She scrounged through several closets, but her keys didn't open everything in the building, only the outer door and the rooms she normally used with the choir. Gabe would have to do without light, but she picked up the cutting tool and took it back with her. As she drove slowly along Main Street, hoping for a parking spot close to where she'd left Gabe and Brian, children and adults seemed to spill out of the shops and stop outside to watch something. Angela lifted her eyes as well.

Two figures were on the scaffolding around the big spruce.

Angela's heart leaped into her throat. One of them was a child.

Brian.

She swung sharply into the nearest open parking spot and jumped out of the car. Gabe promised to take care of the scaffolding. That did not include letting an eleven-year-old child scale its heights.

Where was Gabe anyway?

She narrowed her eyes and peered, all the while jogging toward the scaffold.

Gabe was up there with Brian. Brian must have decided to go up on his own, and Gabe followed to bring him down safely. Yes, that must be it.

From about halfway up, the two of them leaned over a railing, and Gabe swung one arm in some kind of signal. Lights spiraling up the spruce tree went on, and a unanimous cheer rose up from onlookers on the street.

Angela's jaw hung open, and she made several attempts to close it before being successful.

Blue lights. Hundreds of them—no, there must be thousands on a tree that size. Where did he get them and when had he dressed the tree? She'd been with him for most of the day. They'd been together last evening as well, with no ladders in sight.

Brian ran along a platform, his steps clanging against the metal, and found two long ladders to descend.

"Careful!" Angela shouted. She didn't want to explain to the boy's parents or grandparents that he'd injured himself in these particular circumstances.

"That was the coolest thing ever!" Brian glowed in the blue ambiance.

"When? How?" Angela put one hand on Brian's shoulder and looked past him toward Gabe on the ladder.

"My dad and Gabe and me and Mr. Nicholson and some of

his friends." Brian's tone was joyous. "We did it. They let me help. We stayed up practically all night, and I wasn't tired one bit."

Gabe strode toward her, grinning.

"But I didn't see any lights today," Angela said. "You can't have strung them just in the last half hour."

"Of course not," Gabe said. "Pete and I were just finishing up the electrical. The lights aren't meant to be seen during the day. They're deep into the branches and fastened snug."

"Pete?" Angela said.

Gabe pointed and Angela saw Pete fiddling with an industrial electrical box at the back of the thrift store.

"He won't blow out the circuits on the whole town, will he?" Angela said.

Gabe shook his head. "When he says he knows how to manage the lights, he's telling the truth."

CHAPTER 18

The bed sank on one side with Blitzen's weight, and Angela's first conscious thought on Saturday morning was his breathing—more like panting—at the back of her neck. She flung one arm around, doing her best to aim for his mass without having to open her eyes. Her hand found his chest and she scratched it. Blitzen regarded this as an invitation to lick her cheek, which he did with enthusiasm.

"Okay, okay," she said. "I'm getting up."

For the first time all week, Angela hadn't set an alarm, but she should have known the dog would want to go out right on schedule. Grabbing her robe off a hook in the bathroom and looking under the bed for the second slipper, she was ready to stumble downstairs, let the dog out—with a warning not to leave the yard—and make coffee.

She hadn't expected to see snow flurries when she opened the back door and Blitzen brushed past her. The chance that it would amount to anything was remote. Spruce Valley's location sometimes caught the edge of a winter storm lashing most of its vehemence on towns to the north, while being far enough south that many years Christmas Day was dry and a balmy forty-five degrees. Still, snow flurries on the day of A Christmas to Remember added nicely to the ambiance of the event.

Through the window as she sipped her coffee, Angela watched Blitzen romp in the backyard. Carole always said Blitzen liked the snow more than any of the other dogs she'd owned, but in the months since Angela took in Blitzen, Spruce Valley hadn't had enough snow for Angela to witness the joyous phenomenon for herself. The white stuff was starting to stick, and Angela could make out the suggestion of Blitzen's footprints.

She'd slept well, but it was time to get going. Blitzen was content in the backyard while Angela ate a quick English muffin and got dressed. Then she called him into the house with a promise of a proper walk later in the day. Gabe and Brian would be waiting for her at Main Street Church. The last thing to do was hang the lanterns, one above every shop door whose architecture allowed it.

The two of them sat on the front steps of church as if they'd known each other all their lives rather than just two days.

Outside the paper goods shop, Travis stopped for a close look. "You did that with paper from my store?"

"Sweet as, mate!" Gabe grinned.

"I would never have guessed."

They moved on down the street, shop after shop.

At the candle shop, Elinor came outside to watch as Brian went up on the ladder and hung a loop of fishing line on a hook in the gabled entrance.

"Blue," she said. "I suppose it was me who gave you the idea of a Christmas where everything was blue."

Angela minded her tongue. "It's coming together."

"I heard you struck a deal with Buford because he never would have sold this. . .well, I can't call it greenery, now can I?"

"Sweet as, mate," Gabe said.

Elinor pinched her face.

"It's all right," Brian said, descending the ladder. "It means 'yes' or 'awesome.' I think I might start saying it."

Angela and Gabe laughed. They moved on to the next shop, a used bookstore. Gabe leaned his head toward Angela and whispered.

"Kim sighting, ten o'clock."

That was like saying, "Don't think about an elephant." She turned to look. Kim made eye contact, waved a hand in greeting, and headed toward them.

"You seem to have some very different ideas about A Christmas to Remember," Kim said.

"There have been some extenuating circumstances," Angela said.

"I heard about the water in the church basement. Everyone has. But I would have thought you would pursue a more traditional look."

"Garlands, wreaths, paper lanterns, lights," Angela said. "That sounds traditional to me."

"You know what I mean," Kim said.

"Sweet as!" Brian said.

Angela and Gabe laughed. Kim scowled first at Brian and then at Gabe.

"I suppose this was all your idea."

"I'm always glad to help out a friend," Gabe said. "It's going to be a spectacular night. You'll see."

Brian spread his hand and looked up with his tongue out. "It's snowing again. We're going to have snow!"

"Maybe," Angela said. It still seemed unlikely they'd get more than a few minutes of flurries, but she wouldn't dash Brian's hopes with reality. Not five hours before the event.

Soon enough they had hung the last lantern and returned to the church to stow the ladder out of sight.

Gabe rubbed his hands together. "I have a few things to take care of. Angela, can you run my mate here home?"

"Sure. Can I help you with anything?"

"No, ma'am. I will see you back here in a few hours. It will be a great night!"

"Thanks to the two of you," Angela said.

She dropped Brian at the younger Bergstroms' house and drove straight home from there. Blitzen greeted her with his usual ecstasy. After a quick tuna sandwich for lunch, Angela put the leash on him. Blitzen might not know that she had promised him a walk, but she did—and she needed it even more than he did. Elinor and Kim were right. Some of the basic elements were there, but overall the event would be different than what people expected. She made sure to tuck a list of phone numbers and her cell phone in her jacket pocket. If she could make a few phone calls to double-check arrangements, she would have reassurance.

At the top of her list was a family with four children. If she knew for certain they were coming, she'd feel better. Three of them had friends who were hardly ever out of sight. That would give her at least seven children. She still hoped for a couple of dozen, so she called three other families. Everyone confirmed they would be there and knew where to meet.

Simon Masters would be at the south end of Main Street with the horses. The mayor of Spruce Valley was personally making sure the street was blocked off an hour ahead of time.

The sidewalk tables would be set up as soon as the street was blocked off.

The lights already had been double-checked that afternoon and everything worked according to plan.

Satisfied, Angela dropped her phone in her pocket and tugged on the leash to guide Blitzen toward home. Already the temperature had tumbled enough to feel a bite when the wind gusted. Angela dressed in layers for the lower temperatures sure to arrive after sunset.

"Guess what, Blitzen?" She scratched beneath his jowls. "You're coming with me. But you have to wear a Santa hat."

Deftly she put the hat on his head and pulled the elastic strap under his chin. He moved his head in circles for a few minutes before settling into acceptance.

"Time to go, buddy."

Angela loaded the dog in the back of the car and drove into town, parking at the south end of Main Street and waiting in the lot where she'd told all the families to drop off their children. She was more than twenty minutes early, plenty of time to greet even the first family to arrive.

Simon arrived a few minutes later with his horse trailer. Angela kept Blitzen on a short leash while she watched Simon lead one horse out and then the other. He went into the trailer one more time and came out with blankets to hang from their backs.

"Those are beautiful," Angela said.

"My wife was in town the other day and noticed there seemed to be a blue theme this year. We've had these up in the rafters for years."

"They're perfect." She fingered the deep blue velvet with bright white trim. People would have good reason to remember this year as the blue Christmas.

But where were the children? Their parents wouldn't stay home because of light snowfall, would they? She looked at the time glowing on the bank's display. Technically no one was late yet, but she had supposed some would be early. She'd confirmed at least a dozen just a couple of hours earlier, and she'd been very clear about where to meet.

Down the street, some of the businesses were closing for the day, while others would stay open for evening traffic. Spectators were lining the streets. But the Christmas lights weren't on. She'd spoken to Pete, too. The lights couldn't have broken in the last two hours. Could they?

Without the lights, Main Street looked like a sorry excuse for a holiday.

Angela fished in one jacket pocket for her cell phone and then the other. Not there. She unzipped her jacket for access to her jeans. Not there, either.

"I'll be right back," she said to Simon. She searched under the driver's seat of her car, on the passenger seat, on the floor, in the console. Not there.

Still none of the children had arrived and still none of the lights were on. And she had no phone. Her mind's eye saw it clearly on her kitchen table.

She returned to Simon. "Can I borrow your cell phone?"

"I don't carry one," he said.

Angela blinked. No phone.

"I'm just not sure where everybody is," she said. "We're supposed to start soon."

"And we will."

Even with a dozen children, it wasn't going to be much of a parade. But there were supposed to be lights. Two horses and a dog walking down the middle of a dark street—that was an utter failure.

Simon led the horses to the street.

Blitzen tugged against the leash to be allowed to follow, and Angela let him lead her into the street as well. She didn't know what else to do.

A single golden light came on across the street.

And a single voice rang out. "I'm dreaming of a white Christmas!"

Gabe? Angela peered into the darkness, not quite able to fix on the location of his voice as he continued singing the familiar Christmas song. Simon led the horses forward slowly. Blitzen followed, pulling Angela along. Without missing a bar of the music, Gabe stepped into the street to walk beside her, and the song drew her in. Grinning, she sang with him.

Then the children began.

As they passed each building on the street, the lights on either side came on and children slipped out of the crowd to join the parade and the singing. When the song ended, Gabe lifted a megaphone to his mouth summoning more children by name.

Abigail. Patsy. Paul. Rafe. Suzy. Deborah. Jamie. Phil. Tim. Michelle. Bethany. Michael. Eric. Malinda.

The names kept coming, and the kids kept coming. Behind Gabe, a high schooler lifted a trumpet to his lips and another held a violin. The instruments played a stanza of "It Came Upon a Midnight Clear" while Gabe continued to call out names.

Elsa. Ian. Mark. Caleb. Emily. Katie. Lisa. Boden. Rhys. Annalise. Titus. Matt. Eddie. Lilia. Xavier. Aaden. Caspian. Deacon. Galena.

All those names!

The children were singing "O Little Town of Bethlehem" now. Angela had supposed she would be the one to guide their singing, but they seemed to know just what to do without her.

Elsie. Evelyn. Maddox. Tytan. Tucker. Charlotte. Logan. Sally. Eloise. One by one they joined the throng behind the horses. Some pulled red wagons or strollers with younger children tucked in.

Angela could hardly keep up with the names. Somebody with a saxophone joined the instrumentalists, and she wondered where Brian was.

Where did Gabe get this list? The names were all students of hers—some current students and some who were now in college and home for the holidays. Some were older than that and had children of their own. What threaded them together was the hours they'd sat at her upright grand piano learning to play.

The students sang with gusto. The strings of lights came on

block by block, making the blue garland dance. Candles passed through the spectators on the sidewalk, followed soon by the flame. At the towering spruce, blue lights spiraled and twinkled against the night sky.

Gabe had created joy and beauty against impossible odds.

And hope, once lost, was found again.

CHAPTER 19

The glow lasted all evening. Hot cocoa. Cookies. More hugs than Angela could remember ever sharing before in one night. Groups of people stood on street corners, blue candles in hand, singing Christmas carols rather than walking past the carved and painted wooden carolers of years past. Children were intent on scraping together enough snow to at least form one miniature snowball to throw at someone's back. Gabe even set up a table to show people how to fold the paper lanterns. He seemed to have an endless supply of spray-on flocking. Just when Angela thought surely he was down to his last can, he produced more. Angela had come to the task of organizing A Christmas to Remember kicking and screaming, and the debacle of the water damage had lowered her expectations even further. She'd made the phone calls and lists and schedules, but it was Gabe who brought joy to the evening. No longer did Angela think of Christmas Eve, with both its morning service and its late-evening candlelight service, as the last day to get through so Christmas would be behind her.

Angela was in the choir room early on Sunday to make sure the red robe she'd assigned Gabe was long enough. The usual gold collars would be flipped to the white sides for both services on Christmas Eve. As soon as most of the sopranos were present, she huddled with them to explain that they might hear Gabe singing their line.

"Don't let it throw you," she said. "You know when to come in."

"But we haven't practiced that way," someone said.

"I know," Angela said. "And I'm afraid we can't do much more than warm up with the piano right now. Let's have him sing with you on scales just to get used to it."

She had only moments before she had to be at the organ in the sanctuary playing prelude music and the choir would arrange themselves in the foyer, ready to process in while the congregation sang "O Come, All Ye Faithful."

They sang a few scales and a few bars of the morning's anthem. Then it was time.

"Remember," Angela said, "tonight we gather at ten thirty so we can have a brief rehearsal and be ready to process for the eleven o'clock service."

Angela encouraged everyone to take deep breaths while she prayed that their music would bring glory to God and encourage hearts in need of hope.

Like mine.

Then she led them out of the choir room and hurried down the hall to take her place at the organ.

They did well. Both in the processional, which included a descant, and the main anthem, Gabe added just the right vocal touch to support the sopranos when they needed it without taking over or suggesting in any way that they would have been weak on their own. In fact, he surprised even Angela with the range of his falsetto. When she offered to stay after church and run through the other three pieces the choir would sing that evening, he said it wasn't necessary, and she believed him. She was beginning to wonder if he had more substantial musical experience than small-town church choirs.

Then she debated inviting him to her house for the afternoon, but the truth was she wanted a good long nap. With the strain of A Christmas to Remember behind her—as well as the unexpected joy—exhaustion had set in. She pulled some soup from the freezer, left it to thaw a bit while she walked Blitzen, and then ate the soup and stretched out on the sofa under a quilt with Blitzen on the floor right beside her. When she woke, the day's brilliance was spent and nightfall blanketed the neighborhood. She still had most of the evening to pass before going to church, but on Christmas Eve, one holiday movie after another played on television. She liked the old classics. *White Christmas. The Bishop's Wife. It's a Wonderful Life. The Bells of St. Mary's. Miracle on 34th Street.* With Blitzen's head—and it was a huge head even for a dog—in her lap, she propped up her feet and selected *It's a Wonderful Life.* She almost wished she had put up a Christmas tree so she could sit in its gleam.

Angela arrived at church early. The choir's limited warm-up time required intentionality, and she hoped to run through one selection from start to finish. She wouldn't single out the sopranos, though it was for their benefit she carried this hope. The pastor's car was already in the lot, and the church doors were unlocked even though it was only ten fifteen. She saw him lurking in the foyer.

"Merry Christmas, Martin," Angela said, with more brightness in her voice than she'd felt in the entire preceding week.

He glanced at her just long enough for it to feel like a scowl.

"Is everything all right?" she asked.

"Lost my sermon notes, that's all."

"Goodness."

"And I was assured that the candles left from last year were sufficient to use again this year," Martin said. "Have you seen them? Half of them are practically stubs. We may have to skip them altogether."

"No candles on Christmas Eve?"

"Nothing to be done about it at this point." Martin slapped a wall. "I can't think what I did with my sermon notes."

"I can't do anything about your notes," Angela said, "but we do have some candles left from last night."

Martin paused. "The blue ones?"

"Sorry about the color. They weren't my first choice, either."

"Hardly a Christmas color."

"That's what I thought, but they did nicely for us last night."

"This is not the same. Can you think of a single time in your entire life that you sang 'Silent Night' on Christmas Eve holding a blue candle?"

Angela was beginning to resent his tone. She was only trying to help.

"How about this?" she said. "We put the extras in a closet downstairs. I'm not even sure how many there are. But I'll get them out and you decide if you want to use them."

"Fine. As you wish. I've got to find my notes."

Angela shook her head at Martin's departing back. She hadn't thought it possible, but his Christmas spirit was even worse than hers had been before last night.

She hustled downstairs, found the candles, took them upstairs, left them on the usher's table at the back of the sanctuary, and rushed to the choir room. All the margin she'd built into the evening was gone. Most of the choir was assembled.

Everyone except Gabe.

"Where's your friend?" one of the sopranos asked. "Isn't he going to help us tonight like he did this morning?"

"I thought he was," Angela said, "but we'd better get started. Let's run through 'Still, Still, Still.'"

The sopranos had a way of sliding up and down between notes on this old Austrian folk tune. Lea made the transitions cleanly, but without her—and without Gabe?

"Remember, everyone," Angela said, "we want one continuous flow. Sneak your breath when you need to, but not at the end of a line, and not when you know your neighbor is breathing."

She played a few bars of introduction then lifted one hand long enough to cue the choir's beginning. This had always been one of her favorites.

"Still, still, still, one can hear the falling snow.
For all is hushed, the world is sleeping,
holy star its vigil keeping.
Still, still, still, one can hear the falling snow."

She let them go on, even though the sopranos might as well have been sliding and stumbling around a skating rink, and half the choir breathed at the end of every line.

"Sleep, sleep, sleep, 'tis the eve of our Savior's birth.
The night is peaceful all around you,
close your eyes, let sleep surround you.
Sleep, sleep, sleep, 'tis the eve of our Savior's birth."

She cut them off there. They would gain nothing by continuing with the third stanza.

"One last reminder to watch me carefully," she said. "We want clean cutoffs. We want to just let the notes hang in the silence before anyone makes another sound."

They filed out and, for the second time that day, lined up to process into the sanctuary. Angela kept the prelude music simple, playing various familiar carols by memory as she watched for Gabe. He might yet save the night's music. As she started on the fourth carol, she shook away that thought. She was the organist and choir director. If anyone was supposed to save the music, it should be her. This was Christmas Eve. And no matter how many wrong notes they might sing, these dear people would sing with their hearts.

Dim lights welcomed worshippers. There would be fewer families at eleven in the evening compared with eleven in the morning. Only the hardiest families would bring small children out at this hour, equipped with blankets and stuffed toys for small children in Christmas pajamas who would soon go limp in their parents' arms or sprawled on a roomy pew.

No Gabe.

Angela began a fifth carol and started to worry about Gabe. She was certain he'd intended to sing tonight. Something must have happened.

She shifted her attention to watch Martin come in. Usually he left his sermon notes in the pulpit ahead of time, but it remained bare. Either he never found them or they'd turned up at the very last minute and he hadn't had a chance to put them in the pulpit beside his Bible. The time was straight up eleven. She let the organ fade out of the carol as Martin stepped forward.

Martin gave a simple welcome. If he was still annoyed about losing his notes, he covered it better in the presence of the congregation than he had in her presence in the hallway. He even held up one white candle and one blue and reminded worshippers that if they had overlooked picking one up on the way in an usher would be glad to help. The service, which would finish promptly at midnight, would consist of readings and carols and a short meditation. He invited the congregation to stand for the processional hymn.

Angela opened stops to create the illusion of brass instruments in the sanctuary and played a robust rendition of "Hark, the Herald Angels Sing." The choir processed in and took their places in the choir loft at the front of the sanctuary.

The congregation shuffled into their seats, putting away hymnals and arranging themselves comfortably. Martin stepped again to the pulpit to read the first passage of scripture for the evening.

Where was Gabe?

Chapter 20

Martin stood with his Bible in one hand. "As we begin our celebration of the Savior's birth, we hear together these words from the prophet Isaiah, the eleventh chapter:

> "A shoot will come up from the stump of Jesse;
>   from his roots a Branch will bear fruit.
> The Spirit of the Lord will rest on him—
>   the Spirit of wisdom and of understanding,
>   the Spirit of counsel and of might,
>   the Spirit of the knowledge and fear of the Lord—
> and he will delight in the fear of the Lord. . . .
>
> "The wolf will live with the lamb,
>   the leopard will lie down with the goat,
> the calf and the lion and the yearling together;
>   and a little child will lead them.
> The cow will feed with the bear,
>   their young will lie down together,
>   and the lion will eat straw like the ox.
> The infant will play near the cobra's den,
>   and the young child will put its hand into the viper's nest.
> They will neither harm nor destroy
>   on all my holy mountain,
> for the earth will be filled with the knowledge of the Lord."

Angela signaled the choir to stand. The four-part harmony should shine, and it would, though she still wished Gabe were there. Gently, Angela played the starting pitches and then waved her right hand in the motion of four beats to set a tempo that neither rushed nor dragged. The choir inhaled and breathed out the first note in perfect harmony.

"Lo, how a Rose e'er blooming from tender stem hath sprung!
Of Jesse's lineage coming, as men of old have sung.
It came, a floweret bright, amid the cold of winter,
When half spent was the night.
Isaiah 'twas foretold it, the Rose I have in mind;
With Mary we behold it, the virgin mother kind.
To show God's love aright, she bore to us a Savior,
When half spent was the night."

Angela raised one hand from the organ and cut them off. She waited a full five seconds before giving the sign they should sit again, and they did so with a minimum of shuffling and throat-clearing. She smiled and nodded.

Martin's next reading came from Isaiah 9, culminating in the grand words that Handel's *Messiah* had burned into the minds of the faithful with his unforgettable music.

"For to us a child is born,
to us a son is given,
and the government will be on his shoulders.
And he will be called
Wonderful Counselor, Mighty God,
Everlasting Father, Prince of Peace."

Suddenly Angela's fingers itched to play the music of this triumphant piece of choral music. Instead, she turned to the hymn the congregation would be asked to sing, "O Come, O Come, Emmanuel."

A few changes in the organ settings would give the familiar carol a plaintive, yearning tone. Angela played through the full hymn one time, arriving at full harmony at the end of the refrain and slowing just enough to cue the congregation to come in.

"O come, O come, Emmanuel
and ransom captive Israel,
that mourns in lowly exile here
until the Son of God appear.
Rejoice! Re—"

The organ squealed and fell silent. It was a decent organ, but it was an electric organ, and at the moment it was not getting any electricity. Nor was there any light above the hymnal on the music stand. There were no electric lights still burning anywhere in the sanctuary. A few determined voices carried on with the hymn, no doubt assuming the interruption would be short-lived. They were a people living in the land of deep darkness, as Martin had just read from the ninth chapter of Isaiah. Someone began the second stanza of the song, but fewer people sang, either out of less familiarity with the words or distracted by sounds of scuffling around in the darkness.

The only light in the sanctuary came from the four candles lit on the Advent wreath. The Christ candle would have been lit later in the service. Light from a lone streetlamp outside filtered in through a stained-glass window, casting a prism of color over the chancel. When Angela glanced at the choir, she found half its members were already looking at her. She shrugged slightly and raised her hands in a motion indicating they should stay where they were.

A young child called out, "Hey, who turned off the lights?"

For a moment laughter dispelled the oddity of the

circumstances. People began pulling out cell phones and launching flashlight apps.

Martin came down in front of the pulpit. Without a working microphone, it didn't matter where he stood. He stepped to a side aisle to confer with a couple of people and then turned to the congregation.

"Please be patient," Martin said. "Several members of our property committee are here tonight, and they are investigating. Then we'll continue our service." He took a seat in the front pew.

Angela slid off the organ bench and moved to the piano, which required no electricity. Neither did it require light, because she could play Christmas carols from memory. She started with "Away in a Manger," hoping to capture the attention of the youngest and most wiggly people present, and moved on from there. It was hard to tell, but Martin seemed grateful that at least one of them had an idea for a distraction. It wouldn't amount to more than background music. Angela knew that. But it might keep people calm and in their seats rather than lose all focus while waiting for someone on the property committee to find the right fuse to change.

She returned to "O Come, O Come, Emmanuel," keeping the stanzas unadorned but the refrain full-bodied just as she would have on the organ.

"Once in Royal David's City." Gabe had sung that one with her just a few days ago. Her fingers moved steadily over the keys while she watched doors at the back of the sanctuary for his arrival. There had to be some explanation.

"The First Noel."

"Angels We Have Heard on High."

"O Little Town of Bethlehem."

Finally the property members returned to the sanctuary and conferred with Martin. They withdrew and Martin stood up.

Angela let the melody on the piano gently fade.

"Many of you have been coming to Main Street Church for many years," Martin said. "You know that our late service on Christmas Eve is a spiritual high point for the congregation and the many visitors who join us at this time of year. It looks like we will not have electric lights for the rest of this evening, but I wish to invite you to come with me in heart and mind to Bethlehem. Listening to Angela play carols as we waited for lights has given me an idea, and I hope she'll be willing to play a little tag team with me."

Angela nodded. How challenging could his request be if simple carols had inspired it?

"Every year on this night," Martin said, "we read from Luke's Gospel of the night that Jesus was born. Let us do so once again. I know many of you have your phones out and can simply look up the second chapter of Luke. I challenge you not to. Let's go to Bethlehem together and discover how much of the story is in our hearts."

Martin began to pace across the front of the church with no Bible and no cell phone in his hand.

"In those days," Martin said, "Caesar Augustus issued a decree that a census should be taken of the entire Roman world. This was the first census that took place while Quirinius was governor of Syria. And everyone went to their own town to register.

"So Joseph also went up from the town of Nazareth in Galilee to Judea, to Bethlehem the town of David, because he belonged to the house and line of David. He went there to register with Mary, who was pledged to be married to him and was expecting a child."

Martin paused. "How am I doing so far?"

"Terrific!"

"Keep it up!"

"You have a great memory."

"What song do you hear in your head now?" Martin asked.

Laughter rippled, but several responses came in unison. "O Little Town of Bethlehem."

Martin pointed at Angela, and she played a stanza while the congregation sang.

Then Martin pivoted and walked a few rows into the congregation. "While they were there, the time came for the baby to be born, and she gave birth to her firstborn, a son. She wrapped him in cloths and placed him in a manger, because there was no guest room available for them."

He looked up. "What song are you hearing now?"

The answer came quickly. "Away in a Manger."

Angela played one stanza.

"And there were shepherds living out in the fields nearby, keeping watch over their flocks at night." Martin paused. "This is any easy one. Which carol?"

"While Shepherds Watched Their Flocks."

Angela played while the congregation sang.

Martin continued. "An angel of the Lord appeared to them, and the glory of the Lord shone around them, and they were terrified. But the angel said to them, 'Do not be afraid. I bring you good news that will cause great joy for all the people. Today in the town of David a Savior has been born to you; he is the Messiah, the Lord. This will be a sign to you: You will find a baby wrapped in cloths and lying in a manger.'

"Suddenly a great company of the heavenly host appeared with the angel, praising God and saying... What did they say?"

"Glory to God!" several called out.

"Glory to God in the highest heaven, and on earth peace to those on whom his favor rests," Martin said.

Angela played "Angels We Have Heard on High."

"When the angels had left them and gone into heaven, the shepherds said to one another, 'Let's go to Bethlehem and see this thing that has happened, which the Lord has told us about.' So they hurried off and found Mary and Joseph, and the baby, who was lying in the manger. When they had seen him, they spread the word concerning what had been told them about this child, and all who heard it were amazed at what the shepherds said to them. But Mary treasured up all these things and pondered them in her heart. The shepherds returned, glorifying and praising God for all the things they had heard and seen, which were just as they had been told."

Angela played "What Child Is This?"

"I almost forgot to go to Bethlehem this year," Martin said. "I studied well this passage from Luke, and I outlined a strong sermon. And then I lost it. In this day and age, you might wonder how anybody loses a sermon. Isn't it on a computer? Or an iPad? Couldn't I just print another copy? No. My computer is in the shop, and I wrote the notes by hand. And I lost them. I was still festering over my own carelessness when I came into the building tonight. If the notes turn up, perhaps they'll be a sermon for another Christmas Eve. But here, in this moment, despite losing the notes, and despite losing electricity, we have traveled to Bethlehem not to dwell on what we have lost but on what God has given."

Emotion thickened Angela's throat. *We have traveled to Bethlehem not to dwell on what we have lost but on what God has given.*

CHAPTER 21

T his darkness is not what we expected," Martin said. "Many of you hold candles that we planned to light for a fleeting few moments of our service tonight. Instead darkness fell around us."

Angela hoped Martin was finished playing "Guess the Carol." At the moment, she wasn't confident she could coax her trembling fingers to cooperate.

"While I am not always successful," Martin said, "the lesson I learn over and over is to receive even what disappoints as a gift that can enrich me in some way. In these minutes that tick toward midnight, and as we sit in darkness before we light our candles, what is enriching you? Let me challenge you to set your phones down and let the lights turn off. Don't be afraid of a few minutes of darkness and quiet, for there you may find God's surprising presence."

Martin sat down. Angela sat on her fingers, tucked under her thighs on the piano bench. She needed to still them, knowing she would yet be called on for music before the service was over. For several minutes, worshippers rustled in the pews, perhaps looking around to see if others would let go of their phones and the light bearers they had become. Gradually, though, the spots of light around the sanctuary dimmed until only the four pillar candles of the Advent wreath remained. For a few golden moments, the still and silent sanctuary was just the sort of place where one might expect to meet God.

The first disturbance came from the other side of the sanctuary, about halfway back. It caused a hymnal to drop out of a rack, followed by a conflagration of *Shhh* and whispered requests for pardon. Angela couldn't see that far with certainty, but it seemed someone was trying to get to the center aisle. Why not go out the side aisle and cause less commotion? She glanced at Martin. This can't have been planned. Nothing beyond the opening few minutes of the service had gone according to plan. With neither her cell phone nor a candle within reach, Angela relied on her eyes to discern the disruption. Someone stepped into the aisle and began moving toward the front, trailing a finger along the carved oak end pieces of the pews.

A child.

A boy.

Brian.

Angela slid toward one end of the piano bench. Someone should see what Brian needed. Perhaps Martin would. But Brian walked past the front pew, where Martin had sat down and maintained a posture of prayer. Brian reached the Advent wreath and dug in his jeans pocket. Only when he leaned toward the flames did Angela realize what he'd pulled out.

A blue candle.

He tipped it into one of the Advent candles and then lit the Christ candle in the center of the circle. Then he turned around, faced the congregation, and began to sing.

"Silent night! Holy night! All is calm, all is bright."

Angela moved her fingers to the keys again. *That child has perfect pitch.* She'd heard him sing enough times in the children's choir of Main Street Church to have a well-formed opinion. He was singing exactly in the key in which the carol appeared in the hymnal, the same notes she could see with her mind's eye.

" 'Round yon virgin, mother and child, holy infant so tender and mild."

He moved to the pew where Martin sat and illumined the

pastor's features with his flame, though no one but Angela was positioned to see the shock in Martin's face. Angela's fingers entered the music. Even singing alone in the dark sanctuary, Brian's tone didn't waver.

"Sleep in heavenly peace. Sleep in heavenly peace."

Brian continued down the aisle bearing his flame and beginning the second stanza. As light spread through the sanctuary, so did the number of voices rising with the words of the familiar carol the congregation always sang when they lit their candles and prepared their hearts for the Christmas Eve reading of Luke's telling of the birth of Christ and the shepherds. The elements of the traditional service had come in a new order this year, under unexpected circumstances, but a child among them now drew the congregation together. Brian lit the candles nearest the center aisle and the flames were passed outward.

"Silent night! Holy night! Shepherds quake at the sight.
Glories stream from heaven afar, heavenly hosts sing alleluia.
Christ the Savior is born! Christ the Savior is born!"

Martin stood and gestured for others to do the same. In the third stanza, Angela heard, at last, the voice she had sought since the choir had been warming up—not in the congregation, but robed and standing with the rest of the choir at the front of the sanctuary.

Gabe. He'd come.

"Silent night! Holy night! Son of God, love's pure light.
Radiant beams from Thy holy face,
with the dawn of redeeming grace.
Jesus, Lord, at Thy birth. Jesus, Lord, at Thy birth."

The service had taken a distinctly low-key turn once the electricity went out. Angela doubted she would need Gabe's help with the soprano section, after all, but it did her heart good to hear his clear and penetrating tenor coming from among the choir. They were all singing harmonies, she realized, and doing quite well.

Martin stepped forward as the last words echoed and dimmed, gesturing for the congregation to be seated.

"And a little child will lead them," he said, his voice thick. "Thank you, Brian. I wish you could all stand where I stand and see the hope and gratitude lighting your faces. Finding ourselves without the organ tonight—or any electricity—brings to mind the familiar story of how the carol we just heard came to be. I'm sure many of you have heard it. On another Christmas Eve two hundred years ago, in another country, in another church, the organ was in disrepair and not available to accompany the congregation's singing. And 'Silent Night' was offered for the first time. Now that we've had our own Christmas Eve without the organ and held candles in our hands, perhaps we'll all remember this night."

He turned toward Angela. "I wonder if the choir might manage one of their pieces for us by candlelight."

Angela nodded, thinking which selection would be the easiest under the circumstances. But a voice came from the choir loft.

"Still, Still, Still."

Others murmured agreement and began turning pages in their choir folders.

Angela winced inwardly. All those sopranos sliding around. But Gabe was there, and while the piano's accompaniment would not be as seamless and smooth as the organ's, its gentle percussion might be more undergirding with the notes. She caught Gabe's eye. He nodded, and she gave the signal for the choir to stand. Singers seemed to pair off quickly, one to hold the light and the other to hold the music. While she quickly moved to the organ long enough to retrieve her own copy of the music and then back to the piano, wondering what she would do for light, an eleven-year-old boy stood beside her with the solid flame of his blue candle. Brian didn't like to practice his lesson music, but she was certain he could read music and would know where to cast the light.

The congregation settled expectantly. The eyes of the choir turned to Angela, and she beat the tempo in the air before beginning the introductory measures. *Smooth. No breathing when your neighbor breathes. Watch dynamics.* Every admonition she'd ever given about this piece of music raced through her mind. Either they would remember, or they wouldn't, but it was time to sing.

"Still, still, still, one can hear the falling snow.
For all is hushed, the world is sleeping,
Holy star its vigil keeping.
Still, still, still, one can hear the falling snow.

"Sleep, sleep, sleep, 'tis the eve of our Savior's birth.
The night is peaceful all around you,
Close your eyes, let sleep surround you.
Sleep, sleep, sleep, 'tis the eve of our Savior's birth.

"Dream, dream, dream of the joyous day to come
While guardian angels without number,
Watch you as you sweetly slumber.
Dream, dream, dream of the joyous day to come."

They took her breath away. She could hardly believe it! Once again Gabe had just the right touch to lift without intruding on the sopranos, and deep down, it seemed, they had heard every instruction about how to sing the piece seamlessly. If a toddler in the back row of the sanctuary had dropped a pacifier when they finished, everyone would have heard it. Lit by candles, the choir faces flushed with the pleasure of a job well done. Angela was going to hug every single one of them before they left that night.

Martin stepped in front of the congregation one final time. "What a wonderful place to bring our service to a close. I pray you find stillness not only in your body as you sleep and dream of the joy we find in God's gift of His Son, but also stillness in your spirits as we leave this place where we have found the beauty of Bethlehem anew and now journey to our homes, soon to begin another year as followers of the child who lay in Mary's arms. Peace be with you all. Amen."

Angela hit the keys hard with the opening chords of "Joy to the World," and just as she hoped, the choir burst with the words and sang to the last syllable of the last stanza.

Chapter 22

When there's a dog in the house, there's no such thing as sleeping in. Angela could always count on Blitzen to prop his head on the side of her bed. If she didn't respond, the front paws came next as a final warning. If she didn't at least acknowledge him, he would hoist all seventy pounds onto the bed—or more precisely, onto her. Even if she put in a doggy door, she'd have to train him to use it.

He stared her in the eye.

"Merry Christmas," she said.

Since he bore a reindeer's name, it seemed only fair to extend the greeting.

She let him out the back door. The full expanse of the new day—Christmas Day—lay ahead, and she would gladly take Blitzen for a walk later. Yesterday's slight snow, when the thermostat hovered in the mid-thirties, had persisted so that enough of it was still on the ground when the temperatures dipped overnight. In the morning sun, snow glistened like a field of tiny diamonds. Angela made coffee while she waited for Blitzen to be ready to come inside. She hadn't been to the grocery store all week, and the fridge and cupboards demonstrated the growing need. But that was for tomorrow. She knew what she wanted from today.

Blitzen was already at the back door, behavior that suggested the cool temperature and damp ground did not agree with him. He happily followed Angela upstairs for her morning preparations. After a shower, she left her hair in damp ringlets and chose comfortable jeans, a favorite sweater, and thick socks.

Downstairs again, she went into the room where she gave lessons and surveyed the shelf of gifts. There was sure to be a holiday mug among them. There always was. She found two, both large and white, with squares of red and green lettering spilled around them spelling out MERRY CHRISTMAS. She took them both to the kitchen to clean thoroughly before pouring coffee into one. Then she lit the logs arranged in the living room fireplace and picked up her Bible.

She would honor Carole one more way, by reading aloud Carole's favorite Christmas passage, the grand, poetic opening words of the Gospel of John.

"Are you listening, Blitzen?" she said. "You've heard these words before."

Blitzen jumped up on the couch and curled against her, as if he wanted to share in the reading. Angela took a gulp of coffee and began to read aloud.

"In the beginning was the Word, and the Word was with God, and the Word was God. He was with God in the beginning. Through him all things were made; without him nothing was made that has been made. In him was life, and that life was the light of all mankind. The light shines in the darkness, and the darkness has not overcome it.

There was a man sent from God whose name was John. He came as a witness to testify concerning that light, so that through him all might believe. He himself was not the light; he came only as a witness to the light.

The true light that gives light to everyone was coming into the world. He was in the world, and though the world was made through him, the world did not recognize him. He came to that which was his own, but his own did not receive him. Yet to all who did receive him, to those who believed in his name, he gave the right to become children of God—children born not of natural descent, nor of human decision or a husband's will, but born of God.

The Word became flesh and made his dwelling among us. We have seen his glory, the glory of the one and only Son, who came from the Father, full of grace and truth."

The light shines in the darkness. The Word became a human being. And the Word was full of grace and truth. It was easy to see why someone who loved these verses also loved Christmas.

The fire's crackling was the only sound. Angela spread her fingers and laid her hands on the open pages of her Bible with her eyes closed to let the words ring and echo in her mind.

Blitzen jumped off the couch. The sound of him trotting straight toward the front door made Angela open her eyes, and a few seconds later came the knock—and after that Blitzen's bark.

"Take it easy, Blitzen." Angela made sure she had a good grip on the dog's collar before opening the door. "Gabe!"

Angela opened the door wide and Gabe came in. Blitzen's tail wagged in rapid rhythm, and she let go of his collar.

"I brought breakfast." Gabe held up an unmarked gray paper sack.

"First," Angela said, "thank you. It's slim pickings around here, though I do have coffee. Second, where did you find a place open on Christmas morning?"

"First," Gabe said, "I would love a cup of coffee. Second, I struck a deal with Mrs. Glass at the B&B."

Angela picked up her coffee, which needed warming up. "Come through to the kitchen. I have just the mug for today."

She poured coffee while Gabe unpacked his bag of huge blueberry muffins and mixed fruit packed in a large container. Seeing the feast, she laid out plates and silverware.

"I didn't get to tell you what happened last night," Gabe said.

"You were a great help once you got there," Angela said. "Not many would have bothered at that point in the service, and with the electricity out."

"I would never have let you down if I could help it." He cut a muffin in half. "I had double flats on my rental. Can you believe that?"

"Goodness," Angela said, "and late at night on Christmas Eve."

"I'd gone for a bit of a drive. Looking at lights, that sort of thing. I don't even know what I ran over, but it took out both front and back on the passenger side."

"How in the world did you find anyone to come fetch you?"

"It wasn't easy. I'll spare you the long story, but once I had two spare tires on, I went straight to the church."

"I'm glad you came."

"Me, too."

"And the sopranos might not want to admit it, but I'm pretty sure they'd say you were very helpful."

He lifted his "Merry Christmas" mug to his lips, his eyes twinkling as he sipped coffee. Or perhaps it was just the way they caught the light. Either way, Angela wished she could remember this moment for years. Perhaps she would. It seemed a long shot that he would stay in Spruce Valley and live in Carole's house—his house now—but they could always talk by Skype every now and then.

Angela interrupted the daydream by picking up her own mug. She didn't even know what Gabe did for a living, but he must have a life to get back to. His parents? Friends? Maybe a girlfriend?

The doorbell startled them both.

"Who would that be on Christmas morning?" Angela pushed her chair away from the table.

"Could be anyone," Gabe said. "After all, you weren't expecting me."

She allowed a half smile. Not expecting, precisely, but hoping. Since he had fulfilled that hope, she didn't know who else would be at the door now. Blitzen was ahead of her down the hallway. Once again she put a couple fingers through his collar and opened the door.

"Merry Christmas!"

A red and green box moved, and Angela saw the visitor's face. "Elinor! Merry Christmas! Come in out of the cold."

"I won't stay long," Elinor said. "I have a houseful to look after. But I felt so awful about the ruined candles that I wanted to bring something I hope will persuade you to forgive me."

"But A Christmas to Remember worked out beautifully," Angela said. "I hold no grudge."

"Still, I want you to have this." Elinor offered the box.

Angela took it. "Would you like coffee?"

"I don't want to trouble you."

"It's no trouble. Gabe is here, too. It's a morning of surprises."

Angela filled another mug with coffee and handed it to Elinor.

"Hello, Gabe," Elinor said. "I understand you had a lot to do with saving our event as well."

"Sweet as," he said. "Just doing my part."

"I'm grateful that you did."

"Shall I open this now?" Angela said.

"I do wish you would. I promise it isn't blue."

Angela laughed and removed the wrapping paper to lift the lid off the square box. Inside were two golden angel candles twisting and lifting arms upward.

"They're gorgeous!" Angela carefully lifted one.

"Yellow and white beeswax, hand dipped, rolled flat, and

twisted by hand," Elinor said. "These do not come off a factory assembly line. And the wicks are pure cotton."

"Elinor, this is very generous."

"I run a candle shop. I should have known better than to be so careless with seven hundred and fifty candles. I promise you, that will never happen again."

"Thankfully there's plenty of time to sort things out before next year."

"I've got to scoot now. The minions will need their instructions for Christmas dinner."

Angela walked Elinor to the front door and watched her get in her car. Brian was only half a block away, carrying something carefully with both hands underneath it. She went down the porch steps to meet him.

He smiled shyly. "My grandma sent a thank-you cake."

"A thank-you cake?"

"She makes very good cakes. She wins ribbons at the county fair every year."

"Come on inside and let's have a look." Angela took the cake from Brian and was relieved to realize that although it was a round cake carrier under a kitchen towel, it was situated on a solid cookie sheet. "Gabe's inside. I'm sure he'd want to say hello."

Brian nodded. He stepped ahead of her to hold the door open and then followed her through to the kitchen.

"Brian, my mate," Gabe said.

"He's brought me a thank-you cake," Angela said, "though I'm not sure what for."

"Because of what you did for Grandpa," Brian said. "Taking him to the hospital and then checking on him. She thought you were very nice."

"I hope your grandpa is doing well," Angela said.

Brian nodded. "We always have Christmas at their house.

But this year Grandma is bossing him around more than she usually does."

Gabe and Angela let loose with laughter.

"Take the lid off," Brian said.

Angela followed his instruction and was met with a personalized greeting on the cake. "Thank you, Angela!" she read.

"Brian, you were so helpful," Angela said. "You deserve a cake, too."

He grinned. "Grandma always makes three cakes for Christmas. I get to choose which one I want to take home."

"Sweet as!" Gabe said. "She is a fine gran."

Blitzen barked once before trotting to the front door again.

Angela caught Gabe's eye and they both laughed. With all the distractions, her coffee was long cold.

Brian put the lid back on the cake carrier. "Mom told me not to stay too long. She's making brunch for everyone."

"Sounds delicious." Angela walked him to the door only to be greeted by two visitors bearing gifts. "Blitzen, stay."

His tail wagged furiously, but he showed no sign of bolting, so she allowed him to stand at her knee.

"Nora and Jasmine. Merry Christmas to you both." Angela touched the back of Brian's shoulder as he departed. Nora and Jasmine were an unusual duo. She looked from one to the other.

"I won't take up your time," Jasmine said. "The committee just wanted to be sure we expressed our thanks. With this." She proffered a gift basket wrapped in pale silver cellophane and tied with a large blue bow.

Angela took the unexpected basket. "Thank you."

"You did a wonderful job under difficult circumstances."

A few days ago, Angela would have had a thing or two to say about why the circumstances were difficult, starting with how she seemed to be the last person in town to find out it would be up to her to make sure A Christmas to Remember was worth remembering. But she'd come out of that tunnel.

"It's just gourmet teas and coffees," Jasmine said. "My kids had a wonderful time coming out of the dark to sing. They can't wait to do it again next year. How did you ever figure out how to make the lights come on just a few at a time? It was magical."

Angela tilted her head and smiled. Some things were best kept shrouded in mystery—especially since she didn't know the answer.

"Thank you," she said, "to the whole committee."

Nora pressed a package into Angela's hands as well. "Just something for your dog. For Blitzen. Just a throw toy. Maybe he'll like it."

Angela smiled and looked down. "Did you hear that, Blitzen? You got a Christmas present!"

"If you ever need someone to walk him," Nora said, "just let me know."

"Thank you. That's very kind."

"Have a wonderful day." Nora scampered down the front steps. "Merry Christmas!"

"I'll get out of your way, too," Jasmine said. "I was thinking that my older boy might like piano lessons. Do you have any openings?"

"We can work something out. Why don't I call you after New Year's?"

"Thank you. I look forward to it. Everyone says you're the best teacher."

Angela stood there, with her basket of teas and a wrapped throw toy, barely recognizing the woman walking back to her car.

She stepped back into the house, closed the heavy front door, and leaned on it. Gabe came toward her.

"Everything all right?" he said.

"Better than all right. I was expecting a quiet morning, but this was not a bad turn of events."

"I hope I'm not in the way."

"Oh, no, of course not. You could never be in the way."

"I'm glad to hear you say that, and I hope you feel that way in three months or six."

She looked at him.

"I saw my aunt's lawyer the other day," Gabe said. "The lease will be up soon on the house."

Angela held her breath.

"I've always wanted to live in America. I'm going to give it a go."

"But. . .New Zealand. . .your life. . .everything you'd be leaving behind," Angela said. "And won't you need a visa or a green card or something?"

"Got that covered."

"You have?"

Gabe thumbed his chest. "Dual citizen."

The thought hadn't occurred to Angela, but it seemed perfectly plain now. Gabe's grandmother had been a US citizen, and when she moved to New Zealand, she held in her arms her own son. Gabe's father was a US citizen, so of course Gabe was as well.

"And you'll live in Carole's house?" she said.

He nodded.

"She'd like that," Angela said.

"I think it's what she had in mind all along."

Angela smiled and nodded.

"We have seen his glory. . .full of grace and truth."

REFLECTION QUESTIONS
CHRISTMAS IN GOLD

1. As a child, Astrid faced one difficult circumstance after another. In what ways might these sorts of losses shape the spirit and make us more able or less able to respond to losses that come to us later?

2. Inevitably we will all face multiple painful losses. Yet, we also take something forward each time as well. What experiences have you had with loss that you have carried with you, not to diminish pain of loss but perhaps to better understand its meaning?

3. The pain of our own loss can be so encompassing that it's difficult to see what value it may have beyond our own lives. In what ways have you seen your own experiences with loss bear redemptive fruit, as Astrid's did, in the life of someone you did not imagine knowing at the time of your loss?

4. Think back on your own experiences of struggling with difficult circumstances and loss. What does it feel like to give up hope? What does it feel like to recover a sense of hope? What makes the difference?

CHRISTMAS IN BLUE

1. Angela's sense of loss of her friend who loved Christmas led to dreading the first Christmas without Carole. In what ways have you seen your own experience of loss cause you to dread an upcoming season or event? How did you handle your own sense of dread?

2. When the town's celebration landed in Angela's lap, it felt like more than she could handle. Loss can be isolating; it may feel as if no one else understands how you feel, and since grief is an individual experience, the feeling is quite true. How do you manage your own feelings of loss when it feels more like they are managing you?

3. Angela discovered unexpected relationships forming in the bonds of loss. Think back over your own experiences of loss. What relationships have been deepened or brought to you in new ways because of shared grief?

4. Sometimes, like Angela, we think we've figured out just how to bear down and get through the hard time in the middle of our loss. What surprises have come to you and brought healing to your aching spirit to show you that bearing down and getting through is not always the right path?

ABOUT THE AUTHOR

Olivia Newport's novels twist through time to find where faith and passions meet. Her husband and twentysomething children provide welcome distraction from the people stomping through her head on their way into her books. She chases joy in stunning Colorado at the foot of the Rockies, where daylilies grow as tall as she is.

Other Books by Olivia

Amish Turns of Times Series
Wonderful Lonesome
Meek and Mild
Brightest and Best
Hope in the Land
Gladden the Heart

Hidden Falls